THE KEEPER OF SECRETS
A DETECTIVE ARLA BAKER
MYSTERY
ARLA BAKER SERIES 2
by
ML ROSE

Copyright © 2018 by ML Rose

*****

Have you read the first book in the Arla Baker series?
The Lost Sister, Arla Baker Series 1 is out on Amazon now!

CHAPTER 1

Brixton
South London

Gary was a nice nickname for himself, and he liked it. Gary watched the two girls spill out of the brightly lit pub. They giggled and hugged each other, almost falling. The bouncer at the door steadied them with an arm, muttering something inaudible. One of the girls, the taller one, threw her head back and laughed. The light spilled off her rich, brown hair, glittering. She wore a short, pink dress, showing off her bare, long legs in high heels. The dress had a sliver of sequins in the middle, and they caught the light and winked. Gary knew her name: Madeleine. Maddy for short. Her friend was called Maya. They were both seventeen and a half, and they had fake IDs to get them into pubs. It worked, as they looked a lot older. Gary knew about this, because he had been following the girls for a long time. He knew what classes they took at their school, when they met behind the bike shed for a fag and quick snog with a boy, and who they met after school. He knew how long it took them to return home on the bus. Gary liked to know these things. He liked to plan.
The summer night was warm, the glow of the full moon suffusing the air with silver light. There was a dim hubbub of voices and cars, the eternal drone of the city's life, incipient beneath the surface. The sound of crickets buzzed from nearby Brockwell Park. Gary watched the two girls as they lit up fags, inhaling smoke as they tottered on their heels, their backs lit up by the garish light from the pub doors. They laughed raucously, obviously drunk. Gary was lying flat behind a clump of bushes at the edge of the park opposite. He could see the girls clearly. They tossed their cigarettes away, and had a hushed conversation. Gary tensed himself.

The girls turned, and waved and blew kisses at the bouncer. The shorter girl, Maya, went back inside the pub. Maddy, the taller girl, turned and weaved her way down the street, heading for the T-junction, where a bus stand awaited her. Gary breathed faster and slowly stood up. Weeks of planning had led to this moment. He enjoyed the plotting, but the real pleasure lay in the execution. He flitted from tree to tree, brushing himself down. He had to be clean before he stepped out onto the road. The road was long and quiet, lit at regular intervals by limpid pools of light from the lamp-posts. Apart from the tall teenager making her precarious way on the tall heels, there was no one else on the road.

Gary stepped out onto the road and took a quick look around. Behind him, on the underpass, cars buzzed in the distance. The sound was muted by the trees, and the loudest sound here was the clicking of heels on the tarmacked pavement. Silent as a shadow, Gary got closer to Maddy. In the still night air, he could smell her cheap perfume. The lurid smell was intoxicating, and he breathed in deeply, his mouth opening in anticipation.

All for a good cause, he smirked to himself. Maddy was the means to an end, but he would have fun while he was doing it.

Just in time, Maddy's heel caught on a drainpipe cover, and she stumbled. Gary was next to her in a flash. He put on his most winning smile and comforting voice.

"Hey, are you OK?" He extended an arm down to the teenager, who was kneeling on one knee.

Maddy looked up to see a young man, short, dark hair, and a good-looking face staring down at her with concern. He was dressed in a dark suit, and had a small backpack over his right shoulder.

She accepted the hand. It was warm and steady. Gary stepped back after he helped Maddy up.

"I was going home," he explained. "Came off the train, and was going to the bus station. Saw you fall so wondered if you're alright."

"Th...thanks." The words slurred on Maddy's tongue. Gary could smell her properly now, a faint, musky, sweet body odour mingled with her perfume. With an effort he controlled himself. All his planning was coming to fruition.

Take it easy, he told himself.

"I'm Gary," he said as a means of introduction.

Maddy's eyes were hooded. She licked her lips and turned, mumbling her own name. Even in her drunk and drug-addled state, she knew it was not wise to talk to strangers on a dark street.

Gary hurried after her. "Are you going to the bus stop, too?" Maddy nodded without replying. Gary looked up. The girl had speeded up, and the T-junction was a couple of hundred metres away. He could see cars zipping on the road ahead. On either side loomed the dark clumps of trees that formed the fringe of Brockwell Park. He stole a look behind. The street was empty, the lights of the pub at the end of the cul-de-sac now far behind them.

It was now or never.

He reached out and brushed an imaginary fleck of dust from Maddy's shoulder. The girl looked up, alarm on her face. Gary smiled. "Sorry. Just saw an insect land on your shoulder."

Maddy mumbled something incoherent and stumbled forward. Gary got closer, and put his hand over hers. At first the girl didn't react, but when she understood what was happening, she tried to withdraw her hand. Gary's vice-like grip closed over her hand, and he held on tight.

Maddy gasped, alarm suddenly cascading across her features like ripples in a pond. Gary grinned, and pulled her close to him, abruptly. She opened her mouth to shout, but his right hand came across the back of her head, and clamped over her mouth. Gary had large hands, and he put them to good use.

He pressed down hard on her mouth, staring at her eyes, bulging with fear. She tried to scream, but only a choked mumble was audible. Gary felt an icy calm descend upon him, a stark comparison to the terror in the teenager's face. In truth, he didn't like this part. He wished they wouldn't fight. He wished they would give in to his urges, and then to his final wish.

Why did they have to fight?

He held her from behind, and lifted her up at the waist with his left arm. Maddy was a good swimmer, and she was strong. She fought but Gary was stronger.

As he stepped onto the grass, Gary's trainer-clad ankle twisted, and he fell, cursing. Maddy wriggled out of his grasp and cried hoarsely. She got to her hands and knees, but before she could stand Gary lunged forward. Maddy was on her feet, and about to run when she felt him grip her ankle. She fell flat on her face, the breath knocked out of her.

She felt a heavy weight as he straddled her back, and then cried with pain as her hair was pulled back. The same rough, calloused hand closed over her mouth, and a sudden, vicious blow landed on her head. Pain exploded in a yellow-orange fireball in her skull, dimming her vision. Her eyes almost closed, and she felt limp, numb. Vaguely she was aware of his strong hands lifting her up. His fetid breath was on her nostrils, making her gag. "Try another stunt like that and it will be your last one," he growled. "Do you understand?"

Another stinging blow landed on her face, rocking her brain, and her face would have collapsed on the hard ground if he hadn't been holding her mouth.

"Do you understand?"

Maddy was barely able to nod through the fog of terror and nerve-racking pain that convulsed every fibre of her being.

Gary picked her up, right hand clamped around her mouth, dragging her on the grass like a rag doll. The trees and bushes around them grew more dense, and the amniotic darkness claimed their forms as they receded into darkness. Crickets buzzed, and a gentle breeze fluttered with the leaves high above ground. Moonlight silence reigned over the park, but was suddenly pierced by a sharp, breathtaking scream of pain.

CHAPTER 2

Centre for Anatomy and Human Identification
University of Dundee
Scotland

Detective Chief Inspector Arla Baker rubbed her left forearm as she walked down the hallway, following the elderly woman ahead of her. She hadn't taken her jacket off, and the three layers of clothing she wore did nothing to dispel the growing sense of disquiet that was starting to spill around her insides, sloshing around like a storm-tossed boat taking in water. The secretary stopped in front of a light brown oak door, and rapped on it gently, then louder when she didn't get a response.

There was a muffled voice from inside, then the door opened. Arla was ushered inside, and the door closed gently behind her. Arla was in a bright, spacious office, a row of windows on the back wall letting in rays of sunlight. Through the windows, across the campus buildings, she could see Dundee's far undulating, green hills rolling down to the North Sea.

The figure who rose up from the table, blocking her view, was a middle-aged woman wearing a black blouse and matching black skirt with tights on. She was much shorter than Arla's five-eleven, coming up to her chest height. She bustled around the table, sticking out a podgy hand in greeting.

"Professor Hodgson," she said in a clear, no-nonsense voice. They shook hands. "You must be DCI Arla Baker from the London Met."

Arla nodded and took the seat she was indicated. Professor Sandra Hodgson took a seat opposite and took a minute to appraise Arla. Arla met the older woman's gaze candidly, glad she had brushed her jet-black hair back and dressed smartly.

Sandra coughed and said, "I know this is not an easy thing for you. I cannot imagine how you feel."

Arla had sent up the photos of the skeleton to Sandra on VACS – Virtual Anthropology Consultancy Service – so she could examine them and confirm its human origin, and roughly gauge the age and sex. Human, female and aged sixteen. Arla swallowed the knot that had formed at the back of her throat. She had spoken to Sandra on the phone after that, and the London Met's Forensic Office had agreed to release the human remains to be escorted up to CAHID at the University of Dundee. CAHID was one of the world's foremost pioneering centres on the subject of human forensic anthropology, and Sandra, one of its founders, was recognised as a global expert in extracting clues out of human bones.

Arla didn't know what to say. Perhaps there was nothing but silence to offer, words lost, seeping into the earth of shallow graves and memories. She had steeled herself against emotion, because she had a job to do.

She gave a small shrug. "Shall we begin?"

Sandra peered at her closely. "Only if you are ready. Would you like a cup of tea or coffee?"

Arla shook her head. "A glass of water is fine."

Sandra walked to the water cooler behind her, and poured a plastic cup of water. Must be nice to have a water machine in your own room, Arla thought to herself. She clutched the cup when offered, and followed Sandra out of the room. The deep carpet on the hallway absorbed the sound from their shoes. Arla could see white-coated figures moving around in labs through the glass-panelled doors. She passed a door that said 'Crime Writing and Forensic Investigation'.

"You have an office for crime writing?" Arla asked, hooking a thumb towards the door.

Sandra smiled. "This is the era of *CSI*, beamed to every corner of the world. Most crime writers want to sound authentic, and you wouldn't believe the demand for the course."

"I've seen plenty of crime scenes, but couldn't write a word about them," Arla observed drily. "Can you really teach someone how to write stories? I mean it's not like I did a course in policing. I learned on the job."

Sandra didn't break stride. "There is no alternative to learning on the job. But there is a right and wrong way to do things. That applies to writing, as it does to anything else in life. That's what we teach here."

They stopped outside a lab, and Sandra entered a code on the digital keypad. They walked into a sterilising antechamber, with white coats hanging on hooks, and metallic sinks on either side. Arla followed Sandra's example, and picked up a plastic case of sterile blue uniform from the female section on the wall. They walked into a changing room and got undressed. The starched blue uniform, short-sleeved, felt light and crisp on Arla's body. She washed her hands the way Sandra showed her, scrubbing at the elbows, leaving the hands till the very last. Once the hands were washed, they were held up, bent at the elbow. This allowed water to drain down, and the fingers not to get contaminated. They donned gloves, and left face masks dangling from their necks.

Arla walked into a lab with rows of examination desks, a few forensic investigators hunched over skeleton remains or microscopes. Sandra walked to a table where a long box was waiting for them, lid covered.

Arla's throat was dry, and she suddenly remembered she had left the glass of water outside without drinking it.

Sandra sat down in front of the box, and pushed the long-legged, black stool towards her. She looked at Arla. "Ready?"

Arla glanced at Sandra and found something akin to compassion. She swallowed and nodded. Sandra lifted the lid. The bones of a skeleton, almost fully intact, were arranged inside.

A sign on the inside read: Name of Deceased – Nicole Baker.

CHAPTER 3

Very gently, like she was picking up a rare piece of china, Sandra
lifted up a bone in a gloved hand after staring at the box for a while.
She took out a magnifying glass from her pocket, and held it over the
long bone, moving down its length.

"These days we have scanning CT machines to do the work of
magnifying glasses," Sandra said without lifting her head up. "But
for the really important things, I don't think one can replace the
human eye."

"Thank you," Arla said quietly. As she stared at her sister's bone,
she felt an odd and personal connection with Sandra. The blonde-
haired woman was closely examining the bone, as if it held secrets
that she could coax out just by looking. Presently, Sandra lifted her
head.

"This is the long bone from the hips to the knee, also known as the
femur. The epiphyses at the ends, or growth plates, haven't fused as
yet, which means they were still growing. I would put the age at
mid- to late-teens, so sixteen-seventeen years of age. The mass and
width of the bone are much lighter than a teenage boy's, which
leaves the sex in no doubt. These grooves," Sandra touched then
traced her finger gently down an incline on the inside of the bone,
"are to hold the attachments of the quadriceps muscles. They are the
heaviest muscles of the legs, and the depth of the grooves indicates
the muscles were smaller than a man's, which also provides clues to
the sex."

Arla said, "And you have been through the dental records already,
and compared them to her wisdom teeth."

Sandra looked up and nodded. "Yes," she said in a quiet voice. "The
identity is in no doubt. Neither is the sex or age."

There was a finality in that statement, the words hanging in front of
Arla's eyes for a while, before fading like mist in the morning sun.
What was left of Nicole was in front of her. A search that had begun
twenty years ago had finally gained closure.

Sandra stood up and went through the bones of the upper and lower
limbs systematically. She paused at the right foot. She took the bone
to a nearby microscope, Arla following. When Sandra finished, she
had her lips pursed, and an unreadable expression on her face.

"What is it?" Arla asked.

"Trauma. The edge of her big toe is overgrown with white tissues, which implies ossification, or the formation of new bone. That happens where there is a fracture and bone has to fuse back together."

Arla said, "Blunt trauma?"

"Yes. Hard enough to fracture, although bones of the feet can break quite easily. Not much muscle protection." She squinted at Arla. "Sure you want me to carry on?"

Arla nodded. Sandra moved to the hands. "Some bony lacerations, or cuts to the distal phalanges," she murmured. She looked up at Arla and said, "That means cuts like claw marks. Couldn't be done by another human, so had to be a weapon."

"You mean a sharp weapon, like a knife?"

Sandra nodded, her face grave. Arla swallowed hard. "So someone was stabbing her, and she was trying to protect herself, or fight him off?"

In silence Sandra nodded again. They held each other's eyes. Arla was the first to look away. Sandra came closer.

"How old are the wounds?" Arla asked.

"Hard to say. Carbon dating puts the time at less than twenty years." Arla sat down. Sandra said, "Some of the ribs have been broken on impact with a sharp weapon, probably a knife as well. The direction of the bone lacerations indicated the knife perforated the intercostal muscles – the muscles between the ribs."

Arla closed her eyes. A horrible vision of a bastard stabbing Nicole rose like a nightmare in her mind, while Nicole fought back with nothing but bare hands. She blinked, and the cold clinical light of the white halogen flooded her senses. Sandra touched her hand.

Arla looked down at the woman's wrinkled, spotty hand, blue veins arching beneath the old skin. "Think of it as a case," Sandra said. "Otherwise we won't get through this."

Arla exhaled and stood up. She felt a buzz in her pockets and frowned. Her phone was on silent but it was ringing. She took it out, and saw Clapham Common Police Station's number on it.

"Sorry, I have to take this," she whispered. Sandra nodded. Arla stepped out of the lab with the ringing phone. Outside, still in her short-sleeve blues, she answered.

"How's Scotland treating you?" The voice belonged to Detective Inspector Harry Mehta, her trusted sidekick.

"Fine and dandy. This better be something important." She tried to bring the usual hardness to her voice. She knew Harry would see through it, and he did.

There was a pause, then genuine concern. "Hang in there. At least now you know."

"Right. What do you want, Harry?"

"I didn't want to call you. The boss put me up to it."

Arla rolled her eyes. Her boss, the recently promoted Deputy Assistant Commissioner, Wayne Johnson. Only Johnson was still a chief superintendent, his DAC role not starting for another three months. More time for him to pester Arla, she thought resignedly.

"And?" Arla barked, irritated.

Harry continued. "A missing girl. Disappeared after end-of-year drinks from local pub near Brockwell Park. It's been more than a week. Parents and friends suspect foul play."

Arla was silent for a while. She thought about the cold bones on the bare desk inside, all that was left of her once warm and loving sister. Then she thought of the parents of the missing teenager in London.

Harry said, "I have made lists of enquiries already. Johnson has made you Senior Investigative Officer, so as SIO I need your permission to proceed with the list." He put a sardonic emphasis on the word 'SIO'. Arla ignored it, like she ignored most things Harry said. The man was incorrigible.

"Yes, *I* give you permission to proceed," she said archly, matching his tone. Then she dropped it and glanced at her wristwatch. "Its 10.30 now. We should be done here by 12.30. So back by 20.00 hours in London. Meet you at the station?"

"If I'm paid for overtime, then yes," Harry said. Arla hung up, and made her way back inside the lab.

CHAPTER 4

Arla watched the granite darkness pressing against the window as the train plunged through the night. She wanted to get off it, walk, run, do anything to get away. She longed for the familiar lights of London, its grime and oily air, her sense of normality.

Her phone rang. She stared at the screen for a while before answering. It was Harry. He didn't speak for a while, and she appreciated the blank space.

"You OK?" he drawled after a while.

"Been better."

Harry didn't poke, like she had expected. As much as it pained her to admit it, that was one of the things she liked about him. The only thing, perhaps.

"If you won't make it in time, let me know."

Arla checked her watch. It was 18.30, and she was going past Peterborough. King's Cross was 45 minutes away. Theoretically, 20.00 arrival in Clapham was achievable. For some reason, she wanted to get back to work. What else did she have to do? Go back to her one-bedroom apartment in Tooting, and watch the glowing windows from her bedroom? With a bottle of wine cradled in her arm…

No. Not tonight. She craved the oblivion of alcohol, and that was exactly why she didn't want to drink alone.

"Catch you at the nick, by 8," she said to Harry.

"Good." He sounded relieved.

Arla was one of the first ones out of the train. The kinetic energy of human bodies on King's Cross Station was enlivening. She was back in the land of the living. As she joined the queue for cabs, she thought of her dead mother, Nicole, and her only living relative, her father. Timothy Baker had shut himself away from his daughter. Arla had tried in vain to make contact, but he had always refused. On the two occasions when he had seen her, after she discovered who her mother had been, and when Nicole's skeleton was found, he had been silent, withdrawn. A husk of a man, eyes glassy and staring at the world like he can't believe he's still in it.

Arla had forgiven him, but it seemed her father couldn't forget. She ached to speak to him, to find out more of what he knew about Nicole. But she knew he would hold it within, and deny her a look inside his tortured soul.

Arla stopped at her apartment to drop her things off and freshen up quickly. When the Uber cab dropped her off at the white steps of the brown-brick building, it was eight-fifteen. The desk sergeant looked up as Arla walked in. His name was John Sandford, a tall Afro-Caribbean who wore the black uniform of a sergeant.

"Hi, guv, how was your trip?"

Everyone knew why she had gone up north. A tragedy of the proportions that she had suffered couldn't be kept a secret.

"Not bad, thanks, John. Anyone still here?"

A couple of heads lifted from the green plastic seats of the reception. One of them smirked at Arla and said, "Yeah, me. You got something, sweetheart?"

"Shut up!" John bellowed at the man in a deep voice. "Or I'll chuck you inside for the night to cool off."

The man gave John an evil look then looked away. John buzzed Arla in through the steel re-enforced double doors. The cream-coloured corridors needed painting, and the fading carpet on the floor had been replaced by lino. She walked past boards stuck with messages of missing persons. Arla thought of stopping to check if the new missing person was on it, but she didn't know her details. The open-plan office where the detectives had their cubicles was still brightly lit, and a coat or two was still draped around the back of chairs. But she saw only one figure. A long, lanky man, with his outsized shoes up on the desk, leaning back at an angle on his chair that would lose the fight with gravity any second now. His short, black hair was growing longer at the sides, and his fingers were crossed behind his head. She could see the polish on his shoes shining as he rocked them.

"You're late," Harry said when she got closer, his tone disapproving. Arla didn't break stride. Sometimes the best way to deal with Harry was to ignore him. She walked past him to the prefabricated office at the end. It had her name and title on it. Arla walked in, the usual musty smell of old papers and coffee hitting her nostrils. She opened the window at the back. A sultry summer breeze came in.

Harry came and leaned against the door frame, reeking of aftershave. She wrinkled her nose.

"Smells cheap, Harry," she said.

"It's you, actually, and the stuff you get from Primark," he shot back.

"Primark don't do perfumes," she scowled at him.

"If they did you'd be first in line, I bet."

"Are you saying I stink?"

Harry smirked, his chestnut eyes dancing. "Stink so good or stink so bad? You know, sometimes a woman can…"

"Shut up, Harry, I don't want to know."

"I bet you do."

She shook her head at him, frowning. "Sometimes you're like a child." She made a show of opening drawers and slamming them shut. Secretly, she was glad she could take it out on him. Her professional relationship with Harry worked best when she treated the six-foot-three man like a punching bag.

"Rest of the team gone home?" Arla asked, flopping back on her chair.

"Yes," Harry said, closing the door but remaining standing. "Missing person's name is Madeleine Burroughs. Her father came in to file the report yesterday. The boss said the Serious Crime Unit should handle it."

Arla leaned back in the chair. "The SCU doesn't normally handle missing persons, though. That's why we have a national database and specialised teams for missing people."

She didn't like the look in Harry's eyes. But, in a way, she had known from when she had taken the call in Dundee. There was something else going on.

Harry said, "Father is an American diplomat. Close to the US Ambassador. There's pressure from the Commissioner and the rest of the top brass."

Arla threw her head back. "Great." She massaged her eyes with the heels of her palms.

Harry was staring at her when she opened her eyes. She frowned, and a feeling of dread spread like ice-cold water in her guts.

"What?" she demanded.

Harry kicked his shoes, and breathed out. He came forward and lowered his gangly frame slowly into the chair opposite her.

"The dad came for two reasons. One, to report his missing daughter. The other, to show us a letter dropped in through his letter box."

Arla was confused. "What did the letter say?"

Harry scratched his neck. Arla fumed. "God damn it, Harry, will you speak!?"

His next words turned Arla's insides to ice. "The letter was addressed to you. Inside, it said, and I quote – Ask DCI Arla Baker where Maddy is."

CHAPTER 5

Arla shot upright, her heart pounding. If her mind had been suspended in a fog, that mist had now well and truly dispersed. "What?" She leaned over the desk, her face crimson. "And you didn't tell me this over the phone?"

"I didn't want to alarm you. Thought you had enough on your plate."

Arla tried to control her breathing without much success. "Where is the letter?"

"In Secure Evidence. Last I knew, the boss was having a look at it."

Arla groaned. DCS Johnson, the softly spoken, politically astute police officer, to whom rank and career meant more than his own children, would love Arla for this. As if it was even remotely her fault.

She asked, "Where is Johnson?"

"In his office, I think."

Arla skewered Harry with a withering look. "You knew about this but didn't warn me? He told you, right?"

Harry was uncomfortable. "I told you that, didn't I? I had orders, Arla, to call you. So, I did."

"But you didn't think it important to tell me the real news."

Harry shook his head and stood up. "Look, I knew you would be up to your neck dealing with that other stuff." He broke off and looked at her pleadingly. "I'm sorry, but you would have known sooner or later."

Arla felt her anger subsiding. Harry was right. What would she have done with this bombshell in Dundee? Rushed back home with another mindfuck? If anything, her lanky compatriot had done her a favour.

As the rush of blood receded, her mental faculties kicked into gear. She frowned. "What the hell is this? I need to see the letter."

"Yes."

She looked up at Harry, thinking. She could see the wheels turning in his brain.

"It could be anyone," he said softly. "Maybe a prankster."

"A prankster who knew a girl has been missing for more than one week, and decides to drop me in it?"

Harry shrugged. "Why not?" He dropped his gaze when Arla glared at him.

"Think, Harry. My name was specifically mentioned. This isn't child's play. It's not like a bike's been stolen. The person who dropped my name knew the ramifications of this case. They wanted to land me in deep shit. So let's not pretend otherwise."

Harry held his hands up. "Wait a minute. You're charging right into this like you do. Is it hard to find out your name? No. Any freak or nutter could have done this. Hell, it could have been Johnson's name there. That would have seen his Assistant Commissioner job go up in smoke!"

Harry couldn't help but smile. "That would be funny. Him losing his precious job like that."

Arla shared his humour, but the feeling was short-lived. She knew she was impulsive, prone to fits of temper. Emotions ruled her: it was the way she was. She could be headstrong, and make the wrong decision. But her instincts were normally correct. Specially her instincts honed with almost twenty years on the force, seven of them as DCI.

Those instincts were now reverberating, like a weather chime in a cyclone.

Someone wanted to settle a score with her. If so, then the net had to be cast wide. Over the years, she had pulled in a lot of sickos, psychos, crooks. She shivered when she thought of the enemies she had made.

"Why wasn't it Johnson's name, Harry?" she asked softly. "Why wasn't it yours?"

Harry was about to say something when the phone rang. Arla stared at the black phone with trepidation, as if answering it would make it explode like a grenade.

Gently she reached down and picked up the receiver. She put it against her ear. There was silence on the other end, then she heard heavy breathing. Something clutched at Arla's throat. Her pulse rate rose. Harry leaned over the table, a frown on his face.

Then a voice spoke. "Arla, is that you?" The tone was smooth, polished. As she recognised the voice her knees almost buckled in relief. It was Wayne Johnson, the DCS.

"Yes, sir."

"Come to my room immediately." He hung up.

Arla and Harry took the stairs up to the third floor of the five-floor building. She knocked and Johnson told them to enter. The office was much like the man, spick and span, everything in its place. Behind the high-backed, black leather armchair, a glass showcase held his medals, photos with politicians, and certificates. Only one photo of his family was present on the middle shelf.

Johnson was wearing purple non-latex gloves, and he was holding a piece of paper in his hands. He wasn't wearing his uniform. He looked up as Arla came in.

"Sit down, Detective Chief Inspector." He softened his voice. "How did it go in Dundee?"

Arla thought of a smart retort, then bit her tongue. Things were getting weird very quickly, and she needed to see the letter Johnson was holding.

"As can be expected, sir. Not a barrel of laughs."

"No, I suspect not. My condolences, as you know." He held Arla's eyes. There had been bad blood between them, but Arla knew that despite his shrewdness at office politics, Johnson was a bloody good cop. They had worked together for a long time, and Arla knew he was being sincere.

"Thank you, sir." Arla and Harry sat down. She couldn't take her eyes off the letter in Johnson's hand. It was plain white, half a page folded in two.

Johnson took his glasses off. "What do you make of this?" he asked Arla.

"Can I please see the letter, sir?" Arla reached inside her pocket and pulled out a pair of specimen gloves. Johnson leaned over, handing her the paper gingerly.

CHAPTER 6

Arla took the white piece of paper, her heart beating painfully against her ribs. The letters were cut out and stuck on the paper. They were different sizes, all cut out from either a magazine or newspaper headlines. The sentence wasn't difficult to read, despite the strange arrangement.

ASK DCI ARLA BAKER WHERE MADDY IS

Holding the paper with her gloves, Arla turned it over. A simple A4 piece of paper folded in two. She could see a faint trace of carbon dusting on it, from the fingerprint technicians.

"Anything on IDENT1?" she asked. IDENT1 was the national database for matching criminals with their fingerprints.

"Nope," Johnson said. "Forensics haven't had a go at it as yet. It arrived today, and tomorrow it's going over for a DNA and fibre check."

I doubt they'll find anything, Arla thought to herself. Her mind was in overdrive, but she could feel her bones aching. It had been a long day, full of unwanted revelations. Suddenly, that bottle of wine chilling in her fridge seemed an excellent proposition.

"First things first," Johnson said. "You know I have to ask you this."

Arla stared back at him. Eventually Johnson said, "Did you know Madeleine Burroughs, the missing person?"

"No, sir."

"You sure?"

Arla didn't like his tone. She frowned. "If I wasn't sure, I wouldn't be telling you, sir, would I?"

Johnson pursed his lips. "I know. It's just that..."

"Just what, sir?"

Johnson stared at his hands before speaking. "I know you've had a hard time with what just happened."

Arla stiffened without saying anything. She had no wish to discuss the case regarding her sister, and she hoped it had no bearing on the present one. But in the back of her mind, an uncomfortable feeling persisted. And Johnson's silence was ominous.

"What I'm saying is this, Arla. You help out in the community for homeless kids, teenagers under social services, right?"

"So? This is the daughter of a diplomat, hardly a runaway or an orphan."

Johnson sighed. "All I was wondering was if you had come across her at a community event, or maybe you did a talk at her school, you know." He shrugged.

Arla couldn't believe it. She gave a slight shake of her head. "Sir, if I did, don't you think I would have mentioned it? I would be the first one to admit a link between myself and the missing, because that would help to solve the case much quicker."

"Good."

"Can't you see what this is about, sir? The line of questioning you are now subjecting me to is exactly what the abductor wants you to do."

"Now hold on a second…"

"No!" Arla shifted forward, her nostrils flaring. "He, or she, deliberately wants to put my integrity into doubt. Like I know something about where this girl might be. That's why he left this note, right?"

Johnson had to concede the point. "Yes."

"It's like asking me which room in Buckingham Palace The Queen is in right now. I have no idea. I don't know this girl. Do we have a photo?"

Johnson opened a drawer and took a folder out. "This is still top secret. The parents have contacted us only, via the US Embassy and the Home Office. They have not as yet gone to the press. I think we should be grateful to them. You can imagine the stink this will cause if the press gets a hold about your name being involved."

Arla nodded and took the photo. It was a blown-up image of Maddy Burroughs posing in a holiday snap. She was wearing a short, blue dress, and her long, bare legs tapered down to slingback heels. She was wearing bright make-up, and looked older than her teenage years suggested. Turquoise waters of a gentle sea lapped on the sand behind her, and green-grey hills rose in the distance.

"When was this photo taken?" Arla asked.

Harry spoke up. "Last year, summer holidays in Zakynthos island, Greece."

"How old was she then?"

Harry spoke again. "Sixteen and a half."

Arla stared at the confident, pouting face of the teenager. Her dress indicated she was going out for the evening, and her posture held the swagger of a girl approaching adulthood, eager to take on life. Something lurched inside Arla's heart, a somersault that turned into a silent sob.

Nicole had been like this once.

Don't go there. Not now.

She was aware of Harry's long fingers fluttering close to hers, and gently removing the photo from her hands. Johnson was watching her closely.

She cleared her throat and said, "When did the letter arrive?"

"In the morning, after Royal Mail. Mr Burroughs was at work: his wife found it. She called us immediately, after looking up your name on our website."

Arla's mind was whirring. The psychopaths she had come across in her work were all safely behind bars. Who could be playing this sick joke on her?

Johnson seemed to read her mind. "Can you think of anyone?"

Arla spread her hands. "Take your pick, sir."

Harry cleared his throat, and they both turned to look at him. His Adam's apple bobbed up and down in his long neck as he spoke.

"Whoever left this note was aware of the abduction. Her parents haven't been to the press. The mother said the school is aware, and therefore so are the families of her friends."

"You spoke to her?" Arla asked.

Harry nodded. Arla said, "A good place to start our enquiries. First, her family, then the school. From there, we widen the net."

"Who do you want in the team?" Johnson asked.

"Can I decide that tomorrow, sir?" She glanced at Harry. "Everyone's coming tomorrow, right?"

Harry nodded. "Meeting in incident room at 0800."

"Now listen," Johnson said. Both of them looked at the senior police officer. His polished face held a resigned expression.

"When this blows up, it's going to be big. I need a swift resolution. That's why, despite your name being so blatantly involved, I am making you SIO in the case. If I see that we are dragging our heels, or things aren't going to plan, I will have to replace you as SIO. Got that?"

"Yes," Arla said, unfazed. She was used to ultimatums from her boss. "Will the family go to the press? I'd prefer it if they didn't."

"That's the thing. The Home Office, and luckily both the family and the US Embassy, agree with you. But they want it sorted, pronto. You know what the Yanks are like. If they don't see results…"

Like someone else I know, Arla thought to herself. "Yes, sir, I get the picture. How long have we got?"

"Time has not been specified, but there is something bigger on the horizon."

"Like what?"

"A US presidential visit in three months' time."

Johnson was silent for a while, letting it sink in. Arla thought back to the newspapers she had read on the train up to Dundee and back. She remembered the headlines. *Oh no.*

Harry stirred, and Johnson looked at both of them in turn.

"American diplomat's daughter disappears three months before the President visits," Johnson said wryly.

"Look on the bright side," Harry said. "If we don't find her, we can blame the budget cuts. Lack of manpower."

Arla turned in her seat and fixed him with a glare. Harry held his hands up in mock horror and shrank back.

She turned to Johnson. "We will find her, sir. I promise you."

"Promises are meant to be kept, DCI Baker. Remember that."

CHAPTER 7

Arla declined the offer of a lift from Harry, smiling inwardly at the look of puppy dog regret in his eyes. She waited in the station while her Uber arrived. As she waited, Arla thought about where she was heading. Home, certainly, back to her ground-floor apartment in Tooting, South London. But en route lay another place she visited rarely, but it remained at the back of her mind like an itch that never went away. Seeing Nicole's remains had brought those memories back to the forefront. Grainy, distorted images of a childhood she hid in the darkest recesses of her mind. She never plumbed those depths, but she knew it had made her who she was. Impulsive, emotional, short-tempered.

The lid lifted, and some vapour escaped to the surface of her brain. Arla got up and started pacing the front desk area, watched by the duty sergeant. The place Arla had in mind was an apartment in Balham, not far from where she lived, but far enough for her to ignore. Her father lived there. She had no desire to see him. But once or twice a year, she dropped in to say hello. He had said sorry, but it didn't mean anything to Arla. Sorry wouldn't bring her childhood back. Not all of it had been his fault, but his drinking had made a bad situation worse, then out of control. His remorse, and the fact that he didn't touch alcohol anymore, had mellowed him slightly in Arla's eyes.

When the Uber arrived, the blue sky had clouded over suddenly. They came from nowhere, heavy-bellied, laden with rain, and the pulsating heat of the night turned into a warm patter of rain. Arla shielded her hair and ran into the car. She told the driver where to drop her off.

When the car had zoomed off into the rain-slicked, neon-yellow road, she stood for a while under the silent, blinking traffic lights. The railway station was across the road, with the bridge over it. The tall, five-storey Victorian building to her right had been built as a block of apartments, and so it had remained. Off-licences crowded the street around her, and the ground floor of the building was a Co-op supermarket. Some evening shoppers milled around the entrance. Arla ignored the drumming of her heart, or the vacuum opening up inside her, and rang the bell of her father's apartment. After a while, he answered.

"Who is it?" There was no video on the calling system. She didn't answer for a while. A train passed overhead, shaking the bridge. She felt the rumble in her heels, travelling up her body. He didn't hang up.

"Arla," he said, his voice softer. "Is that you?"

She swallowed back the bitterness. "Yes."

There was silence for a while, a pause in which both of them wondered what the other was thinking.

She wondered what he was doing, holding the phone. Standing, sitting? How long would he carry on like this? She cleared her throat, feeling foolish about standing outside, speaking so loud. "How are you?"

"Not bad," Timothy Baker said. "Not bad. And you?"

"I'm fine," Arla said. Great, she thought. Platitudes are over. There was nothing more to say, and it had been the same for many years.

"Would you like to come upstairs?" Timothy asked, his voice hesitant.

Arla thought of what she had to say, and what purpose it would serve. It would cause them both some sorrow, bringing back those days of pain. Then she would go home, and he would stay up all night, nursing regrets.

Really, why was she here?

Now she knew he was alive and functioning. She had done her job. "I should go, Dad. I have work tomorrow." She could hear him breathing, feel his regret expanding and contracting with every wave of sound. It lapped against her ears, the endless pulses of a restless ocean.

"OK," he said. "See you later."

With a click the line went dead. Arla sighed, a kaleidoscope of anger, sorrow and frustration raging through her like a subway train. She crossed the road and looked up at his apartment. The curtains were drawn, and she could see him looking out. Looking at her. She waved, and he lifted his arm slowly, then let it drop. He walked away and turned the light off.

CHAPTER 8

A village in Kent
South-East England

Maddy Burroughs was aware of a piercing pain between her eyes. She knotted her eyebrows, fighting the sharp pain, and her eyelids fluttered open. The sunlight was like shards of lightning, blazing into her eyes. She grimaced and shut her eyes again. Her face and jaw ached, and there was a strange, metallic taste inside her mouth. She tried to move her hands, and found them restrained. Then she felt the burn on her wrists, and knew they were tied together. Her feet were also tied.

Suddenly, the memories came flying back to her like an avalanche. Her eyes flew open, then she blinked as she adjusted to the light. She remembered walking back from the pub, being attacked by that man... Then the memory became sketchy. She had woken up in this place once before, but each time someone had given her an injection, and she had fallen asleep. Had she eaten? A few crumbs of bread, some soup. A man wearing a mask had untied her, and she had relieved herself in a commode dragged to the bedside.

Fear reared up inside her. She cried out, but only a muffled sound came from the tape covering her mouth. When she moved her torso, she was aware of a belt holding her across the bed. She stopped struggling and looked around her. There was one window to her left, above a block of wood with four legs that served as a table. The walls were made of stone blocks, and she could see strands of hay in the corners of the room. Sunlight petered in from the sides of the window, whose shades were drawn. She looked up. Black-painted timber beams criss-crossed the ceiling.

It seemed like she was in a barn or stable. She could definitely smell a whiff of horse manure. She listened for animal sounds, but heard none. She had been horse riding in Richmond Park a few times, and she knew what horses sounded like. This place was empty, and might have been used in the past as a stable. Maddy tried to move around, her shoes clinking against the metal railings at the end of the hospital gurney she was lying on.

A door creaked open behind her. Maddy stiffened. She heard his footsteps approaching. Soft, like he was trying to make no sound. But there was also a sound of something being dragged, a heavier object.

Maddy's heart thrummed, and her chest heaved as she felt him come closer. She screamed and wriggled in the bed as she saw his face appear suddenly over hers. He was wearing a black hoodie, covering his head, and a black balaclava covering his face. All she could see was his glittering eyes, and she turned her head away, sick and repulsed.

"Well, well, we have woken up, have we?" The voice was light, almost sing-song. A strange voice, one she wouldn't forget easily. She could feel him leaning over her, and she kept her head turned away, fear clawing at her throat.

"I'm going to unhook your belt and untie your ankles and hands. Then you can sit in the commode and do what you need to. There will be a loo roll on the floor. I will stand just outside the door. If you try anything funny…" He stopped speaking abruptly and grabbed her chin. She didn't fight as he jerked her face towards him. Her eyes widened when she saw the long kitchen knife. The sharpened tip gleamed.

"I'll cut your fingers off first, then your toes. One by one. Got it?" Maddy nodded vigorously. She could see nothing but his eyes, and they were distant, dark holes in his skull. He unhooked her then, holding the knife in one hand, he expertly untied the rope holding her ankles together with the other. When her hands were free she rubbed them together. He stood in front of her, knife pointed as she sat up in the bed warily. Behind the commode, he had placed a covered plate.

"Bread and soup in there," the muffled, strange voice behind the balaclava said. He thrust at her with the knife and she screamed, falling back on the bed. He loomed over her, and the tip of the knife touched her throat. A teardrop rolled out of Maddy's eye, and she sniffed. She was trying to hold it in like a grown-up, but suddenly she didn't feel it anymore. She felt like a scared, lost little girl.

"Remember what I said. No funny business." The knife came off her throat, and he pulled her up by the collar. She watched him walk to the door, his gait strange, shoulders slouched. He seemed different from the confident young man who had accosted her outside the pub. He opened the door, and left it ajar.

Maddy's bladder was bursting, and she used the commode gladly. She was ravenous, too, and she ate the bread and soup quickly, sitting cross-legged on the floor. He came in as soon as she had finished. Maddy knew the drill. She let herself be pushed back on the bed, face down, hands up. Her ankles and hands were tied swiftly, then she was turned around like a sack of potatoes.

She looked at his dark shape, moving at the base of the bed. An idea came to her. She made noises, muffled by the tape. He came over and examined her closely.

"You want to say something?"

Maddy nodded. "Forget it." He made to move away, and Maddy kicked against the railings. He stopped.

"OK," he said in that weird voice. "I thought you were going to be an adult about this, but it's now time for your injections." He reached inside his pocket and drew out a syringe and vial. Maddy watched in horror as he took the lid off the syringe, and plunged the needle through the rubber top of the vial.

Maddy tried to lift her head, and she shook herself, grabbing his attention. Exasperated, he put down the syringe and vial on the table, and walked over to her. He held the knife at her throat, and his eyes glinted with fury.

"If you scream or shout, I'm going to slit your fucking throat. Got that?"

Maddy nodded. Without ceremony, he pulled back the duct tape that was covering her mouth. She almost screamed in pain as the tape was removed. She felt his hand clamp over her mouth. He had soft hands, she couldn't help but notice. She felt the tip of the sharp knife against her chin, pushing her head back on the pillow.

"Now speak softly, and make it quick."

Maddy swallowed several times before she could get the words out. "My daddy will pay for you to release me." Her voice was hoarse. "I can give you his number. Just call him and say what you want. I swear..." Her words were lost as he pulled the duct tape back over her lips.

He threw his head back and laughed. "You think this is about money, Maddy? I don't give a damn about money. You have no idea what this is about. You," he pushed the knife in a little further, drawing a drop of dark crimson, "are just a pawn in this game."

CHAPTER 9

The incident room on the ground floor of Clapham Common Police Station was buzzing. Arla had arrived at 7 am, and nursing her coffee and croissant from the canteen, she had arranged the paperwork. The incident room was adjacent to the open-plan detectives' office. It seated more than 50, and was lined by a row of computers, printers and fax machines at the corners.

A whiteboard was up at one end, with a projector screen next to it. The screen would not be used today, but the laptop needed to connect to the projector suspended from the ceiling was present and fully charged. Arla had used it often to do a PowerPoint presentation when needed. For most occasions, though, the whiteboard and brainstorming were enough.

Photos of Maddy, and her friend Maya, as the last person who had seen her, had been stuck up on the whiteboard.

The last few people came in, and Arla took her place at the lectern and cleared her throat. "Settle down, guys." From the corner of her eye, she spotted Johnson coming in and closing the door softly shut.

"Name of missing person is Madeleine Burroughs, known to everyone as Maddy. She was last seen at the end-of-term drinks for her school, Brunswick College in Clapham, a private coeducational sixth-form college. By all accounts she was drunk at the pub, but then so were all her friends. At 20.00, she decided to walk back on her own. That was the last anyone saw of Maddy."

"CCTV?" Sergeant James Bennett, a keen detective whom Arla liked, asked, after raising his hand.

"No CCTV in that region of Brockwell Park. You have to walk to the end of the road to the T-junction. We assume Maddy was walking there to catch the bus from the main road."

James spoke up again. "Could she have been meeting a boyfriend? A secret rendezvous?"

"We haven't taken statements from school or friends as yet. All of that will be done from today."

Arla continued. "She had a mobile phone, which has gone with her. We are in contact with the telephone company to get the last signal. She had a laptop at home, and plain clothes are going today with us to collect all her belongings from her home."

Arla held up a finger. "One thing you must all remember. She is a diplomat's daughter, and full credit to the family for not panicking about this and going to the media. We cannot send uniforms or marked cars to her address. The family want this kept from the press while we conclude our rapid investigation."

Johnson raised his gravelly voice from the doorway where he was standing. "The Home Office is watching every move we are making. As you can imagine, this is a transatlantic affair now, and every effort is being made to keep it private. I repeat, no media, no press. If I hear anyone from this room has leaked anything to the media, they will be suspended without notice. If you want your job, keep your mouth shut."

Arla said, "We have to hit the national database for missing persons. I want all the detectives, from sergeant rank upwards, to monitor the database discreetly. If you find anything, please report directly to me or DI Harry Mehta." She pointed to Harry, who was towering next to her.

"I want call logs from the Burroughs' residence for three months prior to the disappearance. We will get Maddy's mobile number and get call logs from the phone company. As you can imagine, that will take some time."

"I can get the Home Office to put pressure on the phone company," Johnson chimed in from the door.

"Thank you, sir," Arla said. "I want call logs from the parents' numbers as well. This will be difficult and intrusive, and it depends on what I can get out of the parents. More importantly, Facebook and Twitter/WhatsApp accounts of the vic… I mean missing person. I want them downloaded as hard copies."

"At the same time, we tackle the school." Arla paused to take a sip of water. "Brunswick High might be a private, fee-paying school, but we need statements from every member of staff who has been in touch with Maddy. Students as well, obviously, and we have to be discreet, because we don't want news to spread too much."

James Bennett said, "I read the prelim report, guv: hope you don't mind." Arla flashed him a smile: she liked detectives taking initiative.

James continued. "In it, the parents have been in touch with the school already, so her friends and their families must be aware."

"Good point, which makes our job more tricky. But it has to be done. I know this is a pain. But we need to merge with the surroundings as much as we can. We need to walk into the school looking like parents picking up the children, not police officers with suits and badges."

"Somebody better tell Harry," Rob Pickering, one of the DIs, quipped. A smattering of laughter swept across the room. Harry was always the best-dressed person in the room. Eliot Ness, they called him, or Smooth Harry. Arla preferred Dirty Harry, which annoyed him no end.

"Who do you want in the team, Arla?" Johnson asked.

Arla craned her neck till she caught sight of Lisa Gayle's blonde locks in the middle of the room. Lisa's face broke into a grin.

Arla said, "DI Mehta, Sergeants Lisa, Rob and James."

"Will that be enough?"

"I'd rather be focused and fast, sir, than waste my time coordinating a big team. Besides, everyone here will keep their eyes and ears open."

Johnson nodded. Everyone stood up and stretched, dragging chairs back into the corners. As they filed out, Arla's eyes fell on the photos of Maddy staring out from the whiteboard. It was still the same holiday photo that she had seen last night, but the AV team had blown up the face and got a close-up. Next to the photo there was an e-fit as well, which would be redundant once the detectives had more photos from the family albums.

Sergeant James Bennett stepped into her circle. "Where do we start, guv?"

Arla liked the fresh-faced young man. She had been like him once, passionate about the job, eager to rise up the ranks. She took in his short, black hair, large and intelligent, grey eyes, and his square-cut jaw. He was a hit with the ladies as well, she knew that. In the office parties she had heard whispers, likening him to an Italian footballer, amidst the usual fit of giggles. His moves on the dance floor had many suitors.

She turned to Harry and raised her eyebrows. He shrugged. "You and I do the house first, I guess."

Lisa and Rob had gathered around them. Lisa said, "That way you don't have to dress like a dowdy 50-year-old dad picking up his daughter at the school, Harry."

Harry scowled at her and the others smirked. Arla said, "Park two streets down and walk in slowly. Lisa and Rob, you hit the school, James, stay here and get Maddy's social media accounts sorted out and the phone call logs." She registered the look of disappointment in James' face.

"The social media accounts and phone logs are critical. They can make or break this case. It's a big job." She looked at James, and suppressed a smile when he squared his shoulders, his eyes lively. "Meet back here at 16.00," Arla said. She glanced at Harry. "Let's move."

CHAPTER 10

The roads that encircle the roughly triangular expanse of Clapham Common contain the best of London's Victorian architecture. Built in the mid- to late-nineteenth century, the red-brick and white-eaved houses are tall and grandiose, built with the residences of the affluent City bankers in mind, when the mansions of Kensington and Knightsbridge became too expensive.

The buildings were still lovingly maintained. Floor-to-ceiling windows of multiple floors reflected the greenery of the Common opposite, whilst effectively hiding the opulence of their interiors. Arla watched from the passenger side window as the terraces appeared. They came off the South Circular, swept around the football fields and ponds of the park, and followed the A24 into a street called Narbonne Avenue. The elegant terraces gave way to grand mansions here, each building with front lawns mown to perfection, red-brick and sandstone edifices separated from each other by curved railings.

"Smell the money?" Harry asked.

Arla didn't answer. Harry said, "I smell the council estates three blocks away. Wonder if these rich people can."

London's juxtaposition of great wealth with widespread, deepening poverty had never made sense to Arla. How could a city where most of its citizens lived at or just above the poverty line boast so many multimillion-pound houses? Entire families were crammed into two-bedroom apartments, while the über-wealthy lived in houses with bathrooms the same size.

"Sure they can smell the estates, Harry. That's why they buy expensive perfumes." She blinked. "You know, like you. You smell like a department store at Christmas. Haven't met a man as vain as you, Harry."

Harry rolled his wide shoulders, and cracked his neck, almost a metre above her head. "I'm special. I got the rough, but hand out the smooth. Remember that."

"Rough with the smooth? Grow up, Harry."

They parked the car in the next street along, then walked back up the road. Arla rang the bell, Harry taking up position behind her. After what seemed like a long wait, the tall, shining black door opened slowly. A small, wizened old lady stood inside, dwarfed by the giant door, which extended a few inches above Harry's head. Her leathery, lined cheeks hung over her jaw. She peered at them.

"Can I help you?"

Arla opened her mouth to speak, but the clickety-clack of heels over the marble floor stopped her. A woman appeared, dressed in a dark maroon skirt, and similar-coloured blouse with cardigan. She didn't have any make-up on, and the attractive, late-forties face was pale and drawn.

"Go inside, Christy," she said. "You must be the detectives."

"Yes, ma'am," Arla said. They stepped inside and the woman shut the heavy door.

The hallway was wide, with a table in the middle that held a massive potted plant. The plant had white flowers that grew luxuriantly, and a few petals lay on the white marble floor.

"I am Mrs Burroughs," the woman said. "Are you Detective Arla Baker?"

Arla took out her badge and held it up. "DCI Baker," she said.

Mrs Burroughs stared at her for a few seconds. "This way," she said eventually, barely glancing at Harry. They passed two lounge rooms on either side, past a sweeping staircase wide enough to fit an elephant, to the end of the hallway into a conservatory.

Tropical plants leaned over them, giving off a pleasant but humid smell. There was a dining table in the middle with twelve chairs. The windows were open and a summer breeze filtered in, playing with the luminous green leaves. The table was empty, and they pulled up chairs to sit down.

Arla took her first proper look at the woman. Her accent was not American. It was English and polished. Southern Home Counties, public school-educated, if she had to put her money on it. She was attractive, her blonde hair tied back in a ponytail, large, hazel eyes over a sharp but small nose. Her mouth was generous with well-formed lips. She didn't smile, and Arla could see the rings under the hollows of her eyes.

"Mrs Burroughs, we better start at the beginning," she said.

"Before we do that, I would like to ask *you* something." Her tone was pointed, and not just because of the emphasis she put on *you*.

Arla stiffened and she heard Harry clear his throat gently. She knew he was trying to warn her. *Keep your cool.*

"DCI Baker, did you know my daughter?"

Arla shook her head. "No, I definitely did not. Look, Mrs Burroughs, whoever left that note is either a prankster or a very sick individual. I intend to get to the bottom of it, I assure you."

"Well, this individual knew that Maddy was..." She seemed to struggle for the word. "...Missing... and then wrote you would know about it. Seems like they were trying to tie you to Maddy."

"Or trying to drop me in it," Arla said.

"That is not my problem!" Mrs Burroughs lashed out suddenly, raising her voice. "Some weirdo who has a grudge against you could also be my daughter's kidnapper." She jabbed a finger at Arla, her jaw set tightly against her now reddening face. "That makes you responsible for what is going on."

"Now hang on a minute," Arla said, anger suddenly surfacing inside her. "What happened to your daughter has nothing to do with me. I understand that my name is involved here, but it could be a prankster from her school who dropped in that note. It could be anyone. All I'm doing is trying to help."

She felt Harry's hand on her arm. He said in a quiet voice, "Mrs Burroughs, we understand this is a very difficult situation for you. We want to do everything possible to get Maddy back home to you safely. To do that we need your help, and right now, this is not helping."

Mrs Burroughs glared back at them, her chest heaving. Then a cloud seemed to pass over her features. She put her elbow on the table and held her forehead, closing her eyes. Harry and Arla exchanged a quick glance. They gave the woman a moment. She looked up at them eventually, and sat back in the chair.

"OK. What do you want to know?"

CHAPTER 11

Arla felt she was being judged, and it was not a nice feeling.
Victims' families could get emotional and angry: dealing with them
was part of every cop's job. But this was uncharted territory. She had
to try and disguise the sense of unease she felt.
"Tell us more about Maddy, please. What sort of a girl she was, who
her friends were, everything."
Mrs Burroughs sniffed. She took out a handkerchief and dabbed her
eyes. "Maddy was just a normal, fun-loving, happy girl. She was
captain of the volleyball team at school, good at her studies. The
teachers loved her. We always had glowing reports."
"Any brothers or sisters?"
"Tom is thirteen and goes to Ridley's, a boys' school in Dulwich. He
is so sad about all this."
Arla said, "We will need to speak to him as well. Do you have any
other children?"
Mrs Burroughs shook her head. Arla asked, "Were you married or in
a relationship before this?"
"No."
Harry asked, "Did Maddy seem bothered by anything in the days
before she disappeared? Was she upset, or did she get any phone
calls? Anything that might seem out of the ordinary?"
She shook her head. "You know what young girls are like these
days. She has her own phone and laptop, and she spends hours on it.
The web server we have at home blocks adult sites, but who knows
what she does outside?" She looked up at them, the defiance in her
face appearing briefly. "But she wasn't that type of girl. I know it."
"Did she have a boyfriend?" Arla asked.
The diplomat's wife pursed her lips. "Once, when she was in the
shower, I went through her phone. She changed passwords often, but
the new text was on the screen, so I could read it."
She continued. "The text said something like I need to see you.
Usual place. Love Michael."
"When was this?" Arla asked.

"Maybe a month ago? Not more than that. She was very particular about her phone. I never saw it left with her clothes or on her desk. She kept it to herself."

"You paid for it?"

"Yes. I got her a £20 card every month. Whether she topped it up, I can't tell."

Arla thought back to the case files. "She didn't have her bag on her that night, did she?"

Her mother shook her head. "No. There was an end-of-year disco at the school, and then some of them went to the pub as it's near the school. Maddy knew that she had to be back home by 10. I did tell her not to come home alone." She paused and her head sank on her hand again.

Arla felt a flutter of sympathy. This poor woman was putting on a brave face to the devastation she was feeling inside. Her features were as thin as her bony hands. Arla doubted she was eating or sleeping much.

"Mrs Burroughs, would you mind if we saw Maddy's room?" Arla asked gently.

The woman nodded and rose from her seat. They followed her up the winding staircase, their feet sinking in the soft carpet. The landing on the first floor was as wide as the hallway, with far fewer rooms. Mrs Burroughs turned right, and paused at the door before the larger room at the end of the hallway. The door of that room was shut, and Arla wondered if it was the master bedroom.

On Maddy's door a sign proclaimed it as her room in red letters on a wooden board. Below it was a sign that read 'No Entry'. Mrs Burroughs went inside, and Arla followed, pulling out gloves from her pocket.

"Has anyone apart from you been in this room?"

"No. I told the cleaner to stay away from it this week."

"Thank you. Would you mind waiting for us downstairs while we have a look around?"

Mr Burroughs looked uncertain for a while, then nodded. Harry clicked the door shut when she left. Arla stared at the posters of boy bands on the walls, and framed works of art. Some of the artworks were beautiful, and she looked at them closely. They were signed Maddy. Arla was impressed.

"Quite the artist, isn't she?" Arla pointed at the pictures. Harry came closer to inspect and hummed agreement. Arla moved to the table top, where the laptop was placed along with the usual teenagers' mess. Piles of pens, notebooks and A4 ring binder folders were scattered on the desktop. Pink friendship ribbons poked out of a drawer, and a tube of red glitter nail polish was left half-screwed on. Arla looked at some of the exercise books, and found homework and school projects in various degrees of completion.

She looked up at the bookshelf, and found paperbacks of vampire novels, a series on a teenage detective agency, all with gaudy, bold covers showing a woman or a group of women. She took one of the books down and looked through it. She repeated the process with a number of books, and stopped at a chick lit novel called *My Little Secret*. Inside there was a scrawl that said – 'To Maddy, let's do it again soon, Maya'. She moved her attention to the ring binders. They were labelled by their subject matter. She took down the psychology folder, and looked at the doodling on the inside of the hard cover.

Arla wrote the name down on her notebook. She tried to switch the laptop on, but it was out of charge. She turned around. Harry was on his knees, peering down below the bed. He reached inside and pulled out a gym bag. He unzipped it as Arla came and stood above him. There were two badminton rackets inside, and a volleyball. Apart from that the bag was empty.

Arla looked at the bedside table, drawers, and inside the dressing wardrobe. Apart from the usual teenage girl's paraphernalia, she didn't find anything else. Harry bagged the laptop and its battery, and they went downstairs. Mrs Burroughs came out of the conservatory.

"Did you find anything?" Her voice seemed hopeful.

Arla said, "We are still very early in the course of our enquiries, Mrs Burroughs. Please be patient with us. Is it OK if we take the laptop with us?"

The woman nodded. Arla said, "If you don't mind, we would also like to see the phones of the rest of the family. So you, your husband and son, if he has one."

Miss B seemed taken aback by this. Arla said smoothly, "It's just to cross-check. We will get the call log off Maddy's phone, and we want to make sure we have records of when you called her and vice versa."

The woman hesitated, then nodded. "You can check my phone, no problems. But my husband might be more difficult."

"Doesn't he have a personal phone that he uses for family and friends?"

She shrugged. "Yes, he does, but sometimes I think he gets work-related calls on it as well."

"We can ask him. By the way, does the name Cindy mean anything to you? As in, did Maddy have a friend called by that name?"

Miss B frowned, then shook her head. "I can't recall."

Harry asked, "What were the names of her close friends?"

The woman thought for a while. "Her best friend was Maya, the girl she was in the pub with. Her other friends were Sandra and Imogen. These were the ones she stayed in touch with, and whose parents we know as well."

"Thank you, Mrs Burroughs. We would like to come back to speak to your husband and son. Maybe sometime this evening?"

Mrs Burroughs nodded without speaking.

CHAPTER 12

Somewhere in the Midlands
Sixteen years ago

The Sisters of Mercy Convent Asylum was a cold, foreboding place at the end of the hill on Church Road. Made of grey-brick stone, it stood darker than a mass of clouds against the fading sky. Candles were lit on the stained-glass windows, the watery light dying quickly in the gathering darkness. Stray yellow leaves blew against the stone façade, dead leaves, spines hardened by three months of winter. Cynthia and Gareth both looked down at their bowls of steaming soup as Father Justinius walked slowly past them. None of the children dared to raise their eyes to Father Justinius. His pale blue eyes seemed empty, devoid of feeling. Cynthia watched from the corner of her eye as he went out of earshot. Both she and Gareth were nine years old. The children at the tables around them were aged between five and ten. After that age they were sent to another asylum, or to a social care centre. If they were lucky, they would be paired with a foster family.

Cynthia wished she could use a hairbrush to her straggly hair that was getting longer. When one of the Mothers used a hairbrush on her, they pulled so hard it made her cry. If she complained she got slapped in return. Experience had taught her to keep her hair greasy and tangled. Washing it once a week was easier, but there was no hairbrush in the toilets.

As she ate, she looked down at Gareth's knuckles. They were swollen from the caning he got last week. He had been the last one to leave the playground yesterday, and Father Justinius had to come looking for him. Cynthia knew Gareth wouldn't be making that mistake again.

Gareth's fingers shook as he broke a piece of brown bread and dipped it in the soup.

"What are you looking at?" he whispered to Cynthia.

"How's your hand?" she whispered back.

Gareth grimaced. "Hurts to make a fist and to hold the spoon."

"Silence!" a loud adult voice roared. There was deathly quiet in an instant. Cynthia didn't have to look up to know who the voice belonged to. Mother Margaret was a buxom, portly matron who was never shy with the whip. She was standing at the top of the stairs, hands on hips.

The rest of the dinner passed in silence. Cynthia, Gareth, and another boy called William shared bunk beds in a room. All the children stood in a line as the matron opened each of the doors with a long, iron key. When they went inside, she came down the line again, shutting each of the doors.

Night was the worst time. Once the candles on the windows were snuffed out, the terror arrived.

Gareth and William were four months younger than Cynthia. When they heard the heavy boots clomping up the stairs, they climbed down from their beds and snuggled into hers. Cynthia was pushed against the wall, but she put an arm around them.

"Shhh, boys, if he hears us he will come in."

"I'm scared, Cynthia," Gareth whispered, his voice broken.

"Shush, then!"

The footsteps grew heavier, then louder still as they came towards their door. The three children huddled even closer together on the bunk bed. The steps grew slower, and then stopped right outside their door. A weight shifted, and the sound of a key chain jangled. The children held their collective breath, wide-eyed with terror.

Then the steps moved on. They became softer, but they knew the man was moving from one cell to the other, trying to decide which child to pick up tonight. He preferred boys: they knew that from the scars they had seen during bath time.

The sound of a door creaking open made their hearts freeze. When the screaming started, they held each other so tight Cynthia thought her bones would crack. The screaming grew louder, then a wail as the body was dragged past their cell by the man. A slap sounded, and with sobs the body was pulled down the stairs into the cellar. A door slammed, and there was silence.

"He's going to come for us, Cynthia. Soon he's going to come for me or William."

Cynthia held them close, staring up at the impenetrable darkness. She stayed awake long after the boys were fast asleep.

CHAPTER 13

Harry's phone buzzed as they walked past the well-tended green lawns and gleaming cars of Millionaires' Row. He spoke briefly, then hung up.

"Lisa's at the school."

"Good. Tell her we're coming."

Harry sent off a text and they got inside the black BMW. Harry loosened his tie and draped his jacket on the headrest of the driver's seat.

"What do you reckon?" Harry asked as he drove out.

"Something I can't put my finger on. She seems like a normal teenager, but some of those books she was reading were for an adult woman. Someone called Cindy had gifted them to her."

"You mean an adult woman called Cindy?"

"Or a friend. Could be either."

With the traffic on Clapham High Street, it took more than half an hour to get to Brunswick High School. They parked in the next block along, and Harry took off his tie, and folded his jacket away. Arla took off her short, black coat, and from the trunk took out a light summer cardigan.

It was past 11, and the school was quiet. The precaution of appearing informal was perhaps excessive at this time with no parents around, but Arla was following orders.

The school was a giant Victorian mansion, mostly red-brick, and taking up a corner block. It had an annex, a glass and white-brick modern construction that contrasted tastefully with the old-style building. They had to buzz at the gates, and Harry said they had an appointment with the senior school principal. He gave his name, but not his job title.

As the gates began to swing open, Lisa and Rob came running from the side road. Arla waited till Lisa caught up with them, walking fast.

"Sorry," Lisa gasped. "We went for a coffee thinking you'd be late."

"Nope. Let's go in," Arla said. They entered the main school courtyard, and walked up the steps to the reception, at whose doors they had to be buzzed in again. Lisa and Rob remained outside.

Harry hung back while Arla asked for the principal, with whom an appointment had already been made. She spoke to the man, who instructed them to attend his office.

They came out of the reception, and walked up to another set of gates where they had to press another buzzer and wait. The gates were tall, with iron spikes on top. Inside, Arla could see a cement courtyard with playing fields, and classrooms arranged around the courtyard.

"Like Fort Knox, this place," Lisa grumbled.

"I know," Arla said. "No chance of anyone walking in here, so we can exclude girls talking to strangers."

They walked across the courtyard into another office block that said 'Senior School Reception'. Arla instructed Rob and Lisa to wait in reception while she and Harry went up to the third-floor office. The door opened before they could knock. Arla saw a slim, well-kept man in a dark suit. He was tall, but shorter than Harry, and had grey hair cut short. Mid- to late-forties, Arla guessed, and from his athletic, toned figure she knew he looked after himself.

"You must be DCI Arla Baker," the man said. "I'm Mr Charles Atkins, senior school principal. Do come in."

Arla was impressed that he knew her correct title. Most people called her Detective. They walked in, and Mr Atkins shook hands with Harry as well. After introductions, they sat down opposite his large desk where piles of paper were arranged neatly, and a desktop PC hummed in one corner.

Charles Atkins had intelligent, intense black eyes, and he stared at Arla with interest. A good-looking man, Arla noted, ignoring the little tingle she felt as she looked back at him.

It was Atkins who opened the conversation. "I take it you are here about Madeleine Burroughs."

They nodded. Atkins continued, a gloomy look descending upon his features. "This is the first time something like this has happened at our school. I mean, every school has pupils who will be difficult. But never has a child disappeared. Have you found anything as yet?" he concluded with an eager look on his face.

"No." Arla shook her head. "We are still at the beginning of our enquiries."

Mr Atkins looked deflated. Harry said, "Tell us about Madeleine."

"She was a good girl. Exemplary student. Liked by everyone. She was captain of the volleyball team."

"What about her friends?"

"She was popular. I'm sure you can ask around for her friends."

"Did she have a boyfriend?"

Atkins shrugged. "This is a co-ed school, Miss Baker. Boys and girls do mix, as you know. Most of it is kept quiet. We, as the teachers, know the least about their private lives. They are older teenagers."

Arla took out her notebook. She preferred the older-style book, despite knowing she could jot down names on her iPhone Notes app. "We have some names here – Maya Patel and Imogen Sparks. Apparently they were her closest friends?"

Atkins said, "I didn't know specific names, but they were the two girls who were contacted when she went missing. Mrs Burroughs got in touch with the parents, and informed us as well."

"Did Maddy – sorry, that's her nickname – have a locker in the school?" Arla asked.

"Yes. All girls have a gym locker. It's been looked in already, and it's empty."

Arla thought back to the gym bag she had seen under Maddy's bed. Something told her she should have taken it back to the station as evidence.

"We would still like to see the locker. Which year and class did she belong to?"

"13E. The form teacher is Miss Macinnes. She is aware that you will be speaking to her today."

"Good." Arla gazed at Mr Atkins. "Anything else you would like to add?"

For the first time, she thought Mr Atkins looked uncomfortable. For a few seconds, the relaxed veneer slipped and his eyes were troubled. He recovered quickly, but Arla knew she had something. "No, nothing else."

"You sure you didn't hear anything else about Maddy?"

Mr Atkins was back to his suave self. "No. But if I do, you will be the first to know, I can assure you." He stood up quickly. "Shall I show you the lockers?"

Was he under pressure from the family? Arla wondered. Maybe the Home Office, or the US Embassy had rung, asking to see him.

Mr Atkins held the door open for them, a hint of a polite smile on his face. They walked down to the reception, where Arla introduced Rob and Lisa to Mr Atkins. Rob and Lisa would hang around, speaking to members of staff and students. They took the tarmac road around the playing fields, and approached the white sports hall building when the doors burst open, and a gaggle of shrieking young students rushed out. In a few seconds, they were in the middle of a crowd of screaming, excited teenagers, waving hockey sticks, laughing and shouting. Arla noted they were all girls.

"Time for an inter-school hockey match!" Mr Atkins shouted to make his voice heard above the commotion. "I'm afraid we didn't choose our time very well."

The navigated past the pummelling bodies, and got to the door of the sports centre, where Mr Atkins pressed his code on the keypad. The row of lockers were on the right, stretching down the corridor. The principal opened one of them, and Arla took a look inside. A poster of a semi-naked boy band group was stuck inside the door, pouting and posing. The rest of the locker was empty, as if it had been cleaned out recently. Too clean, Arla thought to herself.

"Do you mind if we send the fingerprint technicians down to take prints from the locker?"

Mr Atkins pursed his lips. "You can, but is there any need for it?"

Harry said, "Mr Atkins, at this stage, the broader our scope is, the better. As we get more clues, we can narrow our investigation down further."

"No problem," Mr Atkins said. "We must do everything we can to get Maddy back."

"If there is break going on, is it possible to interview Maddy's friends now?"

Mr Atkins nodded. "It's best if we do that back at the office."

When they returned to Reception, Arla took Lisa to one side. "I want you and Rob to go around, speaking to the other teachers and students about the principal. Ask about Maddy as well, obviously. But I want more background on Mr Atkins."

The principal emerged from the reception office as Arla came back. He said, "I have informed the relevant girls' tutors to send them here. You can use the office next door to conduct your interviews."

"Thank you. This is far better than asking the girls to attend the police station."

"Of course."

CHAPTER 14

Imogen Sparks looked nervous. She fidgeted in her chair and kept crossing her arms across her chest, pulling her cardigan in the process. Arla smiled at her, trying to put the teenager at ease. Imogen looked from Harry to Arla, then back at her.

"OK, Imogen, how are you?"

"I am fine. This is about Maddy, isn't it?"

"Yes, she was your friend, wasn't she?"

"Yes." Imogen's eyes sank down to her lap, and she played with her fingers.

"How did you get to know her?"

"We played in the volleyball team in year 11." Her eyes lit up. "We beat Latimer and Wimbledon High in the inter-school cup final that year."

Arla smiled widely. "That must've been good."

"The best." Her expression faltered, eyes losing their shine. "Where could she be?"

"Imogen, I need you to think about this carefully. What happened that night after your end-of-term party?" Arla glanced at her notebook. "The third of June."

"The party at the school was small, in the theatre hall. We had some soft drinks and a disco. Then we went home. Maddy, Maya and I went to the pub."

"Did you walk there?"

"Yes, it's close by. Fifteen-minute walk."

"What time was that?"

"About 6 pm."

"Can you think of anyone following you?"

Imogen shrugged. "No."

Arla pictured three happy teenagers going from one party to another, without a care in the world. Would they be aware of someone following them? Unlikely.

"Did Maddy have a boyfriend?" Arla asked.

Imogen looked coy. "Umm, no, don't think so."

"Don't think so, or won't tell?" Arla asked.

The teenager looked uncomfortable. "I don't know."

Arla sighed. Harry went to say something, but she kicked him under the table and shot him a glance. Arla gestured with her eyebrows. Harry frowned, irritation passing across his features. Without a word, he rose and left.

When Harry had shut the door behind him, Arla focused on Imogen. "Maddy is missing, Imogen. She doesn't have anywhere to live, and she doesn't have any money. That means she is living with someone, or someone has grabbed her. Unless she is living rough on the streets, which could happen, but I doubt it. If you don't help us, then we can't find her."

Imogen stared down at her lap again, fingers entwining. "OK. No one knows about this. But Maddy had a boyfriend."

Arla sat up straighter. "Is he at this school?"

Imogen nodded. Arla asked, "What's his name?"

Imogen hesitated. Arla repeated her question.

"Paul Ofori."

"Which year?" Arla was scribbling quickly.

"13D. Oh please, I won't get into trouble for this, will I?"

"No, you won't. Why should you?"

Imogen darted her eyes around, avoiding Arla's. "No reason, just asking."

"Stay here."

Arla went outside, and almost bumped into Harry standing outside the door. She gave him the boy's name, and Harry went off to ask the principal. She glanced at the sofa, where another girl awaited, looking relaxed and cool with her sunglasses on.

"Are you Maya Patel?" Arla asked.

The girl nodded without taking the sunglasses off. "I'll be with you shortly," Arla said.

Imogen looked at Arla with big, scared eyes. "What's going on?"

There was something about the girl's demeanour that bothered Arla. She seemed more nervous than before.

"Don't worry. We just want to speak to Paul, the same as we spoke to you. Do you know if Paul was supposed to be meeting Maddy that evening?"

"I...uh..."

"Imogen, if you tell us the truth now, it'll be a lot easier later on, I promise you."

Imogen swallowed hard and her chest heaved. She looked down again. "Yes," she said in a very small voice.

"Carry on."

"Paul was with his mates at the pub. He had a plan with Maddy to meet outside, in Brockwell Park."

Arla understood. They were going to go off into the park. Something had happened to Maddy between leaving the pub and meeting up with Paul.

"Thank you, Imogen. That will be all for now, but when you go out, could you please send Maya in?"

Imogen nodded and left quickly. Maya Patel came in. She was an Asian girl who wore hoop earrings and jeans ripped at the knees, and chewed bubble gum. Headphones were fastened on her ears, and sunglasses raised on her head. She breezed in and sat down on the chair opposite Arla without being asked to.

"What?" she asked with a sullen stare.

Arla sighed. She introduced herself, and why she wanted to speak to Maya. She asked the teenager the same questions as she had asked Imogen, and the teenager answered haltingly.

"So, you were the last person to see Maddy before she disappeared?" Arla asked.

Something came to life in Maya's eyes. A new alertness. "There were other people in the pub," she said defensively.

"But you were the only person who came out with her, right?"

"And?"

"That makes you the last person to see her. Where did she say she was going?"

Maya had stopped chewing her gum. She was slouching in her chair and crossed one leg, then played with her hair. Arla repeated her question.

"Home," Maya shrugged vaguely.

Arla leaned forward. "Don't lie to me, Maya, because I can take you down to the station and make you give me a statement. Do you know what happens if you make a false statement to the police?"

Maya maintained eye contact with Arla, but her earlier bravado was gone. She narrowed her eyes slightly, then said, "Like I said…"

"Tell me about Paul Ofori," Arla interrupted. The change of topic worked. From the look in her eyes, Arla knew she hadn't expected that.

"13D. Paul was Maddy's boyfriend, wasn't she?"

"I don't know."

Arla snapped her notebook shut and stood up abruptly, pushing her chair back. "Maya Patel, I want you to come down to the Common police station with me. If you resist, then I will have no choice but to arrest you, as you are a material witness in the disappearance of Madeleine Burroughs."

The teenage rebel cracked. Maya was sitting bolt upright, and her mouth was open, breathing heavily.

"No, wait…"

Arla paused, fixing Maya with a stare. Maya nodded. "Yes, Maddy was going out with Paul. But no one knew about it."

"Why not?"

Maya looked away. "You know."

"Parents? Teachers?"

Maya shrugged. "Of course. Her parents would have a fit if they knew."

Arla frowned. "So when you left Maddy, she was going to meet Paul in Brockwell Park?"

Maya nodded. "And then what happened?"

"Nothing. We stayed in the pub for a while, then we all left. I got back home for ten. My parents can confirm it."

"And when did you hear about Maddy missing?"

"She wasn't at school the next day, or the day after. I rang her phone but it was switched off. Then the principal called, asking about her."

Arla kept her eyes on Maya as she spoke. Something about the teenager bothered Arla. She was too calm and self-assured. Her answers were practised, like someone had told her what to say. It was in marked comparison to the angst that Imogen had shown.

"Are you and Imogen Maddy's best friends?"

Maya sighed and leaned her head back, like she was tired of being asked the same question. "Kind of."

"Maya, you need to help me out here. I need a proper answer."

"OK, OK. Imogen's alright but she's, you know…"

"What?"

Maya lifted both hands, and pointed the forefinger of each hand outwards. Then she drew a square in the air.

Arla suppressed a smirk with an effort. "She's a nerd? Square?"

"Miss goody two-shoes. Butter wouldn't melt. You know the type."

Arla raised her eyebrows. This was a world she hadn't inhabited for almost twenty years. Had she been like Maya when she was seventeen?

"So, what are you? Miss Cool? Got lots of friends? Your phone keeps ringing?" Arla raised her eyebrows, keeping tongue firmly in cheek.

"Nah, I didn't say that." Maya gave that whole teenage body shrug again. "Just normal, you know."

"Normal," Arla repeated. "Did you meet Paul after Maddy went missing?"

Maya shook her head slowly. "Once, in between lessons. He said he hadn't seen Maddy that night. He waited for her in the park, then went home."

"Is this how they normally met, in the park?"

"I don't know, do I? Maddy didn't tell me everything."

There was a knock on the door. Harry jutted his head in.

"You need to hear this," he said.

CHAPTER 15

Arla glanced at Maya. "Can I please have your phone number and
address? We need to speak to you again."
Maya looked hesitant. Gently, Arla said, "I can always get it from
the school. This is a police enquiry now, and the more you
cooperate, the less we have to bother you later."
Arla flicked her notebook to an empty page and pushed it to the
teenager. Maya blew out her cheeks, looking very much like an adult
for a while. Then she grabbed the pen and scribbled.
"Thank you," Arla said. Maya rose and slipped out of the room
without glancing at Arla.
Harry said, "Paul Ofori isn't at school today. He's got a bug,
apparently."
"That usual for him?"
"Apparently not. I just spoke to his form tutor: he keeps good
attendance. But he has had disciplinary issues."
"Like what?"
"Got into some fights that teachers have had to separate, and so on."
"He could well lead us to Maddy," Arla said. She explained to Harry
what she had learned.
"I've got his address," Harry said. "Might as well pay him a visit."
They left Lisa and Rob at the school and walked back to the BMW.
As they walked down the courtyard to the main gates, Charles
Atkins stood framed in the window of his office, watching them.
When they had walked through the gate, he picked up his phone.
With trembling fingers, he dialled the number he needed to.
*****
Harry drove back towards Clapham. It was hot, and he had put the
windows up and turned the air con on. Arla looked at the sun beating
down on the pink and brown bodies tanning on the Common,
laughter and echoes carrying in the breeze, the sultry promise of
summer heavy in the air.
She noticed Harry was heading back towards the council estates at
the border between Clapham North and Stockwell, where the police
station was situated.
"Where are we going?" she asked.
"Well, this is the address I got." He pointed at the sat nav. "32 Union
Square. That's near the nick."

Arla frowned. "Seems like the wrong end of town for a posh, rich family to be living in."

"You never know, Arla." When they were on their own, Harry referred to her by her first name, saving 'guv', or 'guvnor' for the station. She wouldn't admit it, either to herself or to Harry, that she liked it.

"Never know what?"

"Lots of new housing these days. Brand new flats where you wouldn't expect them."

Harry bleated his horn a couple of times to get through a clutch of traffic by the lights at Clapham North tube station, then they finally arrived after streaking down Union Road.

Arla stared out at the row of squat, brown, single-storey council houses. None of it looked privately owned, and as she watched, a ponderous, wide-hipped African woman, decked out in a yellow, red and blue robe with matching headgear, stepped out of one of the houses. She crossed the road in front of their car, without paying them any attention.

Arla said, "You sure you got the address right?"

Harry checked in his phone. "Yup, definitely."

The street ahead ended in a cul-de-sac, and beyond it was the familiar vista of inner-city London, an apartment block of art deco style, several floors tall, one of many built in the 60s and 70s, to house London's growing multiracial and working population. Rap music blared from a nearby window, and colourful graffiti lined the wall. The graffiti was artistic, of various human figures, and served to liven up the drab cul-de-sac atmosphere.

They stepped out and Arla walked to number 32. The net curtain of the window facing the street twitched. After a while, when Arla was thinking of knocking again, a bolt withdrew from inside, and the door opened slightly.

An Afro-Caribbean woman's face peeked out. Her hair was curls, and she was dressed in a T-shirt and slacks.

"Can I help you?" she asked, eyebrows knotted together. She glanced from Arla to Harry, eyes suspicious. She was in her early fifties, Arla guessed, thick around the waist and hips, with a face that had remained attractive despite the years.

Arla introduced herself and produced badges. "Does Paul Ofori live here?"

A look of concern creased the woman's features. She opened the door wider, stepping out.

"That's my son. What's going on?"

"We need to ask him some questions regarding the disappearance of a student from his school."

The woman raised her eyebrows. "The school?"

"Yes. Are you his mother?"

"Yes. You better come in."

Arla and Harry stepped inside. The interior was simple but clean, whitewashed walls, cheap, framed photos of Paul and his mother on the wall. There was a woman in the photos as well, who Arla guessed was Paul's sister. They were holiday snaps of the three of them on a tropical island, and one in front of the Albert Hall.

The hallway was cramped, and a staircase rose from their right onto the upper floor. Miss Ofori craned her neck up and shouted her son's name. After the third shout, loud music floated down from upstairs. There was a sound of a door slamming, then a crashing noise came from the rear of the house.

Arla's head snapped up, her nerves suddenly taut like a steel cable. Miss Ofori was blocking her way, but Arla pushed past her, Harry following.

"Hey!" the woman protested, but Arla was at the top of the stairs by then. The floorboards creaked under her boots as she ran to the end of the small hallway, at the rear, where the sound had come from. The door to a room was shut and locked when she tried to open it. She took two steps back, then kicked it hard with the flat of her shoe. Her thick runner's leg was coiled with muscle, and on the second kick the barrel of the lock snapped out of the door frame.

The box room was tiny, with barely enough space for a small desk after the bed was fitted in. Posters of football players and female rap stars appeared to make the walls shrink even further. Arla had seen hundreds of rooms like this – in drug busts and chasing criminals. This room was a pleasant deviation: it seemed like a normal teenager's room, without the smell of skunk cannabis or smoke. A pile of folders was neatly arranged on the desktop, and three shelves on the wall bore more books.

Arla saw none of this but the open window. She ran to it and looked out of the lifted sash – the roof of the kitchen jutted out, providing a good landing spot. She looked up, and saw a fence at the rear of the small garden, and a row of houses along, all separated by fences, clothes drying on lines. Then she spotted the running figure, scrambling over a fence, and vanishing into a garden.

Harry brushed past her, and sat on the window ledge, dangling his legs down. Then he jumped, landing on his feet on the flat roof.

"I'll cut him off from the other side!" Arla yelled, heading for the stairs. She took out her radio as she ran down the stairs. Miss Ofori was standing on the landing, her mouth open. She began to say something, but Arla was already out of the door.

"Base, this is DCI Baker. Chasing suspect in 32 Union Square, request backup. Repeat, request backup."

She didn't wait to hear the response in the crackle of the radio, shoving it in her trouser pocket. She ran back the way she had come, picking up pace as she came around the corner. A group of young men scattered as she almost ploughed into them. The street lined up with houses whose gardens faced the Oforis and Arla's plan was to run to the end, and wait for Paul to show. He had to exit that way. Harry would chase up behind him, and between them, they had him trapped.

Panting, Arla got to the end of the street and looked around her. Her radio was buzzing but she ignored it. She was in a row of terraced houses, small abodes all stuck together, and she considered knocking on them to get inside one and access their garden. Paul had no way out but through one of these houses.

She heard the distant wail of sirens, and took the radio out, looking at the street address as she did so.

"I'm standing outside 24 Trevelyan Road," she barked on the radio. She strode to the house and knocked rapidly on the door. When there was no answer she rapped on the window. Still no joy. She went to the next door along and had better luck this time. An old man opened the door, and stared in alarm when Arla flashed her badge. She brushed past him into a stinking hovel of old carpets and fading, dark green wallpaper, a house stuck in a time warp from 50 years ago. The narrow hallway led into the kitchen, which was similarly decrepit, but it gave her access to the postage stamp-sized garden. There was a tree in the corner, and she climbed up it to have a look at the neighbours. She saw rows of clothing lines, fences, but no sign of a running teenager. A movement caught her eye, and she caught sight of Harry's long legs straddling a fence awkwardly. He jumped down and dropped from her sight.

"Harry, I'm here!" she shouted, and waved at him. Arla did a 360, but there was no sign of Paul Ofori. She told Harry the house number and then went to the front. Two rapid response police cars had pulled up, and uniforms were spilling out of them. They saw Arla and ran over to her. She explained the situation quickly.

"Fan out and knock on the houses down this street. Aim to have eyes along the back of this whole terrace," Arla said. Harry appeared next to her, panting, sweat pouring down his face.

"Did you see him?" Arla asked.

"Nope. Did you?"

"Great," Arla fumed. This made their job harder now. The uniforms would have to do a search of all the houses. That took up too many men and women, and the force was stretched as it was with the recent budget cuts. She would have to explain to Johnson why she had authorised such an extensive manhunt, and if she had nothing to show for it she would be in trouble.

A thought struck her. She whirled around to Harry. "If Paul has friends here, and I suspect he does, then he could just be hiding in one of these houses."

"Or he might have slipped out, using the same friend's house, before we could get to him."

"Damn." Arla chewed her lower lip. "Let the uniforms do their search still. Shame we don't have a photo of him. Let's get back to his house, before his mother leaves for work or something."

They walked back briskly to Paul's house.

CHAPTER 16

Somewhere in the Midlands
Fifteen years ago

Cynthia and Gareth stood shivering in front of the window. Down below, lamps illuminated a portion of the apple orchard. Flames glowed on kerosene-soaked paper torches, held on a wooden stick. Gareth whimpered. Cynthia held his hand tight and shushed him. Three figures moved below in the cold night, devoid of stars. Cynthia could recognise the shape of Father Justinius and Aiden. The other shape she couldn't make out, but they were all men. Two of them had spades, and they were digging a hole at the base of a tree. When the small, white bundle was lowered into the makeshift grave, a sob caught at Gareth's throat, and he leaned into Cynthia. She put her thin arm around his bony shoulders, drawing her into him.
"Goodbye William," Gareth whispered. Cynthia didn't say anything, or try to wipe her tears away.
Sleep was difficult that night, but for once, the heavy steps didn't shake the narrow corridor. Cynthia didn't know when she had fallen asleep, but when she woke up with a start she realised she was being shaken. The moon face of one of the Mothers was frowning at her.
"Get dressed," the woman said in a heavy Irish accent. "Mother Margaret wants you downstairs, on your best behaviour." She turned to Gareth, who was cowering in the corner. "That goes for you, too." The woman stomped out of the room. They went to the bathroom, then got dressed quickly.
When they arrived in the big hall, they were marched into Mother Margaret's office. Four other children, three boys and one girl, stood cowering in one corner. Opposite them, a man and a woman in a suit. The man held a clipboard, and the woman was asking the children their names.
Mother Margaret glared at Cynthia. "You are late. This is Mr York and Miss Thomson from the social services. Say hello."

CHAPTER 17

Miss Ofori was in the kitchen when they got back to the house. She came bustling out, holding a steaming cup of coffee. Her dress was unchanged, and Arla got the impression she was leaving the house soon.

She glared at them when they came inside. "What the hell do you want now?"

Arla said, "Miss Ofori, we need to have a chat with you about your son."

Without speaking, the woman went into the dining room and Arla followed. Glass cabinets with brown, wooden shelves lined the wall of the room, and there was an old table in the middle, covered by a blue and white-striped tablecloth. At the rear of the room, a door opened out onto the patio, then the garden.

With a clunk, Miss Ofori put the cup on the table, spilling coffee. Arla opened up her notebook. "Could you please confirm your son's full name and DOB?"

When she did, Arla asked her full name. "Ayole Ofori," the woman said, hand on hip. "Would you mind telling me what the hell is going on?" Her eyes had daggers in them.

"As I mentioned," Arla said, "We need to speak to your son about a girl from his school who is missing."

"What girl?"

"Her name is Madeleine Burroughs." Arla took out the photo of Maddy that had been circulated, showing her face only. "Have you seen this girl?"

Miss Ofori came forward and peered at the photo. "Not sure. Paul does have some girls who come around here, but not sure if I have seen her."

"Why did Paul run away?"

Miss Ofori put her hands up in resignation, then let them fall to her sides. "How do I know? I just don't understand any of this. I was about to go to work, it was all peaceful, then you guys turn up and all hell breaks loose."

Harry asked, "Where do you work?"

"At St George's Hospital in Tooting Broadway. I am a midwife. And I'm going to be late for work now, thanks to you."

Arla said, "I'm sorry that you'll be late, Miss Ofori, but it wasn't our fault that Paul ran away. We just wanted to ask him some questions, then we would have left. Him running has made this situation much worse."

Miss Ofori sat down at the table, her face suddenly concerned. "You think Paul has something to do with this girl running away?"

"Why do you think she ran away?" Arla asked.

Miss Ofori looked puzzled. "Isn't that what you said?"

"I said missing. Are you sure she has not been here?"

"Like I told you, I am not sure. Look, I do night and evening shifts. Sometimes I come home in the early morning, or late at night. My job is not nine to five, you get me? I cannot keep an eye on Paul all the time. He can take care of himself, he's close to being an adult."

Arla nodded, it made sense. "Mind if we sit down?"

"OK. But make it quick."

"I will. How long has Paul been at the school?"

For the first time Miss Ofori's face brightened up. "He got a scholarship. He's a clever boy, always did well in school. When he was eleven, I wanted him to try the best schools around here. Lord knows the state schools in Clapham are full of troublemakers."

"So he got in via an entrance exam?"

"Yes. He did so well that they offered him a bursary for the school fees. But I still have to get money for his books and uniform. Also, in these schools they have expensive school trips, like to Val d'Isère in France for skiing." She stopped and stared down at her coffee.

"Does he go on the school trips?"

Miss Ofori took a sip of her coffee. "Well, not always." Her tone was guarded. "I feel bad when he cannot go, as all his friends can."

Harry asked, "Do you give him spending money?"

Miss Ofori avoided eye contact and sipped her coffee again. "Yes." Her tone was not convincing, and Harry met Arla's eyes.

"Do you know where Paul could be now?" Harry asked. "It's important that we find him."

The woman sighed. "Look, I want the best for my son. I always have. I know we don't have much. But I work hard, and I taught that to my children as well."

Arla nodded. "It seems that way. You have a daughter as well? I saw the photos."

"Yes. Adeola is now at university in Manchester."

Arla pressed on. "Have you seen any changes in Paul's behaviour recently? He's obviously a very bright boy. But we have reports at school of him getting into fights with some students."

Miss Ofori nodded, clearly unhappy. "Yes, I was called in as well. Paul, well, like all young men, he has a quick temper and he can be impulsive. His father…" Her voice trailed off.

"Go on," Arla said.

Miss Ofori looked out of the garden door, a vacant look on her face. "His father was a violent man. I was a victim of domestic violence. I ran away with the children, from Liverpool, and settled here." She shook her head. "It was all going so well."

Arla felt sorry for the woman. "Look, if Paul has nothing to hide, then we will not trouble him. But I'm afraid that him running off like this makes it look quite suspect. We need to find him."

Harry asked, "Did Paul have friends who came often? Or any new friends?"

Arla added, "Both from school and around here."

Miss Ofori thought for a while. "There is one boy he has been mixing with lately. I don't like him. He wears a red bandana on his head, and he has tattoos. He comes to Paul's room, and I know they smoke from the window."

"Cannabis?" Arla asked.

Miss Ofori nodded, her face like a storm. "I don't like that stuff in my house. It smells funny, not like normal cigarettes, so it must be that."

"What's this boy's name?"

"He's a man. Name is Sean, but calls himself T."

"T?"

"Yes."

"He's black?"

"Yes."

"Anything else about him you remember? Like what his tattoos are like?"

Miss Ofori frowned. "Actually I do. It's hot now, so he turns up wearing a half-sleeve vest. I see the words 'Z14' in black letters on his arms and going up his neck." She wrinkled her nose. "Odd."

Arla and Harry exchanged looks. Z14 could well be the name of a local gang.

Arla said, "Do you have a picture of Paul that you could lend us? A recent one, please. We will return it as soon as we have made some copies."

Miss Ofori suddenly looked panic-stricken. "Look, Paul's a good kid. I know he's acting strangely now, but his heart is in the right place. He has his whole life ahead of him. He's so young." She looked at them entreatingly. Arla felt a twinge of sympathy, but she also had a job to do.

"Like I said, if he has nothing to hide, then we are not interested in him. Can we please have a look at his room? Then we can let you get to work."

Miss Ofori led them to his room, then went to her bedroom to get the photo. In Paul's small box room, Harry knelt on the floor to have a look underneath the bed. He pulled out a stack of porn magazines. Arla was looking through the drawers of his desk. She found a packet of cigarettes with rolling paper inside. She took the cigarettes out. There was nothing inside the packet, but she could smell the cannabis. One of the cigarettes was wilting, half-empty of tobacco. A sure sign that it had been used to roll a joint.

She showed it to Harry as he stood up, then pulled out a specimen bag from her pocket and bagged the packet. She was going to say something, when she heard a commotion downstairs and Miss Ofori's loud voice.

CHAPTER 18

She followed Harry out into the landing. Three voices were arguing, and Arla thought she could recognise Lisa Moran's. But the loudest voice was Miss Ofori's.

Arla came down the stairs. "They're with me," she said.

"Oh, I should have guessed. Come here to have a party, have you?" the irate midwife said. Lisa was about to say something, her blonde hair plastered to her forehead, face bright pink in the heat.

Arla interrupted. "Guys, let's go outside. Harry, stay inside and finish the room search." She took the Lisa and Rob out onto the street, and Miss Ofori slammed the door shut behind them.

"Rude bitch," Rob muttered.

"Go easy on her. Trying to raise a kid in this neighbourhood can't be easy. And I don't think she knows much of what's going on. But she did tell me about a man who visits, and looks like a gang member." She told them about the man called Sean T. A car pulled up behind them, lights flashing silently. They turned to look and James Bennett came out running from the driver's side.

"I thought you were looking through Maddy's social media accounts," Arla said, irritated that he had overlooked her order.

"It's my fault, guv," Lisa apologised. "When I heard it's hit the fan over here, I thought you might be in trouble, and we needed all hands on deck. I called him."

Arla looked at the bright, enthusiastic face of James and couldn't rebuke him. "I guess you will come in useful. Go inside, wear gloves and don't touch anything. See if Harry needs help upstairs. Show your badge to the woman."

James nodded happily and strode off. Lisa, Rob and Arla walked back to the street where the uniforms were doing the door-to-door. It was more than a simple door-to-door, however. If Paul was hiding in any of these houses, Arla knew they would need a search warrant. Which meant paperwork and a major waste of time. Arla had policed enough in inner-city London to know that the fear of a backlash was a palpable one. No officer in the London Met wanted to get embroiled in the eye of a storm. The last riots had been in 2011, and London had burned for five hot, endless days in August.

As she watched the uniformed sergeants and constables returning to their cars, she felt a spike of fear. People stood at their doorsteps, and faces gathered around street corners, watching them. Arla could feel their indignation. In their view, the cops didn't have a right to come in and search their homes. Many had refused, she could see. Arla walked over to Inspector Wadsworth, the tactical leader of the operation she had authorised. Wadsie, as he was affectionately known, was a stalwart of the Met, and not far from his retirement. He took his cap off, and ran a hand through his sweaty, buzz cut red hair.

"No luck?" Arla asked, although she knew the answer already. Wadsworth shook his head. "We can't just barge in, can we?" He narrowed his eyes at her. "You sure this lad's at Brunswick High? I mean don't the high and mighty send their kids there?"

A shameful look came upon his face. "Sorry, that came out wrong."

"He got a scholarship," Arla said. "Don't worry, it's alright. I just want to know why he ran, and where he is."

"Couldn't have got far," Wadsworth said. "What do you want us to do?"

Arla leaned against the squad car, feeling the hot metal radiate heat. She noticed several men point their fingers at them and talk to each other. The heat was everywhere, blazing from a cobalt blue sky, and slowly gathering strength in the restless, angry hearts of men. These corners of South-West London housed the teeming masses, the ones lured with promises of a new life, then left deprived and forlorn on the city's gutters, their dreams impaled on the glitzy cement and glass buildings that punctured hope like balloons.

Arla said, "Let's clear out. Right now, we need to give them space, and all this visibility isn't helping."

She said goodbye to Wadsworth, thanking him for his help. The three squad cars took off slowly down the road. Arla walked back with the two detectives, and got to the house as Harry and James were coming out.

Both of them had specimen bags in their hands. Miss Ofori appeared at the doorway, arms folded, looking indignant. Arla waved at her, and the woman ignored her, shut the door, then appeared a minute later, locking it. She knocked at the neighbour's house, and Arla noticed her hand a key over. That must be the key for Paul to let himself in, just in case he had run off without it. That gave Arla an idea.

"Good work, team," she said. "Now all of you go back to base and sort out what we have so far. Harry and I are going to stick around here for a little longer."

"Sure you don't need an extra pair of hands?" James asked hopefully.

"No," Arla said. "Have you downloaded all the Facebook and Twitter posts that Maddy made, and her emails?"

"Most of it. Then I got called…"

"Then go back and finish it off, and I'll see you there," she snapped.

As they walked off, Harry said, "Time for some surveillance?"

"And a coffee."

CHAPTER 19

Often Cindy lost herself to daydreams.

She could be walking down a street in beautiful sunshine. But the darkest night would besmirch her mind. The visions rose up like daggers, fangs of a prehistoric monster, saliva dripping from its jaws. She would feel the bite of the nylon rope as it tied her hands and feet. The hands roaming over her young body, pinching her nipples, then that awful mouth bending over hers, that fetid breath…

"Hey, watch it!" Cindy bumped against something, and was shoved backwards momentarily. She stopped and blinked, staring at an angry man looking at her questioningly. He was taller than her, and gave her an evil look, then caught her eyes. Cindy's eyes were a pale blue, and they stared back at him without feeling or expression.

The man went to say something, then shook his head and walked off. Cindy stood there for a while, melting heat from the pavement settling over her in layers. The sunlight was like gas, clouding the air with yellow-stained exhaust fumes. Traffic horns beeped like lost animals, looking for a way out.

Cindy had been six when she first ran away. Her foster parents were cocaine dealers who had graduated to making crack, learning to cook it in their own kitchen. Her blonde curls and pretty looks had endeared her to many of her parents' customers. But she was the favourite of her foster father, who had started abusing her when she was six.

The streets had not been kind to her, and a spate of shoplifting had ended her up back in juvenile prison at Feltham, then to social care again. Once again, the morbid merry-go-round had started: well-meaning counsellors who had no idea of what she had been through, and even when they did, couldn't fathom the ways in which she was changing.

As she crossed the road, running a yellow light, hearing the car almost clip her heels, she remembered her first home. The crack dealer's house. In an odd way, they were all the childhood memories she had. It had been her first home, with a woman and a man she knew as parents. There was a brief golden interlude in her life before the horrors had started, and it was those first few years. Growing up in Nottingham, hazy trips to the park, a sepia-toned movie of laughter and birthday cake.

There had been no birthdays after she was nine. After she ran away. She kicked a stone and watched it skitter away. Birthdays – weren't they weird? Why would anyone want to celebrate the day they were born? Yet another reminder, a celebration no less, of that day. What the hell was there to celebrate about anyone's life? People were born, they lived and died. Get over it.

She lifted her face to the dirt trapped in the gaseous heat, and stared at the men and women of Clapham, always in a rush, brushing past her rapidly, a conveyor belt of humanity. She felt invisible, like she could walk through them and they wouldn't notice. A chain of bodies that lived like machines, and fell apart one day, rusty and broken.

Cindy wouldn't go that way. Her life was different. Ever since she had discovered the Meaning, everything had changed. It all made sense to her now. She was put on earth for a reason. Her chin lifted and her breath quickened, a lacuna of clarity appearing in her mind. She looked at the rushing bodies with pity as she walked past Clapham Common tube station. She was better than them, so much better than they would ever realise.

They might not realise, but they would know. One day, her name would be famous and they would thank her. The thought was like fire in her blood, warming the tips of her limbs, rich and intoxicating.

But first, there was work to do.

Cindy turned left and kept walking till she got to the end of the street. Rows of terraced houses stretched in both directions, then the high-rises began, square, staid, old structures that hemmed in thousands of people in tiny, cramped apartments. She walked to one of the tall buildings, called Sycamore House. The double doors had wire-rimmed glass panels that she could see through. The brown foyer was clean, but the graffiti on the wall was overflowing. Cindy knew the code to the door. She got inside, and the motion detector lights blinked to life. She got into the lift and looked at the address. She needed flat 387 on the fifth floor.

The lift shuddered as it rose. When she stepped out into the corridor it was dark, as the lights weren't working, and there weren't any windows. There was a dank, musty odour, a smell that she knew from her previous life. She stepped into the darkness, feeling a wetness beneath her shoes. She withdrew her feet to find a small puddle. Then she saw the leak from the roof. A solitary drop of water bloomed from the damp patch above her head, and fell, rippling the puddle again. Cindy walked to the green door numbered 387 in white letters.

She knocked and waited. A bolt scraped across, and the door opened cautiously. She showed her ID. A woman lifted tired, hooded eyes and looked at Cindy.

"Who are you?" she slurred in a drowsy voice.

"I'm from the council housing department. You complained about the flat, didn't you?"

"'S right," the woman said. Without another word, she turned her back to Cindy and stumbled her way inside the flat. Cindy followed. It was dark inside. The only light was at the back, where the balcony was. But it was shuttered so the dimness made it difficult to see till Cindy's eyes adjusted to the dark.

The place was a mess. Clothes, newspapers and condom wrappers were strewn all over the floor. Cindy stood in front of the living room, appalled. A stink came from the kitchen to her left. The bedroom next to it was dark. The woman was sprawled out on the beaten sofa, foam spilling out from the cuts. An old TV stood in one corner, a meaningless game show buzzing on the screen. The sound was low. Cindy looked at the woman, whose eyes were glazed and she was already falling asleep.

Cindy looked at the coffee table in front of the sofa. She lifted up the glossy magazine gingerly. Underneath it, she saw a hypodermic needle and syringe, a rubber tourniquet, and a small vial with brown powder inside it. She put the magazine away, and picked up the vial. She took the lid off and sniffed. Her nose curled at the pungent odour. She looked at the woman. The state of the apartment and its inhabitant made perfect sense now. But why did she complain about the condition of the premises?

Cindy was leaning close to the woman, when she heard the voice behind her. "Who are you?"

It was a small voice and came from the doorway. Cindy turned quickly. A boy, no more than five or six years old, stood at the doorway. His face was covered in grime, and his blond hair was streaked in dirt, like it hadn't been washed in ages. He was thin, and his ribs were sticking out. His belly was sunken, and he wore a pair of boxer shorts that hung loose on his narrow waist.

Cindy stood very still. "I am a friend of your mama's. She called me."

"Why?" the boy asked.

"She wanted me to help."

The boy stared at her for a while, then scratched his belly. He walked into the room, his feet scattering paper and discarded clothes. Cindy stared at the spindly spine, and his scapula sticking out from the narrow back. The boy looked at his mother, who was barely conscious. He scratched his hair, then climbed on the sofa next to her. Cindy watched in silence. The sun burned the shutters outside, and a shaft of light fell on his hair. The boy turned and lay on the sofa, ignoring his mother who was starting to snore. For a while he stared blankly at the TV. Then he turned his head to Cindy.

"I'm hungry," he said.

Cindy felt something catch at her heart and squeeze it remorselessly. She put her bag down and rushed into the kitchen. The stench hit her like a wall, stopping her. She powered on, lifting up plates crusty with old food that had littered the kitchen top. She opened the fridge and gagged. Mouldy cheese, going green, and a lump of meat, turning a horrible, putrid black. The milk inside the bottle had curdled a long time ago.

That was when it hit her. She was sent here for a reason. A higher power had done this, the same power that gave her the Meaning. She stood up, eyes shining.

She went back to the boy and held out her hand. He took it without questioning, and her heart broke at his innocence. She had been innocent, too, once.

She took the boy into the bedroom. Bedding was piled up in one corner, and the cushion was ripped in several places. Neither bedsheet nor duvet cover existed. On the bedside table, within the child's easy reach, she found another syringe, this one half-full. She picked it up, ejected the contents into the bin by the bed, and chucked the syringe in it.

She put the boy on the bed. "Stay here." She pointed to the bed. "Stay here, OK? I'll be back soon."

The boy nodded silently and watched her as she closed the door shut. Cindy went back to the woman. She was still dozing. Cindy rooted around in her handbag till she found the little plastic bottle she carried around with her. She put her gloves on, then picked up the syringe from the table and put the needle inside the plastic bottle. She drew the plunger back, getting the needle half-full with a colourless liquid.

She took the rubber tourniquet, and tied it around the woman's arm, just above the elbow. She waited for a few seconds. She couldn't see any veins. She concentrated on the neck. She got closer to the woman, and held the needle just above the jugular vein, two inches away from the pulsing of the carotid artery.

Cindy pushed the needle into the vein. As she depressed the plunger, the woman came to, the pain suddenly awakening her. Her eyes flew open, and her hand came up to her neck. Cindy moved fast, her knee landing on the woman's chest, blocking her movement. She pushed the woman down, while pressing the plunger till it emptied.

The woman's mouth opened in a silent scream, but no sound came. Her eyes opened, wide with terror. They stayed open as Cindy removed the syringe. She took her gloves off, and put them in her pocket. Her job here was done. Exultation and a sense of achievement flooded her being. Her mouth opened in the shock of ecstasy.

She lifted her eyes to the heavens and mouthed thank you.

The bedroom door was still shut when she opened it. The boy was still on the bed, but he was lying down. She felt like Mother Mary as she leaned over the boy, and picked him up in her arms. He smelled vile. He woke up, and she made him stand. He rubbed his eyes and looked at her.

"I'm hungry," he said.

"Come on, sweetheart. Let's get you some food," Cindy whispered. They walked past the living room. The boy looked at his mother lying on the sofa, then looked away. They walked out of the door together, closing it with a click.

CHAPTER 20

Harry had his shirtsleeves up around his elbows, dark shades on his eyes, and a cigarette dangling from his hand outside the car.

"How much longer?" he asked.

Arla took a sip of her coffee, eyeing the cigarette with envy. It was a slippery slope, and she cursed Harry for lighting up in front of her. He had asked her permission, and what choice did she have? Why did men never get the hint?

Clustered, packed, dense rows of houses made the cul-de-sac relatively quiet. There was the preternatural hum of traffic from the A24 outside, running off to the Elephant and Castle roundabout. A breeze tickled the fat leaves on trees, and dead yellow weeds swayed by the roadside. Arla wore shades herself, and was glad of the protection against the sunny glare.

"You in a rush to get somewhere?" She glanced at her watch. Almost 17.00. The team would be waiting at the station. She needed to update them, and have a list of to do's for tomorrow. A tricky list. Without finding Paul Ofori, she doubted she could find Maddy Burroughs. Her phone buzzed and she reached for it. She didn't recognise the number.

After a moment's hesitation, she answered. "DCI Baker. Who is this?"

"Miss Baker, this is Conrad Burroughs," a deep voice said in an American accent. "I work in the US Consulate. It's about my daughter, Maddy."

"Of course, sir, nice to speak to you. Is this a good time?"

"Yes." He hesitated. "I know you wanted to speak to my son and myself. Jenny, my wife, told me. All of us are at home now."

Arla gestured to Harry, and he threw his cigarette away. "We are on our way," Arla said and hung up.

Harry backed up as Arla stared at the house. She knew that she would be back here again, sooner rather than later. She looked up at the neighbour's window, and saw a curtain twitch. Harry did a three-point turn, and drove out.

When they pulled up at the drive of the Burroughs' residence, the front door was ajar. It opened fully when Arla alighted. A trim, athletic-looking man with grey-white hair, six feet tall, stood at the doorstep.

He shook hands with Arla and Harry, his grip warm and firm, but not crushing.

"Conrad Burroughs, how do you do?" he said in a flat voice matching his expression.

They went inside, through the opulent hallway, into the conservatory at the rear. It was warm, sunlight flooding in through the open windows, but cool as well, surrounded by living plants. Arla wondered at how different the heat seemed out in the concrete jungle, pouring from the sky like magma from a volcano. Then she spotted the small air-conditioning machine on the back wall. She had missed it the last time.

They sat down and the maid came in. Arla and Harry politely refused offers of tea and coffee. Mr Burroughs was watching Arla closely, his dark eyes reflecting the concern biting away inside him. Like his wife, he had a haunted look on his face.

"Any news of Maddy, Miss Baker?" he asked.

"We are pursuing several leads at the moment, Mr Burroughs. It would be premature to speak of any particular one at the moment."

Mr Burroughs crinkled his brow. "What does that mean? Do you know what it feels like to have your daughter abducted? It's all very well for you to sit here and give me the standard answer, but that's not enough, damn it!"

Arla felt the heat rush to her face, but she had expected this. "I can assure you, we are trying everything at our disposal."

"So what have you found?" Mr Burroughs insisted. "Jesus, I just want a straight answer!"

Harry pressed on Arla's arm before she could speak. He took over. "Mr Burroughs, we went to Maddy's school today. New Brunswick High. We have been informed that you want to keep this news to ourselves, so we are being discreet. We met the principal, and spoke to Maddy's friends. That has led to several lines of enquiry, and DCI Baker was just referring to those."

"We know who Maddy's friends are. We are friends with the parents of her friends. We socialise with them. I can tell you, they don't know anything."

Arla and Harry exchanged a glance. Arla asked, "Mr Burroughs, did your daughter stay overnight at any of her friends' houses?"

"You need to ask my wife but…" He seemed lost in thought. "Yes, she has a friend called Maya Patel. Nice girl, I know her dad, he's a banker. I dropped her off at Maya's house, I think, two months ago. It was only for one night. But my wife will know more." He rose from his seat and picked up an intercom phone on the wall. He spoke into it briefly, then came back.

Arla said, "Did she go to Maya's house often?"

He shrugged. "Once in a while. Not that frequently. Can't remember the last time she went."

"What about nightclubs, discos? Did Maddy go out often?"

"She's seventeen and thinks she is 25. Of course she went out, and yes, I picked her up from clubs late at night. But these are rare and well-controlled occasions, Miss Baker. My daughter wasn't some party animal going out clubbing every night, if that's what you're implying."

Arla got the sense he was being defensive. "Did you think Maddy was sad or acting strangely in any way in the days and weeks leading to her disappearance?"

Mr Burroughs sighed and flopped back in his chair. His face wore a tortured, pained look. He looked exhausted, and despite his grating attitude, Arla couldn't help but feel a surge of sympathy. The man looked like he had lost a part of his body.

His voice caught as he spoke. "She's growing up now. What can I do…? My work keeps me busy, and I… I don't see her as much as I'd like to. You know?"

He looked up and stared at Arla. Nothing but pain marked the deep lines in his face now.

"She was my little girl, and now she's almost an adult. She won't tell me if something's bugging her, will she? I'd like to." He covered his head in his hands. "Oh God."

Arla didn't say anything, but visions from her own childhood rose up like black shadows at the back of her mind. Images of holding her father's hand, and the day she had to let it go. The day she had been led away by the social workers. She remembered her father's face, sunken, white, staring out of the window as she got into the car. He held her eyes till the car went around the bend.

Arla swallowed and squeezed her eyes shut. When she opened them, Mr Burroughs was leaning in the chair again, a vacant look in his eyes. She noticed Harry examining her with a frown. She nodded at him quickly. There was a movement at the conservatory door, and Jenny Burroughs walked in with a boy who was almost up to her shoulders.

CHAPTER 21

Mother and son sat down next to Conrad Burroughs. The boy still had the innocence of an early years teenager, childhood misting his wide-eyed stare. Arla smiled at him, trying to put the boy at ease. He looked uncertain, then his lips twitched. She wondered how he felt now that his big sister wasn't there anymore. Had he been close to her?

The thought came to her like an explosion, knocking her sideways. How had *she* felt when Nicole had disappeared? The morning she woke up and looked for her... and went to school alone. Later, the slow death of hope, staring at the door, watching out of the window. Nicole never came back. Neither did the part of Arla that vanished with her sister, leaving her broken, like a butterfly with one of its wings ripped off.

Is that what this boy felt like now? If she couldn't find Maddy, would he become broken, like Arla had?

A heavy weight lodged at the back of her throat, and she stared at the three people sitting opposite her. A father, a mother and a child. A trinity of trust, a locus of love. Something Arla had never had, no matter how much she had wanted it. And now they were being ripped apart just like her own family had been. And it was down to her to try and... do what? Save them? Bring Maddy back? Like Nicole had come back... No. No.

The pressure built to a dead, bludgeoning force in her throat, and suddenly she couldn't breathe or swallow. She was staring between Mr Burroughs and his wife, and she caught them looking at each other, a puzzled expression on their faces. Arla felt the rage in her chest, a loud knock as her heart hit a rib in slow motion, and bounced back, quivering. Heat swarmed to her face like a fan, and the world tipped sideways, suddenly wet, drenched with tears.

She stood up quickly, scraping the chair back.

"Excuse me, I…" She didn't finish the sentence. She walked around the table and literally ran out into the hallway. Her rubber-soled shoes whispered on the marble, and then she was wrenching on the door handle, the heavy oak door opening out into the yellow sunshine. She stepped outside and gasped, leaning against the wall. Visions were swimming in her head, pounding against her skull like rain against a window pane on a stormy night. She closed her eyes, and wanted to sink to her knees, letting the earth eat her up.

She felt a strong arm steady her, and hold her gently around the waist. She knew that physique well, and allowed herself to fall back into Harry's soft clothes.

"Shhh," he said, rocking her. "It's OK. Go and wait in the car." He gave her the keys.

Arla put a hand to her fevered temple and stood up straight. "No. I should go back." Her breathing was returning to normal, but she still felt the panic fluttering inside her. She breathed in and out deeply, and walked out towards the road. Harry stayed where he was, watching her. Arla came back and nodded.

"I'm alright. Let's go back in."

"Like hell you are. If you go in there again…"

"I said I'm fine, Harry. I'm the SIO, aren't I?"

They stared at each other for a while, his chestnut eyes full of concern, probing, asking. Harry was one of the few people who knew. And perhaps the only person who cared. For once, it was she who looked away. She stared at the ground for a few seconds, then brushed past Harry and went in.

To her relief, the family had remained seated at the table. They looked up curiously as she entered. Arla felt embarrassed. What she had just done looked unprofessional. But she hadn't been able to help it.

Dear God, she needed help. That was the whole point of the psychiatry sessions last year, and maybe she just needed to start them again. By herself this time, and not being forced to by the bloody London Met. She needed to get it back together.

"I'm sorry about that," she explained to the Burroughses. "We have been very busy and I have had no sleep recently, so a bit tired." She tried to smile and it felt like pulling teeth out.

Conrad Burroughs gave her a brief smile back, but Jenny's eyes were boring into Arla's. She sat down, Harry joining her. Arla gestured to him and he started the questioning.

"Tell us about that evening. What were you doing?" Harry addressed the question to the whole family.

Conrad answered. "I got back from work around 7 pm, which is early for me. We had dinner, and then I worked in my study, took some calls. When I came down, Tom was watching TV and Jenny was in the kitchen."

"What time was it?"

"8.30, and before Tom's bedtime," Jenny said, giving her husband a quick glance. "We normally go to bed around 11, and Maddy sleeps around 10. Tom is in bed before that."

Arla wrote the times down in her diary. Harry asked, "Apart from Maya and Emma, did Maddy have other close friends?"

Jenny said, "She was popular. Yes, she had lots of friends but the two you mentioned were her closest."

Arla spoke up. "Do you have the numbers of their parents? I have spoken to the girls already, but we would like to speak to the whole family."

The couple glanced at each other, then nodded in silence. Conrad cleared his throat.

"Why was your name mentioned in that envelope, Miss Baker?"

Arla stiffened and Harry gave her a concerned look. She paused for a while before answering.

"In my line of work, Mr Burroughs, it is easy to make enemies. I suspect someone was playing a prank."

"Do you know who it might be?"

Arla noticed Jenny was watching her carefully. "We are keeping our options open. We don't have CCTV cameras on your street so we cannot get a visual on who dropped the letter off. And we didn't find any fingerprints either. But whoever it is, eventually we will find him."

Harry took a statement from Tom Burroughs, then it was time to leave.

CHAPTER 22

Shadows were lengthening on the Common as Harry drove back. The air con was off, and wind brushed her hair back as she kept her face by the window. Wisps of pollen floated in the air, and Arla stretched out one hand to catch one as it drifted close to the car. It brushed past her fingers with a feathery kiss, gone before she could grasp it. Distant cries from the players filtered through the still summer air, hearts racing, ripening to gold and brown in the sun. Harry parked at the carpool, and sat still after switching the engine off. Arla waited.

"Can you see this one through?" Harry asked.

Arla took her time to answer. "I've done it before."

"This one's different."

"Why? After what I did last year, this one should be peanuts." Last year she had come to know the truth about her family. But even as she said the words, Arla knew how hollow they sounded.

"For starters," Harry said, "I don't like this letter that says your name. I know you don't either. But the more I think about, the more worried I get. Someone has it in for you, Arla, and I don't know who or why. Yeah, we all have enemies. But most are behind bars or dead."

She knew he was right, and didn't know how to respond. Harry continued. "Then there is the case itself. I saw you looking at the boy today. His elder sister's gone, just like…" Harry stopped speaking. There wasn't much to say, really.

"Trust me, Harry. I got this covered." Arla got out of the car and walked towards the entrance. She held the doors open for Harry, and they walked into their open-plan office. Arla's desk phone was ringing when she walked into her office at the end.

"DCI Baker," she answered.

"Where have you been?" Wayne Johnson barked.

"Catching a witness who did a runner, and interviewing the missing person's family. Sir. Didn't realise I had to ask your permission."

"Don't get smart with me, Arla. I don't have a progress report as yet, and I have the Home Office breathing down my neck, as well as bloody MI5."

That got Arla's attention. "MI5?"

"Are you deaf? Yes, it's sodding MI5. There's only one, last time I checked."

"Bloody hell."

"I need to see things happening, Arla. We need witnesses brought in for questioning, new lines of enquiry. Stop this bullshit at her school. There's nothing happening there."

"With all due respect, sir, I think there is. I think the principal is letting on less than he knows. We need to get the boyfriend, and I'm pretty sure there's a side to Maddy not many people knew about."

There was a pause on the line. When Johnson spoke, his tone was guarded. "Come to my office."

Arla went up the stairs to the fourth floor and knocked on the door. She heard a muffled voice telling her to come in. Johnson was on his own. He waved at her to sit down. Arla remained standing.

"If you don't mind, sir, I need to get on. You want a report and I have a shedload of evidence to wade through."

Johnson leaned back in his chair and fixed Arla with a stare. "What did you mean by another side to Maddy?"

"Well, her boyfriend, who no one seems to know about, including her parents, is almost certainly friends with a gang member and smokes cannabis himself. Whether he does other drugs, I don't know. Maddy used to get served at pubs, which means she had fake ID."

"So do a lot of teenagers. Hardly makes her have a dark side."

"I mean an alternative side to her, which her parents might not have been aware of…" Arla broke off and stared at Johnson hard. "What's this about, sir?"

"She's the daughter of a US diplomat. You know what that means."

"No, I don't. My job is to find her, and get her back safe and sound to her parents. I don't care who her parents are."

Johnson shook his head, exasperated. "Think, Arla, for once in your life! If we don't find her in a couple of days, someone will have leaked news to the media. Do you really think the US Consulate will be doing cartwheels of joy? And then if you put in bombshells like her darker side, God help us. We're gonna have another feeding frenzy at the zoo."

"So, it's alright to be worried about what the press will say, but we shouldn't explore Maddy's personality more, see where it leads us." She smiled grimly. "Is this tied in to your promotion as well, sir? Wouldn't do if your last big case, before you got the Deputy Assistant Commissioner job, was a mayhem, would it?"

Johnson stood up, his face turning purple. "Watch your tongue, Arla," he hissed. "Remember the times I covered your back. If it wasn't for me, you'd be directing traffic right now."

"And I never failed you in getting a conviction for the bad guys. I always came through, didn't I, sir?"

Johnson banged his fist on the table. "For fuck's sake! Why do you have to be so difficult? You know, Arla, there was a time when I saw you, yes, you," he pointed a finger at her, "as someone who would climb up the ranks in the Met. I saw you as an Assistant Commissioner, despite being a woman. But you know what your problem is? You don't know what to say, and when. You can't control yourself. You're a brilliant detective, maybe the best I've ever seen. And I've seen plenty, believe me. But you have no tact. You piss off the wrong people."

"The truth is often the wrong thing, what people don't want to here. And I don't tolerate fools."

"And they don't tolerate you. So, you have a really big fucking problem when one of those fools, as you call them, is the boss of your boss!" Johnson's chest was heaving. He turned his back to her and walked over to the window. Arla sat down and studied her fingernails. Johnson had given her a start in the Serious Crime Squad. They clashed often, but he also knew her better than most people, bar Harry.

Johnson spoke in a quiet voice. "This case is bigger than you, me or my bloody promotion. Yes, I do want to leave with my reputation intact. But that's not the point here. The point is that we are..."

"Diplomatic about the diplomat's daughter?" Arla finished.

"Something like that, yes. I cannot imagine the parents would be overjoyed when they learn their daughter has another side to her."

Arla stood up. She was feeling exhausted all of a sudden, and she wished she could dump everything on Harry and take off for the evening. "If that is all, sir..."

"Do what you have to, but just remember what I said."

"Roger that, sir."

Her phone buzzed as soon as she said the words.

CHAPTER 23

"Where are you?" Harry asked.

"Upstairs with the boss. On my way down." Arla hung up. The incident room was buzzing when Arla entered it. The buzz subsided as she took up her place at the whiteboard next to Harry and Lisa, both of whom stood back as she approached. James stepped up from his seat and handed her a steaming paper cup of Costa coffee. Arla accepted it gratefully and took a long sip.

Maddy's photo stared back at her from the white screen, and next to it, Paul's. It was the first time that she had seen Paul's photo. He was a handsome young man, curly, black hair cut close to his face, with a pair of sensitive, intelligent eyes that stared out with a mischievous expression on his face. Photos of Emma and Maya had also been stuck on below Maddy's.

Arla gave the assembled detectives a quick rundown of the day's events.

"Do we have any plain clothes at Paul's house to keep watch? He could be back anytime."

Anderson, one of the uniformed sergeants, who was also black, raised his hand. "There's a team there already, and I'm heading down there with another one for the night."

"Thank you," Arla said. "Have we searched the grounds in Brockwell Park where she disappeared?"

One of the Scene of Crime women raised her hand. Her name was Gabby, but she had a longer Polish name that no one remembered. "All the samples came back to the lab last night. We found some hair follicles that belong to Maddy, and some bloodstains that have her DNA. There is another DNA in the bloodstains, but nothing that matches in our database."

"So she was injured at the site where she was last seen. Anything else?"

"Patterns in the grass show that a body had been dragged along it. But it doesn't really give us much to go on."

"CCTV?"

Lisa spoke up beside Arla. "No CCTV there, only in the main road."

Arla thought to herself, then aloud. "We know that she had a rendezvous with Paul. It stands to reason that he was somewhere in the park and close by. Maybe he was watching her, and walked towards her when he saw her. In that case, Paul should have the perfect view of the person who got Maddy."

James Bennett lifted a hand up. "If Paul did see something, then why is he hiding?"

"That could be the very reason why he is hiding. He doesn't think that we will believe him. That we think he abducted her."

"Could he?" James asked. "I see no reason not to treat him as a suspect. He can't be on the run just because he's scared. He knows something more."

Arla nodded. "Yes, that makes sense. We need to keep open minds. Find Paul, and a lot of this puzzle falls into place."

"Anything from the phone?"

James spoke again. "Got the call log today. She made several calls to an unknown number the day before she went missing. Also some calls to Paul Ofori."

"Are we any closer to getting transcripts, or voice logs?"

"Nope. That will take time," James said.

"Last location of phone?"

"Brockwell Park, then the A23, heading down towards South Surrey. On the night she went missing."

"Really?" Arla frowned.

"Yes. Whoever had the phone must have realised it was still with them, and threw it out. That's what I think," Harry said.

Arla brooded over this. "Anything unusual happen over that stretch of the A23 recently?"

Blank eyes met her gaze. "Can we look for it, then, please?" she urged. "And get a map of the A23 southbound and that part of Surrey. I want it on the board. If someone did abduct Maddy, then chances are they were driving down the A23 that night with her."

They didn't have a large Ordnance Survey map they could stick on the wall, but they did have Google Maps. Arla used Harry's phone, and looked at the map.

"This stretch of the A23 goes down to the M23, which then carries on all the way to Brighton," Arla said, almost to herself. "Do we know the exact location of the phone that night – before or after they joined the M23?"

Blank faces regarded her again. She looked at Harry, then Lisa, both of whom raised their eyebrows. Arla shook her head, frustrated. "People, come on. Let's get this ball rolling, right?"

James piped up from the front row. "I volunteer to contact National Highways and Motorway Police, and ask for CCTV feeds from that region."

"No, you have too much on your plate at the moment." She looked behind James and pointed to John Sandford, the tall, broad-chested black sergeant. "Can you…?"

Arla didn't have to finish her sentence. "Yes, boss, I got this," John said.

Arla turned to the rest of the team. "Can everyone please give John a hand with this? There is likely to be lots of CCTV footage from the motorway cameras."

"But guv," James cut in, "what exactly are we looking for? For starters, will the A23 even have that many cameras? The majority of CCTV is going to be on the M23, and we don't even know the car went that way."

Arla suppressed a smile. The young man's enthusiasm was heartening, but he was also smart, following the lines of her own logic.

"Good question, detective," she said. "No, we don't know if the car where Maddy's phone was last located joined the M23 from the A23. It could have joined the M25, for instance. For that matter, why should it be a car? It could be a truck, or even a service station on the motorway."

Arla continued. "But we need to think logically here. If someone did abduct Maddy, then they had to remove her from Brockwell Park. She was a tall girl, sporty, and wouldn't have been easy to move. The abductor didn't just carry her on his back, did he?"

All the faces in front of her shook their heads. Arla said, "Therefore, we check CCTV on the T-junction of that road coming out of the park. That road only has one exit. We have an approximate time, and we can use the CCTV images to see what car came out of that road at that time."

Harry spoke up. "Unless he, or they, carried her across Brockwell Park, into somewhere like Herne Hill and had a car waiting there."

"Possibly," Arla said, "but what do you do on a warm summer's night, with strollers in the park everywhere? Would you risk a chance of getting spotted?"

"Good point," Harry agreed.

Arla turned to James. "Have you got the Facebook and social media accounts downloaded?"

"Yes. She was more on Twitter than Facebook, to be honest. She posted on Twitter regularly, mostly photos."

"I want to see them. Have you downloaded them as hard copies?"

James nodded. Arla looked at her watch. It was almost 8 pm, and the team had been working for almost twelve hours already.

"That's a wrap, folks. You know what you have to do. I want the CCTV images, anything else from the SOC guys, and keep up the surveillance on Paul's house."

One by one, the team drifted out. Harry turned to Arla. His face was grave. "It's been eight days. Nothing on the missing persons database. Not looking good."

Arla knew the statistics on missing people well. Sooner or later, most were spotted. Somewhere, somehow, they left a trail. A credit card payment, asking for a lift. If they went totally off the grid, it was bad news. And Arla was beginning to have a bad feeling about this. The first three days were critical for any missing person. Most called back home by that time. Those that didn't were seldom found. Arla stared at Harry's face and read the concern in his eyes. She said, "Something has to give. I hope she either makes contact in the next two days, or we have a breakthrough."

The door of the incident room opened and DCS Johnson walked in. Harry and Arla straightened.

"Sir," Arla murmured.

Johnson planted himself in front of them. "It's come to my notice we have a surveillance team outside 32 Union Square, where Maddy's boyfriend was last seen."

"Yes, sir."

Johnson didn't have to say anything else. He stared silently at them for a while, then nodded. "It's a sensitive region. We need to have a very good reason to be there."

"This is the best lead we have, sir," Arla said. "It might even crack the case."

"I hope you're right, DCI Baker," Johnson said in a low voice. "For your sake, I really do."

CHAPTER 24

Arla went to the coffee machine at the rear of the station, near the corridor that led to the carpool at the back, and poured herself a mocha. She needed the hot chocolate. Then she got a double espresso, and poured it inside the mocha. Sipping the hot liquid gratefully, she walked back to her office. She took out the folder that contained the Facebook and Twitter posts of Maddy.

She flicked through them, noting the dates and times of posting. Maddy was a surprisingly mature girl. She cared more about animal rights and global warming, it seemed. Most of her posts were about the ozone layer, depletion of rainforests around the world, and warming seas causing worsening hurricanes. Arla had not seen a pet dog around the house, but there were many posts of an adorable Golden Retriever called Rambo. Arla spotted a photo of Maddy's brother, Tom, running with the dog on Clapham Common. She could see the common's bandstand in the background. It was a winter photo, the ground was frosty, and Tom was wearing hats and a woolly scarf. Several more close-ups of the dog followed with its tongue hanging out or chewing food – it was quite clear that Maddy was very fond of Rambo.

She seemed fond of shoes as well, especially high-heeled and expensive ones. She had posted several images of Christian Louboutin, Manolo Blahnik and Dolce & Gabbana shoes. Arla couldn't help but stare at a pair of blue leather pumps that would fit perfectly with a blue evening dress she had purchased last year. It would fit well with her blue glitter clutch bag, and the aquamarine pendant necklace… Who was she kidding? When was the last time she had a date or been on a night out?

Arla kept flicking. She noticed the paucity of photos that contained either Maddy or her friends. A Twitter post of a shoe that had garnered 50 hearts had a caption – 'for Maddy B only!' – with several heart and open mouth emojis. Arla looked at the name again. Maddy B. Sounded like a cool name for a teenager.

On an impulse, Arla flipped open her phone and opened up the Facebook page. She typed in Maddy B, and got a page full of hits. She narrowed it to Maddy B, London, and there were only two. One was an older woman who seemed to be a DJ. The other was Madeleine Burroughs.

"So, this is where you hide," Arla murmured to herself.

Under the moniker of Maddy B, and looking very different in baggy street clothes, Maddy had several photos of herself with Paul Ofori. This Maddy was virtually unrecognisable from the clean-cut, polished public school girl image that Arla had in mind. Her shoulder-length ginger hair was dyed black, unless she was wearing a wig. On a selfie with Paul, Maddy had black lipstick on and black mascara, and Paul wore a string vest, showing off his muscled physique.

In another, Maddy reclined in Paul's arms and someone else had clearly taken the photo. Arla noted a tattoo on Maddy's upper right shoulder. She saw a similar tattoo on Paul's forearm. Arla zoomed in, and Paul's tattoo bore the legend Z14, but she couldn't see Maddy's tattoo well. She flicked through several more of the photos, and finally got one that had a close-up of Maddy's shoulder. Her tattoo also said Z14. Arla thought hard, and it came to her.

The friend of Paul's, called Sean T. He had a similar tattoo. Arla came to a photo of Maddy and Paul flanked by young men, wearing baseball caps and baggy clothes, with tattoos on their arms, and one quite clearly with a handgun tucked in his front belt.

Whether the gun was a replica or not Arla couldn't decide. But it was something the forensic lab could determine for her. She looked at the young men in arrogant poses, with Maddy in the middle. The tattoos were similar for all of them, and spelled out the same letters, Z14.

Arla took a deep breath and closed the folder. She picked up the phone, called switchboard, and asked to be put through to Trident, London. Originally set up in 1998 to monitor the rise of gun crime in the Afro-Caribbean communities of London, Trident had since morphed into a city-wide operation that pursued gun crime in general.

The switchboard operator lady said, "Only the on-call duty sergeant is on now for Trident. Who will I say is calling?"

"DCI Baker of the SCU."

"Hold on."

After a buzz of static, a male voice came on the line. "Detective Sergeant Goodwin here."

Arla introduced herself quickly. "I'm afraid I cannot discuss the details of the investigation, but I need urgent information on a gang who could be called Z14, and active in the South-West London area – in Clapham, Brixton, Herne Hill."

"I need to log this request, DCI Baker, are you OK with that?"

"Please do."

"Who is your superior officer?"

"DCS Wayne Johnson of SCU."

"Hang on." The voice vanished, replaced by the buzz again. Arla held on, tapping her feet. She hated hanging on on the phone. She put the phone on loudspeaker and leaned back in her seat, putting her feet up on the desk. She took her flat rubber-soled shoes off. Damn, that felt good.

The receiver crackled. "DCI Baker?"

"Yes, I'm here."

"There are reports of two arrests in the last six months. Both related with possession with intent to supply Class A drugs, crack cocaine. One also had possession of a firearm. Both of them confessed to belonging to a gang called Z14."

Arla digested this news in silence, alarm growing inside her. "Why did they confess?"

"They faced jail terms, and their lawyers cut a deal with the Crown Prosecution Service, from these notes. CPS allowed them out on parole after six months, pending good behaviour."

"Can I have their names please?"

Arla wrote down the two names, neither of which meant anything to her. She looked up the address of the first man, named Mark Dooley. It was an address in Brixton. She tapped the pen against her lips. Then she called Harry on the phone.

Harry answered on the first ring. "The wine is chilled, and I've made an avocado and prawn salad with chilli garlic flakes. Did you know avocado is an aphrodisiac?"

"Shut up, Harry."

"Tell me you're not tempted."

She was tempted, but she wouldn't admit that to him. The man was beyond reproach. "Some of us have work to do, Harry. You, on the other hand, have too much time on your hands."

"I just know about work-life balance. So should you, Arla." His voice wasn't jocular anymore.

"I've got a lead in the case." She changed topic quickly. Before he could open his big mouth, she explained further, going into the details.

"So, what are you suggesting?"

"We check out the address of this Mark Dooley in Brixton."

"The guy with a gun? We should take a firearms officer with us."

"And risk getting into a firefight? All I want is surveillance, Harry. And there's no time now to arrange a plain-clothes unit."

"Forget it. Come to my place and have the wine instead. I've got a three-year-old Sancerre…"

"Harry! Are you listening to me?"

"I like it when you talk dirty."

Arla face palmed her right cheek. "Jesus, Harry," she groaned.

"This is getting better."

"I just want to watch the house and have a look around. Are you coming or not?"

Harry sighed. "No. And you aren't going either."

"I am," she said and hung up.

CHAPTER 25

While Arla strode out to the rear corridor, and then to the double
doors that led to the carpool, a dark figure stole across an alley
between two houses in Tooting Broadway. The figure stopped, and
in the darkness, took a deep breath, smelling the diesel-streaked
night air. The detective inspector's house was right across, on Hoyle
Road. Detective Arla Baker. The figure had been observing her
closely. She was passionate about her job, and didn't spend much
time at home. Which gave rise to this opportunity. The figure walked
calmly across the road. Hoyle Road didn't have any CCTV. The
road was deserted. The detective lived in the garden-floor apartment
of the split-level Victorian house. The windows were dark, and the
figure knew the place would be empty. After watching for five
minutes, the figure approached the door and took out the Swiss
Army knife. Using the credit card to slide across the door jamb, the
figure used the hook from the knife inside the lock. Within a minute,
it was inside, and no one had walked down the road behind it.
The figure took out the flashlight and shone it to the ground, cupping
the mouth. Across the corridor, the bedroom door was ajar. The
figure stepped in and smelled Arla Baker's fragrance.

*****

Arla drove her Ford Fiesta through the broad avenue of Brixton High
Street. She passed by the huge promenade of the old Morleys
department store. In the 1920s Brixton was the centre of London's
new shopping malls, with three of the largest shopping centres in the
country, Morleys being the largest. The bombing in the Second
World War put an end to that, and Brixton never recovered from that
decline. The first Afro-Caribbean wave of immigrants were lured to
post-war London with the promise of new jobs in 1948, and most
settled in Brixton and surrounding areas. The Brixton that Arla now
drove through was still affectionately known as Little Jamaica, and
most of the population were of Afro-Caribbean ethnicity.

Arla drove to Southern Street, a road off the long, narrow Coldharbour Lane. She parked her car a few doors down from number 17. According to the Land Registry, that was where the Dooley family lived, and Mark was the youngest son. Arla sat in her car for a while, then noticed a tall figure slouching up the road. A cigarette tip glowed near the man's mouth. As the figure got nearer, Arla observed closely, finding the gait familiar. Then she smirked and shook her head.

The figure stopped on the pavement, and leaned over the passenger side window. There was a knock. Arla put the window down.

"Are you going to let me in, or what?" Harry asked. He took one last drag on his cigarette, then threw it away.

"What are you doing here?" Arla asked, keeping her voice even. She didn't want Harry to think she was glad to see him.

He sat down, and took out a small lunch box from his jacket pocket, with a plastic spoon.

"Got you some food."

Arla frowned. "What?"

"Remember the salad I made? Shame to let it go to waste. So I brought you some."

Arla was touched. "You shouldn't have."

"When was the last time you ate? Bet you skipped lunch."

Lunchtime had been the emotional roller coaster she had suffered at the Burroughs house. Of course she hadn't had any lunch, and didn't miss it either. Too much caffeine did that to her.

She shrugged and reached for the lunch box. It tasted divine. She devoured the whole box, then put the spoon inside and handed it back to Harry.

He put it back in his pocket without further comment.

"Thanks," Arla said, trying her best not to look at him. She had needed that.

"No problem. Any sign of our man?"

"I don't know what he looks like, but there's no sign of anyone."

"Lights on downstairs," Harry observed. It was a typical London residential street, terraced houses stuck onto each other like postage stamps, lives and deaths shared across two flimsy rows of bricks, stretching across the oceans, from one end of the world to the other.

"Did Trident not send you the case file?" Harry asked.

"Apparently I need clearance from a superior rank for transfer of files."

Harry shook his head. "All this bloody box-ticking. Gets us nowhere. Let's hope we don't get the wrong guy."

Arla didn't answer. She watched the light in the downstairs window of number 17 go off. The house was now sunk in darkness. The street light created pools of yellow halogen light on the ground below. She watched and waited, feeling Harry sitting still, doing the same.

She almost missed the shadow that walked in from behind. It was almost upon them, on the other side of the street. She watched the shape in her wing-view mirror.

"We got something," she whispered to Harry.

The shadow walked up to number 17. It was a man, and he was wearing a hoodie, his features hidden. His trainers were white. The man stood at the doorway, and took a key out from his pocket. He turned the key and went inside.

Harry was sifting through Google Maps. "There's another row of houses at the back. I can go around…"

Arla knew he wanted to avoid the mistake of last time, when Paul had escaped. But there were only two of them.

"No," she said. "One of us has to stay in the front when the other goes inside. He could come out the front as well."

"OK," Harry said, "I'm going in, and that's not up for discussion. You stay here, and radio for backup."

He opened the door and sidled out, shutting the door softly. Arla stayed in the car, and pulled out her radio. She called for a uniform unit, asking for Wadsworth who she knew was on duty. She wanted to call Sandford, who was keeping watch on Paul's house in Clapham, but couldn't risk missing Paul in the process.

She watched Harry pause at the doorway, then turn the handle and go in. She frowned. Had the door been unlocked, or did Harry pick it? She got out of the car quickly, feeling for the flashlight in her pocket. Her fingers closed around the cold, metallic surface as she crossed the road.

She arrived before number 17 just in time. The front door burst open, and a man ran out, heading straight for her. He saw her and stopped. He jumped over the brick fence, heading for the road. Arla shouted for him to stop, and ran after him. The man was quick, but he had to jump over the fence. He landed on the road when Arla flew at him, tackling him like a rugby player, grabbing him by the midriff. Momentum was on her side, and they slammed against the brick fence.

Arla felt a surge of pain as her hand hit the bricks, and a grunt from the man as his body bounced against the wall. The man fought her, trying to escape from her grip. He reached up and punched Arla. She moved her head away at the last minute, and the blow hit her shoulder, pushing her back. The man kicked with his leg, catching Arla in the belly, and pain blossomed inside, but she didn't fall over. Her hand pulled out the metallic Maglite, and she raised it high and brought it down as hard as she could. She hit the side of his head, above the ear, and she heard a curse of pain. She hit him again, and his face slumped down to the ground, dazed.

Arla whipped off the handcuffs from her belt and grabbed his hand. She turned him over, ignoring the pain in her belly and wanting to vomit. She wanted to read him the Miranda rights, but she didn't know his name, and the nausea was almost gagging her. She finished cuffing him, then sank back against the wall, breathing heavily, sweat drenching her body.

She heard shouts and cursing, and two bodies staggered out from the house into the street.

"Be quiet!" a voice boomed. It was Harry. He tussled the man he had cuffed down to the ground, then looked at Arla.

"You OK?" he panted.

"Not bad," she gasped. "Who is he?"

"Don't know his name yet, because he won't give it to me. Him and his friend were too busy counting up money when I got to them."

Arla got to her feet, and turned over the man she had cuffed. He was lighter than she thought he would be. She flashed the light on his face, and recognised him after a beat. He was young, barely a man. There was an ugly bruise on his right forehead where the Maglite had hit him, and he still looked dazed.

It was Paul Ofori.

CHAPTER 26

Arla heard the footsteps and looked up. Several people had come out
of their houses, and more were coming up the street. She looked
behind Harry and saw similar movement. A crowd was gathering.
"Did you call for backup?" Harry grunted as he pulled up his man.
Arla looked around her wildly, chest heaving. "Yeah, but they might
be the last thing we want."
With an effort, she pulled Paul to his feet. "Move, Harry," she
ordered.
He had started already, but the inquisitive crowd was now hemming
them in.
"Make way!" Harry shouted. "This is the police!"
A murmur arose from the crowd, which wasn't very thick, Arla
noticed. But the longer they waited, the worse it would become. Arla
wondered if either of the men had a chance to use their phones. She
hadn't even searched Paul. She leaned him against the fence, and
quickly patted him down. Then she turned around with him. Harry
had moved ahead and he was closer to her car. She knew that Harry
had driven down as well, and she got the impression he would leave
his car here. As Arla stepped onto the road, a Rastafarian man
stepped forward.
"Where you takin 'im, mon? 'E's only a boy!" The man was angry.
His shout created another murmur from the crowd.
With one arm, Arla steadied Paul, and with the other hand she
whipped out her badge. She held it up in the air for all to see,
especially for the man who was now standing a couple of feet away
from her.
She shouted her name and ID. "This man is under arrest. Now stand
back, and let us do our job."
"What's he under arrest for?" someone shouted from her left. Arla
had no time for this. She pushed Paul along with her, then looked up
in alarm as a group of men stood in her way.
"You need to move," Arla said, trying to shove past them.
"Just tell us what he is under arrest for? He's a kid: why don't you
arrest some of the real criminals out there?" a woman shouted from
somewhere, and another murmur rose from the crowd, a dangerous
hubbub of dissent.

Arla gritted her teeth and pushed and shoved her way through. A shout rang out from in front of her – in a voice that she recognised – and relief ran through her. It was Harry.

The crowd parted to an extent as Harry's long frame pushed its way through. But it also created its own problems. Some of the assembled took exception to a man pushing them around. The Rastafarian man raised his voice again.

"You think we all criminals, mon? Our children, dem criminal, too?"

"Fucking pigs!" someone shouted at the back. Harry pushed his way to Arla and gave her a hand. He grabbed Paul at the waist and took him off Arla.

The crowd was denser now, and the chanting was spreading.

"Fucking pigs! Fucking pigs!"

"Pig dem! Pig dem!" a chorus answered back.

"Leave our boys alone!"

Arla was sweating profusely. Her heart thudded in her mouth. A sea of bodies was now pressing close to them: hands reached out and touched her hair and face. Blindly, she pushed on, holding onto Harry's coat. Someone grabbed the back of her shirt, and she shrugged it off, but another hand pulled at her belt. She kicked out, and heard someone swear.

A blare of sirens suddenly pierced the melee, and flashing blue lights lit up the entire street. The squad cars drove right up towards the crowd, dispersing it to an extent. The cars screeched to a stop, and Arla saw uniform officers peel out. John Sandford, the black sergeant, was the first one to reach them.

"Take the prisoner," Harry said, thrusting Paul towards John. He reached behind and grabbed Arla's hand.

Arla shouted at the uniforms. "Get out of here, meet back at the nick!"

Somehow, Harry managed to get her back to the car. The other guy was still handcuffed in the back seat, but he was awake. He was on his back, trying to kick the window. The car was shaking with his blows.

"Oi!" Harry roared and beeped the car open, then chucked the keys to Arla. "Drive," he said, then ran and opened the back door, and piled inside. Arla saw him grab hold of the man and pull him up to sitting. By then, Arla was in the driver's seat and the engine had revved to life.

She drove out and zoomed down the road, blaring the horn as a couple of men blocked her way. They scattered, but not before they threw something at the windscreen. The missile landed with a heavy clunk on the windscreen, and Arla winced. She ducked and the car swerved wildly. The windscreen had spider's web cracks that spread rapidly. Arla tried desperately to get control of the car, but the back-end fishtailed out, and slammed into a parked car. A back window shattered on impact, showering shards of glass on Harry.

"Shit!" Arla shouted. She spun the wheel and slammed on the gas. The tyres spun on asphalt, letting off a screeching sound. With a jolt, the car came off, and Arla had to rotate the wheel again to stay in control. She zoomed down the road, scattering people as she rushed. She could hear more sirens in the background. She took a hard left as she got to Brixton High Street, and raced down the road towards Clapham.

"You OK?!" she yelled at Harry. Wind whipped past her ear, and she could hear the roar in the back of the car.

"Fine, just drive," Harry shouted back. In the rear-view mirror she could see he had the man pinned down.

She set her jaw and concentrated on the road.

CHAPTER 27

Arla stumbled back into her flat, exhaustion making every movement an effort. Paul Ofori was in lock-up for the night with the other man who had confessed to being Mark Dooley. The night staff would take a statement from them, and have it ready for Arla in the morning.

As she turned the light on in the hallway, the first thing she noticed was the heat. The flat was positively baking. Had she left the thermostat on? It was attached to the wall on the hallway, so she walked over to it. It was on. How could she have been so careless? She tried to think, but in her current state of mind, nothing appeared with clarity. The mirror was opposite her, and she caught her face in it as she turned the thermostat down to 16 degrees. Her face was deathly pale, black hair strands poking out everywhere, sticking to her sweaty forehead. Make-up had bled from her eyes. She looked a complete mess, and felt like one, too.

Her eyes fell on the digital keypad of the alarm on the wall, and her eyes narrowed. Why hadn't it gone off when she came in? Had she forgotten to set it? She jabbed some buttons, but the screen remained blank. Arla sighed. The fuse must have gone.

The apartment was still boiling. She opened the door to the living room, and from the darkness another cloud of heat wafted out. She stepped inside. It was pitch black, and she stumbled around, fingers groping on the wall. It felt like a sauna inside. Rivulets of sweat poured silently down her forehead and the nape of her neck. She wiped her face, and finally found the switch. The room was suddenly bathed in a yellow glow. Arla blinked several times. This room faced the street, and was her study and living area. Her desk with the laptop on it stood by the bay window. The curtains were drawn, as she had left them. The brown leather sofa set and TV, the two criminology textbooks she had left by the laptop, and the magazine on the coffee table were all undisturbed. Arla wasn't especially house-proud: the relative neatness in this room stemmed from the fact that most of her "living" was done in the bedroom.

"Solitary living" was a better phrase to describe it, she thought to herself with a lonely sigh, as she parted the curtain to open the casement window, which had a side panel with a handle. She pressed on the handle and it turned easily. Arla frowned. She normally locked these before she... In fact she never opened them, as they faced the street. Her brows tightened and the corners of her eyes flickered.

Ask DCI Arla Baker where Maddy is.

The message left at the Burroughs' residence.

Arla snapped around on her heels. The hallway light was still on. The silence was almost total, and she knew where the creaky floorboards were under the carpet, so she tiptoed around to avoid them. From the coffee table she picked up the brass candleholder. A strange weapon, but it was all she had currently. She padded out into the hallway, then stared at the darkness of the kitchen. The front half was illuminated, and she could see the legs of her dining table and the chairs. The door at the other end, which led to her small, ten-foot garden, was closed. Or was it? Would it be open when she tried to open it?

Arla suppressed the fear that was gnawing away at the back of her mind. She breathed open-mouthed, trying to control her surging pulse rate. The bedroom door was ajar. With one foot she prodded it open, then shrank back against the cleaning cabinet. A triangle of light opened onto the black carpet. No sound came from within, save her heart beating so loudly she could swear it was audible to anyone listening.

She could see the light switch on the wall. Arla took a deep breath. She flung herself inside the room, crashing against the door with all her strength. Her hand was on the switch, flicking it on. She fell on the floor, carried by her momentum, and crouched against the dresser wardrobe. The candleholder was still in her hand, raised. The room was empty. Her bed was covered with the duvet, like she did every morning. Two red, heart-shaped cushions rested on top, with her initials carved on them in white. They were a gift from the station when she had reached the DCI grade. Her bed was undisturbed. Arla flung open the wardrobe, and brushed through her hanging dresses. It was empty, too.

She went to the fuse box, and looked at the switch for the alarm circuit. It was turned down, which meant it hadn't tripped. Arla frowned and went back to the alarm. She went outside, and stood for a while on the porch, watching. The streets lights cast gloomy penumbras of yellowness on the street. A few pedestrians walked past, but none stood watching. She looked at the houses opposite: either most of the curtains were drawn, or she could see the neighbours moving around.

She bent down to the flower bed, where the earth was freshly overturned. She did it every morning before she left. She put her hand inside and rooted around till she found the alarm cable. She lifted it up, trying not to dislodge the planted dahlias.

Arla's breath caught in her chest. The cable had been cut halfway through. That's why the alarm wasn't working. She stood, panting, looking feverishly around.

She slammed the front door shut, locked it, went to the kitchen, and turned the lights on. She tried the back door and, to her relief, it was locked. She took out the key from the drawer, then went back to her coat in the hallway. She took out the Maglite, then went back to the kitchen and opened the door. Sounds from the street filtered in. Hoyle Road was a quiet road, but the larger Tooting High Road lay at the other end. Traffic growled in the distance.

Arla switched the light on and swallowed heavily. The beam pierced into the dark. She swung it around the corners, picking out the blooming flower vases. In the middle of the paved space she had put a garden table, a cheap one from Ikea, and all that she could afford after rent. Next to it lay a small coal barbecue. So far, it hadn't been used this year.

The beam from the Maglite lit up dust motes as it traversed into the farther ends of the garden. Arla stepped out, swivelling her eyes around. Her throat was caked and dry. Even the sweat felt hard, saline residue against her skull. The garden was empty. At the end there was a small, wooden seat for three people. Nothing in the garden had been disturbed.

She was on her way back when the flashlight shone on something metallic. There was something under the barbecue. Arla directed the light on it, and picked out a small steel box with a hook on top. Her heart hammered in her chest. She had definitely not left anything here. Not recently, and not before either. The barbecue had not been used.

She approached the barbecue, bent down, and pulled out a pair of gloves from her pocket. Then she picked the box up. She put it on the table. It glared in the light of the Maglite, the brightness radiating back like an open, evil eye.

With a trembling hand, Arla reached out and grasped the hook on the top. She lifted it and the lid opened. Inside there was a green felt cover, the type used to store jewellery.

In the middle there was a purple amethyst earring, with small golden ringlets arranged in a circle around the central stone. Only one.

As Arla recognised the earring, a frozen scream rose and then died in her throat. This had belonged to her sister Nicole. She stepped back, gasping, fear galloping like a racehorse in her heart. She swung the Maglite around, jerking it everywhere. Into the ground, the fences, the houses opposite and above.

She closed the lid, picked up the box and ran inside the kitchen. She shut and locked the door, then sank against it, sliding down to the floor. Her breath was heavy, wild, scratching around in her lungs like a wild animal.

No one knew about that earring apart from her. It had been a gift from Nicole when they were teenagers, and Nicole had a matching pair. But Nicole was long gone, and she was never coming back.

Ask DCI Arla Baker where Maddy is.

Arla gritted her teeth, and this time she did scream, a wounded, primeval sound ripped out from her vocal cords.

CHAPTER 28

Cindy had returned to the council flat with the little boy, and called the police. The cause of death was a drug overdose, which wasn't surprising given the mother's state. The boy was taken into care. Cindy took a sip of her wine, and thought of the boy's face before he walked away with the social worker. He had turned, just to look at her. Cindy had held his eyes for a few seconds. She knew that boy would get lost in the maze of social care, sent to foster homes, and if he ran away, to juvenile care homes. She couldn't imagine a worse fate for the little soul, but what options did he have? Her hand tightened around the stem of the glass. Maybe she could have given the boy a better life. No, that was madness. She drained her glass and tried to concentrate on the TV, trying to stop the voices starting to speak inside her head.

A soap was on, and a man and a woman were arguing. The woman was shouting, red in the face.

"Leave her alone, you bastard! How could you do this to her?"

The man said something and the camera zoomed into his face. Cindy didn't hear what the man was saying anymore. His face had morphed into the bushy eyebrows and spiky hair of her abusive foster father. He was leaning over her bed, his breath fetid in her mouth… Cindy started breathing faster, panic surging inside her like a geyser. She pulled her legs close to her, and her knuckles whitened around the stem of the wine glass.

His eyes bulged out, and he reached out with his hand, and the hand perforated the screen of the TV, that horrible, hairy hand: it smelled of metal and fire, darkened at the tips, and it clamped over her mouth.

"No!" Cindy screamed, standing up. She threw the wine glass at the TV, and it smashed against the screen. But his face was on the screen still, only it was different now, the face of another of her abusers.

Fear and rage mixed into a lethal cocktail inside her skull. She grabbed her hair with both hands, pulling strands from her scalp, and her voice bellowed out like a whiplash, "Stop it!!"

The screen changed into the woman's face, then it broke into a commercial, as if it had just heard her command. Cindy closed her eyes and knelt down on the carpet. The remote had fallen off the sofa. She used it to turn the TV off. Her face was hot and painful like someone was poking daggers at it from inside. She got up and stumbled out of the room.

She lived in a small, ground-floor flat, council-owned. It was a 1920s house, art deco style, divided into two. She went to the small kitchen at the back and unlocked the back door. She stepped out into the garden. It was paved with cement blocks, and weeds grew between the cracks. An old water drum, the type that stored water drained from the gutters, stood in one corner, holes punctured in its sides. The night was sticky and warm, a smell of grease, cooking oil and diesel heavy in the air. The sky was clear, and over the yellow lights of the street corner she could see pinpoints of starlight in the black sky. She breathed the night air for a while, then went back inside.

She went to her table drawer and opened it. She took out the steel box inside and put it on the table. Inside, she had a stack of photos, a phone number, and an earring. She held the earring up to the light, examining it closely. She put it to one side. She took a newspaper sheet, and armed with a pair of scissors, she set about cutting out numbers. When she had the phone number digits all cut out, she picked up an A4 piece of paper. With a glue-stick and wearing her gloves, she stuck the digits on the A4 sheet. When it was done, she looked back at her handiwork. It was perfect.

She had prepared her dinner already, a ready meal cottage pie that she stuck in the microwave. After eating, she finished off the rest of the cheap wine bottle. That made her sleepy, but not enough. She opened the box of medicines she got from her GP. She took out the small blue pills of Diazepam, and swallowed two of the 5mg tablets. She wanted to be ready for tomorrow, and for that she needed a good night's sleep.

She couldn't have the voices disturbing her tonight. She read the rest of the newspaper for a while, and when her eyes drooped, she got into the bedroom and crashed, still fully clothed.
*****
Cindy arrived at the library at ten the next morning. She was the first one to get there, and that's how she liked it. She went to the study area at the back and sat down to read the newspaper.

It was in the back aisles of the study area, behind a row of journals, that she had first seen the boy and girl snogging. They were oblivious to her, and Cindy had silently replaced the bound journal she had just picked up, and watched them. They kissed passionately, and seeing their closed eyes and rapt faces, she had felt a strange sensation. A blunted, headless force that made her knees weak and heart palpate. And then she felt shame. Shame that she wanted to do it herself. There was no pleasure in it, because for her it had always been buried under a mountain of shame.

Every Wednesday it became a ritual. They would come, after their lessons, and meet up here when they thought no one was watching. She learned their names and followed them around.

When Cindy learned who she was, it had not been a surprise. She knew that the girl had been chosen for a reason.

Everything was falling into place.

Cindy was stacking a row of books when she felt her phone buzz. She picked it up and frowned. The LogMeIn app was flashing. The app allowed her to remotely control her computers. In the safe house, she had hooked the CCTV cameras to a desktop PC, and uploaded the LogMeIn software on the PC. The app on her iPhone allowed her to access the PC from her phone, and thereby she could see all the feeds from the CCTV cameras.

The cameras were motion and infrared light detectable. The screen on her phone divided into four panels, showing the front, back, her office, and the barn room where the girl was kept. Although she was strapped down, she was lifting up her head and looking around. The rattling bed had tripped the cameras with the movement of her body. Cindy stared for a while. The girl couldn't move, despite wrenching her body in every direction. She looked pathetic, trapped like a worm. Cindy tapped on the screen and zoomed in. The girl looked at the camera, her hair was stringy and hard, and her cheeks sunken. Her eyes widened in terror.

Cindy smiled. She had a lot of work to do today.

CHAPTER 29

Arla woke up with a headache and a dry mouth. The alarm was
jingling on the bedside table, and she reached out a heavy arm and
slapped it. It was 6.00 am and sunlight was already visible through
the gaps in the curtains. Memories of last night diffused through the
fog of slumber and registered on her consciousness.
Her eyelids snapped open, and she looked around the room. Then
she sat up in the bed, drawing the blanket up to her chin. She was
alone. She sighed and closed her eyes.
Jesus, this was stupid.
She took a long glass of cold water from the kitchen sink, then
stepped into the shower. She hated cold showers, and the hot rush of
water soothed the grime from last night, drumming against her head.
As she dried her hair, she glanced at her phone. Harry had left a
message.
"Had the wine by myself last night. 🙁"
She thought of the day ahead and took a deep breath. It was going to
be busy, and she would also have to deal with Johnson. As she
brushed then sprayed her hair, Arla wondered about the earring. The
steel box, with the ring inside, was already in her jacket, inserted last
night so she didn't forget this morning. For the hundredth time, she
wondered if it could have been the same person who left the message
and put the earring in her garden.
Why? Who could possibly gain anything from this?
Whoever it was, they knew the most secret aspect of her life. At
work, only Harry and Johnson knew the whole story about Nicole's
death, and what happened to her family. Arla stopped brushing. And
her father. When was the last time she had seen him? She didn't
want to, but he was still alive, and just for this, she had to see him.
She made a mental note of dropping by where he lived that evening.
She pushed the thought away from her mind. Seeing her father was
not a prospect she relished.
Before she left, she made sure all the windows were locked, and the
back door. She peeked at the garden and the barbecue. No more
surprises. She thought about Harry's remarks about having CCTV
and motion sensor lights for the garden. She did have a light, but it
was operated by a switch from the kitchen.

Sunlight was warming up the streets as she walked down, commuters appearing from their houses. Traffic was light as usual, although schools were still open till the middle of July. It was the end of June, so no more than two weeks away. The sky was a brilliant, scrubbed blue already, with majestic palaces of white clouds. She walked past the overflowing rubbish bin in the corner, and the mingled smell of diesel fumes and frying food from the café hit her nostrils. Students ran to catch the bus, and older, wide-hipped Caribbean women walked slowly towards the Broadway Market. Arla joined the rainbow rush, getting overtaken by suited professionals en route to their City jobs. She stopped on the way to pick up an almond croissant and a café latte from Starbucks, then joined the human flow descending underground.

By the time she got to the station, the brisk walking had created a sheen of moisture on her forehead. She nodded at Sandford, the black sergeant at the desk, then buzzed herself in with her ID. It was 7.20, and none of the team had arrived as yet. She sat down at her table with a new cup of coffee, and went through the statement that Paul and Mark Dooley had submitted to the uniforms who had kept them in overnight cells. It wasn't much. Mark Dooley had admitted to belonging to the Z14 gang, but Paul had been non-committal. He had hardly said anything, actually, apart from revealing that Mark had helped him escape.

Arla thought back to the photos of Maddy with Paul, and the tattoos. She stacked the folders away, and walked down the green lino floor to the secure detention area. The white-shirted constable rose from his chair when she showed her ID. From a chain dangling at his waist, he removed a thick set of keys and opened a grilled door. They walked down the corridor of cells, all heavy, steel doors with an eye slit 1.5 metres from floor level.

"Paul Ofori?" the constable, whose name was PC Dickson, asked. Arla nodded. Then she put her head in the eye slot. Paul was lying in the cot, one arm draped over his eyes. His chest rose and fell, but his body was still. He seemed to be sleeping.

"Open the door," Arla said.

PC Dickson asked, "Are you authorising, guv?"

"Yes."

He had a blackboard in his hand, with a white sheet of paper clipped onto it. "Sign here, please, guv."

Arla signed, then stepped back as the keys turned and the heavy door clanged open. Arla walked into the cell. It was small, five by six feet, with a cot and a jutting shelf stuck to the wall. It was a holding cell for overnight stays only.

The door remained open. Paul opened his eyes, and sat up slowly, blinking. Arla spoke over her shoulder. "Close the door please, Dickson."

The constable was uncomfortable. "I'm not supposed to, guv. You know that."

Arla turned around. "What do you think I'm going to do? And don't worry about him. One night in a cell is enough to cool him off. Isn't that right, Paul?" she asked, turning around to face the youngster.

Paul looked crestfallen. His hands were gripping the edge of the cot, and his head was lowered. He looked up as he realised he was being addressed.

"There's not going to be any trouble, is there, Paul?" Arla asked again. He swallowed and nodded.

Arla said, "Dickson, would you please get him a glass of water?" Dickson huffed, but ambled off to comply. Arla closed the door without shutting it, and pulled in the chair that was outside the cell. She faced Paul and took out her ID badge.

"DCI Arla Baker, in charge of investigating the disappearance of Madeleine Burroughs."

Paul's eyes flickered at the mention of Maddy's name. He held Arla's gaze for a little while, then looked away.

Arla said, "There's no lawyers here, and this statement is not being recorded. Do you understand, Paul?"

"Y...Yes, I do." He licked his lips. Arla was looking closely at his hands, his posture, what he did with his feet, and his expression. His thumb and forefinger rubbed against each other, under the cot. He pursed his lips and looked around. He looked anything but calm and cool like a seasoned criminal.

"You can talk to me, Paul. Nothing you tell me now will be treated as evidence."

PC Dickson came back with the water. He handed the paper cup to Arla, gave her a look, then walked away.

Paul took a sip of the water. "I don't know anything."

"What happened the night of 3rd June?"

Paul didn't answer. He swallowed more of the water. "Nothing. I was with my friends."

"What friends?"

"Eh... school friends."

"If you give me their names I can check with them."

Paul nodded and started to move his feet. Arla said in a gentle voice, "You were waiting for Maddy outside the pub, weren't you? Why didn't you see her inside?"

Paul looked at Arla, like he was debating whether to trust her or not. He looked scared and lonely, and Arla felt sorry for him.

She said, "It doesn't have to be this way, Paul. You tell us the truth, and if you haven't done anything wrong, we will let you go. I can promise you."

Paul suddenly blurted, "It wasn't me. It's not my fault."

"What's not your fault?"

"Any of this. I'm innocent."

"Then tell us what happened, and we can let you go."

He stared at her and she held his eyes. Paul rubbed his face, then stared at the floor before replying. "You're going to twist my words. Make me out to be the bad guy. You guys plant evidence to convict people like us, don't you?"

Arla was shocked, but she tried not to show it. But the indignation she felt was tinged in her voice. "No, Paul, we don't plant evidence. We want to catch the real bad guys. And I don't know what you mean by 'people like you'. You go to one of the best private schools in the whole of South London. Is that the kind of people you mean?"

Paul was silent. After a while he said, "Leave me alone."

Arla stared at him, then got up. As she was leaving, Paul said, "I want a lawyer."

Arla nodded, and walked out with the chair, shutting the door. She waved at PC Dickson at the end of the corridor, who stood up and walked over.

"Bring him up to the interrogation room at 8.45, as soon as we have a legal aid solicitor ready."

"Yes, guv."

CHAPTER 30

Cindy was sweating underneath the black hoodie. Thank God it was cotton. She shrank further back into the awning of the shop as a car whizzed past Balham High Street. The street was deserted at this time. It was still warm, that early predawn summer chill still a few hours away. A train creaked noisily over the bridge to her left. Cindy had covered her face with a balaclava, not visible when she had her hoodie up and over half her face. It was a man's size, XXL, and, although she wasn't thin, it covered her adequately. She also had a pair of sunglasses to wear when she walked out into the high street, where the CCTV cameras could pick her up. She walked with a limp as well when she was in public. The cops would be looking for a sexless invalid if they did manage to pick her up on CCTV. Cindy looked at the row of shops opposite, and right next to the bridge, the tall, once stately Victorian house that was now a dilapidated block of flats. All owned by the council as well. There was one window she was focused on. On the third floor, facing the street. The old man lived there, and one day, Cindy knew, they would meet each other. She had followed him around a few times, and once, he had turned around to look, sensing her behind him. Cindy had enjoyed that. He hadn't seen her face, covered under her hoodie.

The shadow of the shop's awning hid Cindy effectively. A drunk lumbered past, and she could easily have leaned across and struck him over the head with a brick...

She stiffened as a flash of light caught her eyes. She looked up, and her heart beat faster when she saw the third-floor window lit up. It was prominent, as the other flats around it remained in darkness. Cindy stepped forward. She wanted him to see her. Let him realise that he was being watched.

The blind on the window lifted slowly, and the shape of an old man was framed against the window, lit up from inside. He looked down, and for a moment Cindy was sure that their eyes met. She made no effort to move or hide away. She stared up at him, and watched him looking down.

After a while, he lowered the blind and retreated into the room. The light went off, plunging the window into darkness.

CHAPTER 31

Harry was at his desk when Arla walked back into the open-plan detectives' room. He rose from his desk. She smelled woodsmoke and burned spice, and saw a questioning look in his chestnut eyes. His coffee-coloured cheeks were smoothly shaven as usual. He towered over her as she got closer.

"My office," she said. She had hesitated about telling him. But the discovery of Nicole's earring had put a different twist on everything. Now she knew whoever had left the note at the Burroughs' residence was playing a strange, dangerous game.

Harry's eyebrows were knitted together as he leaned against the closed door of her office.

"You sure they are the same earrings as your sister's?"

Arla went to her coat and slipped on some gloves. She took the box out and showed the earring to Harry.

"In the early 90s they were all the craze. All sixteen-year-olds wore them. Nicole was no exception. And only I had these. I looked last night, and both of mine were present. Mine and Nicole's." She dropped her eyes. She only ever had one of Nicole's. Harry knew the grisly details of how she got the other one. Only because he had been there.

Harry looked at the rings critically. "What about your father?"

"What about him? Even if I did contact him, what would he be doing with his daughters' earrings?"

"So you have both pairs? All four of them?"

"Yes. And none of mine are missing."

Harry frowned. "So, let's assume this is a replica. Whoever did this knew what earring Nicole wore."

"Yes, and that's what is scary. No one apart from me, and now you, knows."

"Johnson might do."

"Yes, but he won't know the exact type." Arla got up and started to pace her office. "Either they found my pair, or they knew..." Arla stopped. Her sister's life after she had run away from home had always been a mystery to her. When her remains were found some of the gaps were closed, but not all. She gripped her forehead.

Why was this coming back to haunt her now?

"Hey," Harry said in a soothing voice. "Don't let this get to you. Let's take this one by one. We need to send an SOC team down to your house to look for clues. And we send this box down to the lab for the same reason."

Arla shook her head. "I don't want this to become a distraction when we are in the middle of a big case. And I need to tell Johnson about this in order to get the SOC guys in."

Into my flat, she thought. My own home, now a crime scene.

"I don't think we have a choice," Harry said. "If you don't want it to become a distraction, then deal with it properly. Otherwise you'll keep thinking about it."

Harry was right. She didn't have much time. Arla looked behind Harry. Detectives were beginning to drift into the office.

"OK," she said, "hold the fort here while I speak to Johnson." She rang her boss while Harry went outside to prepare the incident room for the morning brief.

In his office, Johnson listened to her carefully, a troubled expression on his face. "And you think this is the same person who left the message at the Burroughs' residence, about you?"

"I have no proof of that, sir. But leaving my dead sister's earring, something I kept for years till I found her body, definitely fits a pattern. If this person wants to torture me, then..." Arla looked away, embarrassed by her use of the word "torture". She certainly felt tortured now, and the word had just slipped out.

Johnson tapped his finger on the green felt of his desk. Above his head, photos of himself with David Cameron, the ex-prime minister, smiled back at Arla from the glass cabinet.

"This person knows a lot about you. Don't they?"

"I would say that's an understatement, sir. We kept the real news about Nicole secret from the media, the bit about us being related. How the hell this person knows, I have no idea."

Johnson said, "OK, open a case, and send the SOC guys to your place for prints etc. And the box to the lab, with its contents."

"Yes, sir." Arla rose to leave.

"Just a minute. I heard about the fracas in Brixton last night. I thought we were going to tread carefully."

"We are, sir." Arla shrugged. Johnson nodded, a sympathetic look in his eyes. "Keep me posted. Are you interrogating the main suspect today?"

"Definitely."

It was 8.20 on the big white clock on the wall in the incident room, and everyone was present. A smell of coffee and doughnuts was in the air. A hush fell across the room as Arla entered. She glanced at Harry and gave a slight nod. The look of relief on his face was palpable.

Arla looked at the whiteboard, where a photo of Mark Dooley had appeared next to Paul Ofori.

"OK, people." She turned to the room. "We have some news about Maddy. She has another social media account which shows a different side to her." Arla told them about Maddy's alternative lifestyle, and whistles and catcalls filled the room.

"OK, that's enough," Arla said. "Have we interviewed the pub employees and punters who were present that day?"

Lisa said, "As many punters as we could. I showed photos of all her friends to the pub staff. Only a handful were there."

Arla asked, "And they remembered Maddy?"

"They did when I showed them the photo. She left the pub at 20.00, going to wherever. According to her friend Maya, she had an appointment with Paul Ofori." Lisa looked up. "He's in today, right?"

"Speaking to a lawyer right now," Arla said. "I'm taking the official statement in fifteen minutes."

Arla asked, "Did the phone logs from the parents' handsets show anything?"

"On the night, they made multiple calls to her phone," James piped up from the front row. "Before that, occasional calls from her mother's phone to hers."

Arla said, "As far as I remember, Maddy made some calls to the same number the night before, right?"

James said, "Yes. We got the IMEI details of the number. It's a pay-as-you-go. We're trying to find out which phone mast it connected with. That should give us an approximate location, within 500 metres."

"Alright," Arla said. "We need to keep an eye out on this number, then. Any news on Maddy's phone?"

James groaned. "Boss, do you know how much CCTV I have to go through? It's me and Rob, and there's no way we can get through it all even in one month." Arla knew he was referring to the motorway CCTV images.

"Our approximate time of Maddy's abduction is 21.00. Any CCTV images of a car coming out of the cul-de-sac?"

James face brightened. "Yes, that we do. There are three cars that left the pub car park, it seems. Unfortunately, all of them went in the same direction, between 9 and 10."

"Which direction is that?"

A map of Greater London and South-East Surrey was up on the wall. James got up and walked over. The map was large, ten by ten feet, and the cul-de-sac where the pub was situated in Brockwell Park was marked with a red pin.

James pointed with his finger. "From here, they went down towards the A23, heading south."

Arla felt a clutch of excitement. "And the phone was last on while it was on the M23?"

"Yes. But which one of the three cars went down that route?"

Arla fixed James with a stare. "You will have three more pairs of eyes now, to help you look. All three cars couldn't have headed down in the same direction. Even if they did, not all would be on the M23, unless we are really unlucky. So find out which one of those three cars went all the way down to the M23, and we probably have our man."

Arla raised her voice. "Anything from the SOC guys?"

Dean Lambert, one of the technical officers from SOC stood up. "It might be nothing, but we found some fibres where we found her blood and DNA. Now, the fibres could have come from anyone's clothes."

"Get to the point, please," Arla said impatiently.

"Sure." Dean, a senior technical officer, didn't look pleased at being rushed. "There are some pollen grains on the fibres that we have sent to the forensic botanist at Kew Gardens. She will shed some light on if these pollens are native to Brockwell and Clapham, or from further afield."

Arla asked, "And these fibres were found where we got Maddy's DNA?"

Dean nodded. "Good work, team. We're getting somewhere. OK, you all know what to do."

The meeting broke up, and Arla headed to the interrogation room with Harry.

CHAPTER 32

Paul Ofori looked scared. He glanced at Arla, then at Harry, and back at Arla again. Harry checked the camera and the DVD player were on. He pressed the remote to turn the recorder on, then introduced everyone present. Next to Paul, a bespectacled older man in a pinstripe suit sat impassively. Derek Smith was a veteran solicitor. He had his notepad out, and Arla knew he would have had his ten-minute chat with Paul in private already. Derek was also the legal aid solicitor for Mark Dooley. Arla had no time for solicitors, who acted in their clients' best interests, even when it was bloody obvious they were guilty. She was tired of seeing seasoned criminals get off the hook on technicalities – a lack of evidence in most cases. Arla started. "Paul, where were you on the night of 3rd June?"

"With my mother, watching TV. You can ask her."

"We have already, but we need to ask you as well. If that is the case, then why do Maddy's friends say that she was supposed to meet you that night?"

A look of annoyance flitted across Paul's face. "Maddy and her friends."

"What about them?" Arla asked.

Before Paul could speak, Derek leaned over and touched him on the arm. They spoke in whispered tones before Paul straightened. "They always made things up about me," he said.

"In what way?"

Paul glanced at Derek and the lawyer gave him a slight nod. Arla concealed her irritation and focused on Paul.

"That we were close and that. It wasn't true."

"Really?"

Paul nodded. "Yes."

Arla picked up the A4 envelope in front of her, and shook out the photos she had enlarged from Maddy's other Facebook page. She picked up one that showed Maddy and Paul showing off their tattoos in each other's arms, and turned it over to Paul.

His eyes widened, and a look of panic overcame his face. He leaned back in the chair. Derek leaned towards him and whispered something in his ear. Paul appeared not to have listened.

Arla said, "Is your answer still the same?"

Paul didn't answer. Arla asked, "I'm going to ask you again. Where were you on the 3rd of June evening, between 8 and 10 pm?"

"I told you," Paul said, his nostrils flaring. "In the house watching TV. Ask my mum!"

"You were not in the Wrangler's Arms pub, outside Brockwell Park?"

Arla already knew from Lisa and Rob that the witnesses who had seen Maddy didn't recall seeing Paul.

"No, I wasn't."

"So where were you?"

Derek Smith cleared his throat noisily. "I think my client has already answered that question, DCI Baker. Can we move on now, please?"

Arla ignored him and stared at Paul, who avoided her gaze. Arla needed to know if Paul had seen anything that night. But he could only do that if he had been at the park. The way in which he was sticking to his guns didn't bode well for that theory. And Miss Ofori had already provided his alibi.

Arla flexed her jaws. If Paul had been a witness to Maddy's abduction, then she would have hit the jackpot. Right now, she was losing cards. She decided to change tactics.

"Did you love her, Paul?"

Startled, the youngster raised his eyes to hers. He looked surprised, then a stricken look came over his face. His eyes darted around like a trapped animal, and he swallowed.

Arla said, "You did, didn't you?"

An expression of pain flitted across Paul's face, then he looked away. Derek leaned over to him again.

Arla said, "Where is she, Paul?"

Paul craned his neck back and shook his head, staring at the ceiling. "If I knew, I'd tell you. God, just leave me alone!"

"Why did you run the day we came to see you, Paul?"

Again, a quick whisper between lawyer and client. Paul seemed to have some difficulty in getting the next words out. Arla noticed Derek staring at his client, then giving him a nudge. Paul nodded, looking resigned.

"Kids in school got money, right? Go to five-grand ski trips twice a year, and even more expensive holidays in the summer. School arranges trips once a year abroad. I can't go on any of them."

"Because you don't have the cash?"

Paul nodded, a doubtful look on his face, like he didn't know if he was doing the right thing. He glanced at Derek, who encouraged him to speak.

"So, I started selling dope on the side at school," Paul said. He looked as if he had got something big off his chest. "I told the right people I was their man, and pretty soon I had regular business."

"And one of these right people was Maddy?" Arla asked.

"Yes. She was the first one I spoke to, 'cos I knew she was cool. Her friends, too."

"Maya and Emma?"

Paul nodded. Arla exchanged a glance with Harry. A dope-dealing gang inside the exclusive Brunswick High School. Wonders would never cease.

Harry spoke up. "What sort of dope?"

"Cannabis."

"Maddy got into this, didn't she? Both of you were members of the gang, Z14."

To her surprise, Paul shook his head vigorously. "I never wanted to become a member. Sure, we had the tattoos to look hard, you know. It's good for street cred. But to actually become a member you have all this bullshit initiation stuff to do – like beat someone up, steal a car, all that rubbish."

Paul said, "Maddy wanted to become a member. But then she realised it was crap."

"What about Mark Dooley?"

Paul became quiet. Derek leaned over again. Their chat went on for longer this time. Paul looked unhappy, but he talked.

"Mark was supplying me. He made a gangbanger's life look like Heaven. I sort of went along with it, but I always knew it wasn't for Maddy or me."

"Is that why you ran, because you thought we were there to arrest you?"

Paul looked shamefaced. "Yeah. And I knew that Maddy was missing so I figured you were out to get me for that as well."

"Did you and Maddy ever talk of running away?"

A faraway look came into Paul's eyes and then he blinked. "Bitch!" he suddenly said with venom.

Arla and Harry looked at each other, surprised. "Excuse me?" Arla asked.

"It all changed later on. Things fucked up. She started two-timing me."

Arla leaned over. This was getting interesting. "She was seeing someone else?"

"Yes. She wouldn't tell me, but I knew. She was always on the phone to someone. When I asked, she said it was her parents checking up on her. She was lying, man."

Arla's mind was racing. She thought of the phone calls to the pay-as-you-go number that Maddy had made from her phone the night before 3rd June. A faint cone of light was appearing in her mind, lighting up the end of a tunnel.

"Paul, I want you to think very carefully now. Why didn't you see Maddy the night of 3rd June?"

"She said she had to go home from the pub."

Harry moved and Arla looked at him. They both knew it. Maddy had told everyone that she was meeting Paul. Could she have lied, instead meeting up with her other lover?

Arla asked, "Paul, everything you tell me here will be used in a court of law if this case proceeds to charges. Think carefully now. Are you sure Maddy told you that?"

Paul shook his head, exasperated. "I told you already. She said she was going back home."

But she wasn't, Arla thought to herself.

CHAPTER 33

Arla and Harry stepped back into the side room and watched Paul and Derek through the soundproof triple-glass barrier. A speaker above transmitted the whispered conversation they were having.

"Do you believe him?" Harry asked.

"Either he's a great actor, or he was truly shitting himself."

Harry nodded. "I got that impression, too. And he's a bit young to be that good an actor."

Arla had noted the pressure of speech when Paul had spoken. Like he had kept things bottled up inside him for too long, and needed to let go. There had been genuine regret in his eyes.

Arla knew she had to keep an open mind, but her gut instincts were screaming at her that Paul was not her man. He was a kid, in fact. A terrified kid.

But she also knew fear could make people do strange things. What if Paul had been hiding in the park, saw Maddy being abducted, and was now denying it to save himself more trouble?

She felt Harry's eyes on her. They looked at each other in silence, each feeling for what the other was thinking. Harry shook his head.

"Really?" Arla asked.

"Never say never. But I don't think he's part of any plan. He's too green."

"He's selling green in the school." Arla grinned despite herself. Hell, she could do with some green!

"If anything," Harry said, "that shows his immaturity. A pro would never make a childish move like that. He would have bigger fish to fry."

Arla shrugged. "Let's move on. Going to be a long day. Is Mark Dooley ready?"

Harry nodded and reached for the intercom hanging on the wall. Fifteen minutes later, they were sitting in the interview room next door, opposite Mark and Derek Smith again.

Mark had a confident smirk on his face that Arla didn't like. His short, curly hair was buzz cut, and he wore a black jumper, dark jeans and trainers. He slouched in the chair in an arrogant manner. Harry did the introductions for the DVD player, and they began.

Arla said, "Mark Dooley, where were you the night of 3rd June?"

"With my bitch," came the insolent reply.

Arla pursed her lips. "Can your partner verify that?"

"She ain't no partner." Mark's smirk was wider. "She's my bitch. You know what I mean?"

"No, I don't," Arla said evenly. "Are you saying you don't have an alibi?"

That got Mark's attention. He rolled his eyes. Arla noticed Derek try to tell him something, but Mark shrugged him off.

"Yeah, baby, I got an alibi."

"My name is DCI Baker."

"Whatever. Baby."

Arla's jaws clenched and she was about to grind out a reply when Harry intervened. "Do you want to head back in the cell, Mark?"

He shrugged. "Whatever, mate. You get to let me go without any charges, right?"

"How about obstructing arrest, assaulting a police officer, being in possession with intent to supply?"

"You can't prove the last one 'cos you didn't find any on me." Mark's arrogance was grating. "As for the first two, go ahead, slap charges. My man here will get me out with parole." He pointed to Derek, who sat still, looking uncomfortable.

Arla wondered at the contrast between Paul and Mark. Paul had been nervous, worried. It seemed like he would do anything to get out of there. His record was clean, he had never seen the inside of a police station. Mark Dooley was different. His record boasted of several charges of affray, drunk and disorderly, and once caught with possession of cocaine, a Class A substance, which was more serious than dealing cannabis. He had got off the last one, as the solicitor had argued the supply of four grams was for his own personal use.

"Just answer the question, Mark," Arla said, controlling her anger.

"Like I said…"

Arla cut him off. "What's her name and number? If you don't give us that, we have the right to treat you as a suspect, and start searching your residence."

Mark sighed. "Name's Samantha. Number's on my phone. You've got the phone, so don't ask me for the number again."

"Did you know Madeleine Burroughs?"

"I saw her around, yeah. Bitch wanted some."

Arla stayed impassive, not rising to it. "What do you mean?"

Mark shrugged, a relaxed cockiness all over his features. "These rich girls, they don't get out much. Not like we do, anyhow. So she wanted to party." A knowing smile came to his lips. "Bitch was with Paul, but she was sharing her love, know what I mean?"

"Are you saying you had sexual relations with her?"

Mark yawned, like he was bored. "I ain't sayin nothin, you get me? I don't know nothin, either."

"Then why did you try to run when we got to you?"

The first look of animation crossed Mark's face. "'Cos you be the pigs, man. Oink, oink! You see a brother crossing the road you want to put him in handcuffs. What you expect me to do? Make you a cup of tea?"

This wasn't the place for politics or refuting his argument. "We just wanted to talk to you."

Mark snorted. "Yeah, right. You barged in without a warrant."

"The door was open," Harry said. "And I did call out, but you were too busy listening to loud music."

Arla asked, "What do you know about Madeleine?"

He shrugged. "Rich bitch. Wants to be cool, so hangs around with us. Only saw her a few times."

"Was she with anyone else other than Paul?"

His smile widened. Arla shut him up before he could get any further. "No, I mean outside your group. Did she meet or talk about anyone else?"

"You need to ask Paul. She was his bitch." His eyes narrowed, then gleamed at Arla. "Did Paul snitch on me? What's he told you?"

Arla felt happier. "That's what you'll have to find out in court, won't you, Mark?"

Derek intervened. "So, are you charging my client?"

"Yes," Arla said firmly. "For possession and resisting arrest."

Mark slapped the desk, making a loud sound. Harry raised his voice an octave. "Cut that out, now!"

Mark looked at Harry, curling his lips. Harry leaned forward, meeting his gaze. "You need to behave, Mark. Do you understand?"

"Fuck you."

CHAPTER 34

Arla was seated in the fourth-floor office of DCS Johnson, facing the man himself. Next to him, wearing his uniform, was the Deputy Assistant Commissioner Nick Deakin. Harry sat next to Arla, and she could feel the tension in the room. Deakin was there for a reason. The top brass wanted answers they could feed to the Home Office and American Consulate. So far, they had precious little.

Arla told them what she had gleaned from the suspects. She stared apprehensively at Nick Deakin, then looked away when he glanced at her. Deakin was known to be a hard taskmaster, but he had always been tough but fair with Arla.

Deakin was shorter than Johnson, and he was wiry, athletic. His glasses were thin-rimmed, and the intensity in his eyes was apparent through them. The uniform fitted snugly on his muscular shoulders. He said, "If you don't think Paul Ofori, the boyfriend, is a suspect, then do you consider Mark Doyle to be one? He is the more seasoned criminal."

Arla cleared her throat. "Yes, sir, he is. But I don't get the impression he's a psycho. I mean, what would he have to gain by kidnapping Maddy? It's not like anyone's asked for ransom."

"Therefore we have nothing," Deakin said with a sigh.

"That's not true, sir," Arla said. "We are pursuing several leads. The phone log to this pay-as-you-go number, for one. We are trying very hard to get the exact location. Then there are the three cars on CCTV. One of them has to be the one we want. And thirdly, I want to interview Maddy's parents again."

Both senior officers shifted in their seats at the last comment. Deakin narrowed his eyes and exchanged a glance with Johnson. "What for?"

"I want to know more specifics about Maddy. What she wore, if she had favourite shoes or a necklace, things like that."

Deakin pressed his hands together on the desk. "In fact, I wanted to talk to you about that."

"Oh?" Arla felt immediately uncomfortable.

"The last time you were at their house, you acted strangely."

Heat rose to Arla's face. She gave a furious look towards Harry, who shook his head, protesting innocence. Johnson seemed to have read the exchange between them.

"It was Mrs Burroughs who told us, Arla," Johnson said quickly. "Apparently, you were quite emotional, if that's the right word." Arla was silent. Deakin prodded. "Is that correct, DCI Baker?" Arla tucked a loose strand of hair behind her ear. "I… Well, it was sad seeing the little boy and the family suffer, sir."

Johnson dropped his voice an octave. "And I know what you went through last year. I mean, finding Nicole and all that. Are you sure you can cope with this case, Arla?"

She felt her cheeks warm up again. Harry moved next to her, leaning forward, getting into her eyeline. She was glad of his familiar presence, and knew that he was silently supporting her.

"Of course, sir. Why wouldn't I?" Even to her own ears, her voice sounded shaky.

Johnson said, "There are similarities between this case and what happened to you last year. That was…"

"I said I'm fine!" She hadn't meant to raise her voice, but it slipped out, harsh and cold. Arla raised appalled eyes to both of her senior officers. "Sir," she mumbled quickly, "I am the SIO of the case and I want to finish my job."

There was an urgent series of knocks on the door suddenly. Johnson frowned. "Come in."

James Bennett burst in through the door. He said to Arla, "Guv, you've got to come downstairs now. There's a crowd outside."

"Hang on," Johnson said. He rose up and went to the side window, raising the blind. "What the…"

Arla, Harry and Deakin rose to join Johnson. When she looked down at the front of the courtyard facing the main entrance, Arla couldn't believe her eyes. There was a group of people, taking up about half of the courtyard space, waving placards and shouting. She read one placard. "Free my son!"

"Our boys are innocent!" read another. The crowd were chanting something they couldn't hear from up here. "Students are not Criminals!" a new placard went up, bouncing up and down in the air. James said, "This is about Paul, sir. His mother's downstairs at the main desk, wanting to speak to her son immediately."

Johnson groaned. "Oh Jesus, this is just what we need." He turned to Arla. "Secure the perimeter. No one leaves the station, and no one gets in. Last thing we want is a nosy reporter filling columns about this."

Arla said, "No, sir. If you hem these people in, you make the situation worse. They're angry, let them protest."

Johnson looked doubtful. "The numbers will grow."

"But if we lock them in there's a chance of this getting violent, sir. And much worse."

Deakin said, "I agree with Arla. We need to defuse the situation quickly."

Arla said to Deakin and Johnson, "Leave this to me." She turned on her heels and left the room.

CHAPTER 35

Arla ran down the stairs, followed by everyone apart from Nick Deakin. Harry and she went up to the main desk, which was in pandemonium. A mass of people were banging on the doors that had shut, making the glass panels shake. Another dozen were already inside, crowding the desk, standing on the chairs, waving their hands. They were mostly middle-aged and older citizens of the local communities.

John Sandford, the desk sergeant, was shouting and gesturing at them, and the crowd were stabbing fingers back at him. Arla came around behind John.

"What do they want!?" Arla shouted.

"God knows!" John shouted back.

A woman leaned over the desk, her hair hanging down in long braids. "You cannot lock up our kids! They are children who have done nothing wrong! Let them go!"

"Who are you?" Arla shouted to make herself heard.

The woman said something but it was lost in the chanting that started. "Let them go! Let them go!"

Arla looked wildly around. Then she spotted Mrs Ofori, her expression haggard, holding onto the main desk corner by her fingertips. Arla lunged forward, touching her fingers. The woman looked at Arla and her eyes widened, then anger creased her face. She shouted something to the man next to her, pointing towards Arla.

Arla didn't care. She screamed as loudly as she could, "Do you want to see your son?" She had to say it twice before realisation dawned on Mrs Ofori's face. She nodded quickly.

Arla gestured with her hand to come forward, and Mrs Ofori pressed through the heaving bodies, pushing her way closer.

Arla said, "I will take you to Paul. If you want my honest opinion, I think he's innocent. I am not going to charge him with anything." The relief on Mrs Ofori's face was evident. Arla continued. "But you need to do something for me." She pointed to the desk. "Stand up here, and tell them your son is free. Then tell them to go home. I give you my word he will be free. Do that, and I will take you to Paul."

Mrs Ofori hesitated. She thought for a while, then nodded. Arla spoke in John's ear, and he nodded. He reached out an arm, and almost half-lifted Mrs Ofori onto the desk, with the help of Arla. Seeing one of their own on the desk, the crowd quietened. John raised his booming voice.

"Listen to the lady! Listen!" He had to say it three times before the crowd's chanting subsided to a hubbub.

Mrs Ofori raised her hands. "My son is free," she said in a low voice, and cleared her throat. She shouted out. "Paul is free! They just told me that!"

A cheer went up from the crowd. "Now go home!" Mrs Ofori shouted. John pressed the button, and the gates swung open. The crowd outside surged in, but the previous anger had dissipated. They met a calmer bunch inside, and rapid explanations did the rounds.

"My son is free!" Mrs Ofori shouted again at Arla's insistence. "Thank you for your support. Now please go home."

Arla held her breath. This had the potential to become a serious disaster. A full-blown riot. The media would feed on this like vultures on a juicy lump of meat. She closed her eyes and prayed, something she hadn't done in years. She heard the voices die down, and the shuffling of several feet. Mrs Ofori was still standing on the desk, and on hearing her words, the crowd seemed to have calmed. One by one, they began to leave the station.

Arla breathed out with the rest of her colleagues. She exchanged looks with John, Harry, Lisa, Rob and James. Everyone was out here, braced for the worst. This had been an extraordinary event, one that Arla hadn't expected. She thanked her lucky stars it had been defused without violence, arrests or, God forbid, bloodshed.

John and Harry reached out hands to help Mrs Ofori down. The woman was still agitated. Arla felt a flare of anger at her. She could have called her, or Harry, and demanded answers. Did she really have to go and stir the community up? Her behaviour had been reckless, Arla thought, but she kept it to herself.

Stressful situations were nothing new to Arla. In fact, she thrived on the adrenaline rush, the buzz of doing her job in the face of danger. But that also meant keeping her cool, something she didn't always perform very well. As she faced Mrs Ofori now, with an effort, she controlled herself.

"Where is my son?" the shorter, buxom African woman said. Her wavy hair shone in the light, and she was dressed in deep blue trousers and a matching blouse with cardigan.

Harry whispered. "Best to take this inside, guv." Arla nodded. She mouthed thanks to John Sandford and the rest of the uniform officers manning the desk, and followed the rest of her team inside the station. She entered one of the interview rooms off the main corridor with Harry and their guest.

When the door was shut, Arla glared at Mrs Ofori. "Why did you have to do that?" she asked in an even voice.

"Those people? They are my friends. I called the London Met Liaison number, and also your Community Liaison Officer. All I got was answerphone messages, promising to call me back. I never got one."

"I left you my card and number," Arla said. "You could have used that."

"Look, Miss Baker. My son is in prison, and he's a good boy. He's never been in trouble before." She waved her chubby fingers in the air. "Do you know what it's like to have your son in prison?"

"I understand this is a stressful time for you…"

"No, you don't." They were standing, and the older woman stepped forward. Her voice quivered with emotion. "After we ran away from that terrible man, we made a new life. My children are academically gifted. They study hard. You have no idea how hard it is for me, living in that area, to send my kids to a good school."

Arla sighed, her shoulders drooping. Harry stepped in from the sides. His voice was gentle. "Why don't we sit down, Mrs Ofori? Would you like a glass of water? Tea or coffee?"

Mrs Ofori nodded, and they scraped chairs back. Harry left to get some water.

"It is so hard. All the kids there, they have no role models. Many of them join these stupid gangs and throw their lives away." Mrs Ofori frowned. "And my son, he's a god boy. OK, he might have made some wrong choices recently." She looked at Arla entreatingly. "He needs help. He has such a bright future…" Her head lowered, her voice choking.

Arla leaned forward and touched the woman's hand. "I know. I think your son will get through this. But next time, please call me first. We could have resolved this much more easily."

Mrs Ofori sniffed and wiped her eyes with a brightly coloured hanky. "I'm sorry. I am working nights right now. It's just shattering, you know? The labour ward at the hospital is so busy, we are overworked, not enough midwives or nurses…"

Arla smiled ruefully. "Same here. I could use a team twice the size of what I am allowed. But there's not enough policemen or women to go around."

The woman wiped her nose. "But it's OK for some people to earn million-pound bonuses and live in five million-pound homes."

Yes, Arla thought to herself. But this was not the discussion she had time for right now. The door opened, and Harry's lanky form filled the doorway. He handed glasses of water out for both of them. Arla accepted hers gratefully and downed it. Mirth appeared on Harry's face when she caught his eyes. She frowned at him.

"Can I see Paul now?" Mrs Ofori asked.

"Yes, of course. Stay here, and we'll bring him over," Arla said.

As they walked over to the holding cell, Harry asked, "You sure about letting him go?"

Arla shook her head. "I can't fit him in the picture, Harry. He has an alibi. He has no motive. He's crapping himself being arrested."

"He did run away. What if he and Mark Dooley planned to kidnap Maddy, and were about to ask for ransom?"

Arla stopped. Harry's words had triggered something at the back of her brain. She touched her forehead. "The other person," she whispered to herself.

"The one Paul mentioned?"

"Yes. My gut tells me Maddy was meeting him that night. But she didn't want anyone to know. So she lied to her friends about meeting Paul."

"What did she tell her parents?"

"That she would be back by 10. She left the pub at 8, right?"

Harry nodded. Arla said, "That gives her enough time for a rendezvous with this mysterious stranger."

"Careful," Harry warned. "Is this the line we are going down now?"

"If she had been kidnapped, Harry, where is the ransom demand? It's been nine days now. Ransom demands are quick, they don't give parents or police time to get organised."

"True, that."

Arla said, "I want to interrogate Paul one more time. Can you inform his mother that she might have a wait on her hands? And we hold onto that idiot, Mark Dooley, for as long as we can. Let him stew in a cell. Teach him to be rude."

Arla asked Lisa to bring Paul to Room 1. He looked as nervous as before, and couldn't shed any further light on who Maddy's other contact might be. Arla felt frustrated. She didn't even know if this person was a man or woman, boy or girl.

"How do you know she was cheating on you?" Arla asked impatiently.

"'Cos the way she spoke to him!" Paul frowned. "I overheard her. She said I miss you, too, can't wait till tonight. Does that sound like a friend to you? Bitch was two-timing me."

Arla thought back to what Mark Dooley had said, and the explicit photos of Maddy she had found. Arla had no problems with it. The girl was six months away from being a legal adult: she could do what she wanted. But it was clear she had a hidden, alternative side that she carefully kept from her parents, and possibly her friends as well.

Arla left Paul, and told Lisa to start the paperwork to let Paul go, with a verbal caution for evading interrogation.

She went to the coffee machine and got herself a cappuccino. As she waited, her phone buzzed. Arla took it out of her trouser pocket to find a photo image on her screen. She picked up the cup of coffee at the same time as her screen went blank. She sipped on the coffee and reopened her screen.

As her brain registered what she was seeing, her mouth opened in shock. Her pulse surged, heartbeats exploding against her ribs. She felt dizzy, air compacted inside her lungs like a brick, unable to breathe.

Waves of nausea hit her like a tsunami. The cup fell from her hands, landing on the floor with a splash, splattering against her trousers. Arla reeled backwards, stumbling against the vending machine, her knees buckling.

CHAPTER 36

"Sweet Jesus," Johnson whispered as he stared at Arla's phone.

The whole team had gathered in Arla's office downstairs. Johnson was sitting in Arla's chair, while she stood, her face the colour of the white wall. Harry stood next to her, his grim face cast in stone. Lisa, Rob and James stood with identical expressions.

The photo showed a girl's body and face. It was mottled grey, eyes open wide and staring. It was Maddy and she was obviously dead. The clothes on her body were a short, pink dress and high heels, the dress in which she disappeared. The photo was taken in a park, and the body was placed near the roots of a tree.

"Where is this?" Johnson asked.

Harry answered. "Forensics have had a look at it, and it looks like Brockwell Park. Maybe near where she was last seen. Two squad cars are on their way to check."

Johnson said, "And this is your phone?"

Arla cleared her throat. "Yes, sir." There was a feeling of unreality about this. Her words and actions were projected through a vapour, a mist-like aura that surrounded everything she did and said. Her head felt woolly, hazy.

"Have we traced the number?"

Harry had taken over from her effortlessly. "Pay-as-you-go. Not been used before, and not on our records. This was not the same number that Maddy had called several times on 2nd June."

"Any more data on the phone?"

"I have to say the technical guys did wonders to get this info so quickly," Harry said. His voice dropped. "We have the IMEI number, and the call was from a local mast."

Johnson looked up, frowning. "How local?"

Harry swallowed before answering. "Our mast, sir."

Mobile phone signals were sent remotely to the nearest cellphone mast, and a string of these cellular masts bounced the message around till it got to the phone it was intended for. Each police station in London had their own mast to make communication easier for the forces. Any caller within a five hundred-metre radius could also use their mast.

The phone on Arla's desk started to ring. Johnson reached out a hand and answered. He listened for a while, then hung up.

His voice was grim. "They found the body in the same location where she was abducted from. Initial appearances are consistent with Maddy Burroughs. Uniform have secured the area."

Arla closed her eyes, then exhaled. It was still difficult to speak. But she had to push against the fog that was surrounding her, hemming her in. It was the only way to get through it.

"Tell them we are on our way, sir," she said to Johnson.

She didn't say a word as Harry drove, and ignored the several concerned looks he gave her. Lisa and Rob sat in the back. As the car turned into the cul-de-sac, Arla saw blue and white tape being strung from the base of a tree around the corner. White-suited SOC guys were on the scene, getting changed by their van. The white tent was already being erected over where the body lay.

Grey plastic, sterile duckboards had been laid on the grass. Arla stared at them, and then at the pub at the end of the street. It stood lonely and forlorn at this time of the day, only the black sign sticking out from its yellow-fronted exterior. The sign said 'Wrangler's Arms' in white letters, with an image of two sailors playing tug of war with a coiled rope.

Arla thought back to the night Maddy disappeared. What had happened that night, where she was standing now? A drunken Maddy had stepped out, and then approached by a stranger. Or had it been someone she had known? Most homicides were committed by an individual known to the victim. This person had assaulted her, and dragged her over the grass. Then it got murky. Was she put into a car and driven off? Or as Harry suggested, she was taken across the park? Arla thought it was unlikely. Maddy's phone's signal had been picked up on the M23, and it had to be inside a car. Was Maddy inside the car when that happened?

Arla felt drained, shaken. She couldn't think anymore.

"Penny for your thoughts," Harry said. Then she felt his arm on her back, long, heavy. Without thinking, she leaned into him. He smelled of the familiar aftershave and faint cigarette smoke. A transient cocoon of comfort, and she wanted to stay there for longer. She knew it, and didn't make herself suppress it like she normally did. Layers had been stripped off her, and for some reason, she felt exposed, threatened. Harry being there made it easier to deal with. Moments later, she separated. She was at work, and she was the senior officer. Briskly, she stepped on the plastic boards, making her way to ground zero, as she liked to call it.

The technicians erecting the white tent smiled at her, and she tried to make her lips move. It wasn't successful. The uniformed sergeant made her sign the visitors' log with her rank, time and signature. Inside, a partition blocked an immediate view of the grisly scene. She walked around it to find the pathologist crouched over the body, wearing the white uniform and gloves.

Dr Banerjee looked up with his thick glasses. His lips parted in a smile when he saw Arla. Dr Banerjee was an old veteran of the London Met, and long-time conspirator with Arla. They had worked scores of cases together, and the older man looked upon Arla with almost paternal fondness.

"Ah, the intrepid detective approaches," he said.

"Hi, Doctor," Arla said tonelessly. She rustled up a smile: it felt like someone was manually stretching her lips to either side. Banerjee stood up and shuffled over, his gait reminding Arla of Detective Columbo in the TV series.

"Are you well, my dear?" he enquired, peeling his gloves off.

He knew her well enough to discern her discomfort, Arla knew. But she wasn't in the mood for a chat. Not that she could chat to anyone save her close team about what had happened.

"Any ID on her?"

"Yes," Banerjee said gravely. "A student ID. It says she's 21, and a student of Roehampton University, but from what I gather that's a fake one."

Arla nodded. The name and photo on the ID wouldn't be a fake. Banerjee asked, "Is it true that she is the US diplomat's daughter?"

Arla nodded in silence. She could see the bluish glaze now spreading up from the neck of the dead body, combining with the mottled grey. Maddy's head was turned to the left, and the lifeless eyes were staring at the ground.

"Time of death?" Arla asked.

"She's thin, so she would have lost heat quickly. Rigor mortis hasn't set in yet, so less than twelve hours. I haven't taken the rectal temperature, but in this heat, body temperature would fall very slowly."

"Have you checked her?"

"Nope, was just getting started. On visual inspection alone, no sign of trauma or laceration. No ligature or hand marks on her throat, so she didn't asphyxiate."

Arla frowned. "How did she die, then?"

"I don't know right now. Maybe poisoning? We need to send blood and tissue for toxicology."

"Can I have a look?"

"As long as you follow protocol, yes." Banerjee smiled, but Arla didn't respond. The mirth faded from the pathologist's lips as Arla moved past him, and crouched down by the body. The ground was hard and dry, and the smell of the body, decomposing fast in the present heat, hit her nostrils as she bent over it. The neck was untouched, but Arla could see some scrape marks at the frontal hairline, like someone had pulled her hair back. She was tempted, as always, to reach out and close the eyes. Her gaze moved down the body, at the soiled and dirty pink dress. It clung tightly to her body, accentuating the breasts and the bones of her hips.

"Where was the ID?" Arla asked Banerjee.

"Around her neck."

Arla's glance fell on the pockets at the side of the dress. The dress had one on each side. On the right, the side closest to her, Arla could detect a bulge. She looked at the pocket on the left. A white piece of paper was sticking out from it. She craned her neck back again, and told Banerjee what she had found. Both Harry and the pathologist shuffled forward, intrigued.

"Can I remove it?" Arla asked the SOCO technician crouched opposite, collecting samples from the ground.

"No, wait," he said. His ID badge named him as Tom Lindquist. Tom pulled out a pair of plastic tongs from his bag, and picked up the piece of paper, putting it on a slide. With the tong, he smoothed the paper on the slide, which would later be looked at under the microscope.

"It's a phone number, written out by hand."

"Can you read it out to us?"

Each number was like a knife wound to Arla's stomach. It was her number. Not the phone she carried at work, but her personal number. Where the photo had been sent in the first place. Her head fell back on her chest. She felt a warm hand squeeze her right shoulder, and without looking up, she knew it was Harry.

"There's something else in this pocket," Arla said when she had recovered. She got up and moved away to let Tom take her place. Tom reached inside the pocket with his tongs, seized something. It was a necklace on a chain. He pulled it out, and the pendant dangled from the chain.

It was a gold cross, held against a distinctive blue and white square. The chain was silver.

As Arla stared at it, a pressure grew inside her head. A raging horror spread in her bones, making them numb, frozen. Her insides felt hollow, like she had been punched so many times in the gut her organs were macerated to liquid. She stumbled backwards, falling against Harry, who caught her as she fell.

CHAPTER 37

Cindy parked her car outside the dilapidated terraced house in Brookstone Road, a run-down corner of Lambeth. She checked the email on her screen to ensure she had the right address. As she did, a text message buzzed on her phone.

Gary: Is it all done?

Excited, Cindy replied immediately.

Yes. No one saw me, I made sure.

Gary: What time did you do it?

Cindy: About five in the morning. Then sent the photo almost five hours later.

Gary: Good. They'll have found the body by now.

Cindy: When are we meeting?

Gary: It's getting interesting now, we have to be careful.

Cindy tried to hide her disappointment. Gary meant everything to her, and when they had set off down this road, she had followed him without question. That meant to listen to him now, even though she was dying to see him.

Cindy: I wish I could see you.

After a pause, the words pinged back.

Gary: Me, too.

Gary: Don't worry, we are near the end.

Cindy: Then we can be free.

Gary: Exactly. We will make sure we have justice.

Cindy: There is no justice in this world. But I know what you mean.

Gary: What are you doing now?

Cindy: On my job. Seeing a family.

Gary: You have to be careful with that. Any slip-up can alert the cops.

Cindy: I know that. Don't worry.

Gary: Just looking out for you. X

Cindy: I know. X

Cindy put the phone in her handbag and got out. Cars went up and down the street, and at the top of Brookstone Road they joined Brixton Water Lane. Cindy knocked on the door. After a while, a rough voice answered.

"Who is it?"

"Lambeth Housing Officer. Here to inspect your premises."

The door opened and was left ajar. Darkness loomed beyond it, despite it being a bright day. Wallpaper was peeling off the walls, scattered on the floor. Cindy's boots crunched on something, and she lifted her feet to see a small glass vial, reduced to dust. The familiar stench of decay and sickness made the air thick like smoke.

Through the narrow corridor she walked into the lounge. A man was sprawled on the sofa, watching TV. He didn't look up as Cindy entered. Images of a holiday channel flickered on the TV. The man's eyes were half-closed, his cheeks sunken, eyes colourless, dry orbs retracted deep into the bony sockets. In the middle of the room, a toddler played with some plastic toys. The baby turned around as he sensed Cindy. He stood up on his chubby legs and sucked his thumb. He couldn't have been more than two and a half, Cindy reckoned. After staring at Cindy for a while, he flopped back on his bum, and went back to his toys.

Cindy went to the next room along. It was a bedroom, and a woman lay on it. She had passed out. Next to her, on the bedside table, smoke still lifted from a long glass tube, broadened at the base, with a small aperture covered by silver foil. It was a bong pipe, used for smoking crack.

Another drug user's den. The father looked like he had just injected, and the mother was enjoying her high from a snowball – injecting heroin, then smoking crack. Neither of them deserved to be parents. Cindy's lips twisted in hate. She searched the rest of the property. The kitchen looked like it hadn't been touched in years. Microwaved meal wrappers littered the floor.

Cindy went back to the living room, where the man was still staring at the TV. This time he looked up at Cindy.

She said, "Do you have any other children?"

"No," the man mumbled. He pointed to the baby, who was still playing on the stained carpet. "'S not mine."

Something tightened inside Cindy's heart. The man's eyes glowed brighter, then suddenly he was reaching for Cindy. He stood up, swaying. He took a step forward, and Cindy stepped back in terror. His hand reached for her again. Cindy saw the yellow nicotine stains on the nails, the bristling black moustache on his lip, and smelled his fetid breath. She screamed but no sound came from her throat. The man opened his mouth, his teeth were jagged and broken, and saliva dribbled down his throat. His eyes bulged out, and the saliva turned red, flowing down his neck to soak his shirt. He lunged for her, and Cindy jumped back, her back slamming against the door.

The baby turned on the carpet and began to wail. Breathless, Cindy looked at the man on the sofa. He hadn't moved. His rheumatic eyes were still focused on the TV. Cindy walked over to the baby and lifted him up. She cuddled him and he stopped crying. She pressed the baby softly against her, feeling his tiny ribs and chest beneath her palm. One of his hands was nestled against her neck, and she felt his little fingers move.

She looked at the man on the sofa, and saw his hooded eyes staring at nothing. Rage flared against her chest like a flapping sail in the wind. She had the liquid inside her handbag, with the hypodermic syringes, pre-fitted with needles. She wanted to take them out and... but there were two of them. Cindy was confident she could do it, but she had to be careful. Two more dead drug addicts might arouse suspicion.

Cindy walked out of the apartment with the baby, closing the door shut.

CHAPTER 38

Arla couldn't breathe. She groped and stumbled her way out of the tent, pushing Harry and the sergeant outside, out of the way. She put a hand against the tree, panting. Her eyes were closed, air clawing inside her lungs to be let out. She sank to her knees, then turned around and leaned against the tree stump.

She felt someone sit down in front of her. Harry's voice said, "What is it, Arla?"

Arla gripped her forehead, feeling the hard, craggy surface of the tree against her back. She desperately wished this was a nightmare she would wake up from. Reality was turning itself inside out, a shadow within a shadow. The world was tilting, becoming unhinged.

"Arla? Talk to me."

"That necklace. I need to see it again," she whispered. Harry got up and came back with Tom, who looked at her strangely.

"You can't touch this, but look all you want," Tom said. Arla stared at it, heart in mouth. There was no mistaking it. That chain belonged to her mother, Katherine Mendonca. Her throat constricted as she remembered how she had first seen the necklace. On the throat of a dead woman. Since then, it had become a cherished heirloom. Kept inside a box, locked safely inside her wardrobe at home.

Not that safe, obviously. How the hell had she not checked after she found the earring in the garden?

Arla felt bile rise inside her throat. She sprang to her feet, and walked away as fast as she could, wishing she could run. She heard footsteps and turned. It was Harry.

His face was flushed from running. The heat was beating down on them from a blue sky, not a cloud in sight. Grass blades were parched to yellow, every corner of the park was basking in the sweltering heat.

There was nowhere to hide.

"What is it?" Harry asked.

Arla told him.

"You sure it's the same one?" Harry asked.

"Portuguese church necklaces are easy to spot. They all have that design. I know what is."

Harry was silent. Arla looked around her at anywhere but the white tent.

"Who could be doing this?" she whispered. A sudden restlessness filled her. She needed to find out more, get things moving. Sitting and thinking about this would make it worse.

She strode back to the tent, determined. Harry grabbed her arm before she went in. "You sure you want to do this?"

Arla stared at him for a while, then snatched her arm free.

Banerjee and Tom were leaning over the body, surgical masks over their faces. The smell from the body was slightly stronger, and Arla knew they would have to remove it soon.

"Anything else?" Arla asked.

Banerjee glanced up at her, using the back of his wrist to push his spectacles up his nose. "Rectal temp is 28 degrees Celsius. Outside temp is now about 25. I think she's been dead for five or six hours."

Arla made a mental note. "Any trauma?"

"No signs of recent sexual activity. But I would have to examine her properly. Her muscles are very flaccid, after taking death into consideration. She has been incontinent rectally as well, and relaxation of that sphincter is unusual. No injury anywhere that I can see. Which leaves one manner of death as the prime suspect."

"Which is?"

"Poisoning."

"And you won't know the answer to that till you send the samples off."

"Exactly."

Banerjee had stood up. He came closer to Arla. "Are you alright?"

"Not really. Got a lot of pressure from the boss on this. He's getting it from the Home Office. Not to mention that this photo was sent to me."

Banerjee listened to everything with a frown. "Oh dear."

"Putting it mildly, yes. I need you to make this super-urgent, Doc. Like, tomorrow morning."

He nodded. "The morgue is not too busy, this being summer. I'll get it done, then call you. But remember toxicology won't come back till three or four days at best."

Lisa and Rob had gone back earlier in the squad car. Harry drove them back through the customary light traffic of summer. Arla leaned back in her seat as the breeze rippled through her hair.

Maddy's death changed everything. But whoever was doing this had a score to settle with her. Arla knew it. He or she was sending her a message. Arla could feel the secrets chafing at her throat, suffocating her.

What did they want?

An impotent rage surfaced inside her, born out of frustration. She swore and slammed her fist on the door.

"Take it easy," Harry said.

"Easy for you to say," she shot back.

"I know. This is a headfuck for you, I get that. But can't you see that's what this person wants to do? They want to make your life a misery. Put you under pressure."

"So what do I do?" She spoke more to herself than to Harry.

"Focus on the case. Who killed Maddy? Why? That's the way we get to the bottom of who's harassing you."

She knew Harry was right. She had to make an effort and stop thinking about whoever was behind this. What they were trying to tell her… and why.

The traffic built up the closer they got to Clapham High Street. Harry put the windows up and turned the AC on full blast.

Back in the office, she sat down with the team. James was sitting directly opposite her, and she picked on him first.

"Any news from the CCTV?"

"It's painstakingly hard work," he complained. "But we're getting through it. All three cars are heading down to Surrey, in the same direction so far."

It was frustrating, but there was nothing that could be done. "OK, keep at it."

"What about the phone number?" Arla asked. "It's vital now that we get a current location of the number. Has it rung again?"

Lisa said, "Not as yet, no. We are scanning that mast for any calls made. But to be honest, guv, the phone could be in a different location, using a different mast."

"We need to get lucky here, folks," Arla said. "We have to believe that phone will call from the same location again."

Lisa said, "And Maddy's phone could be anywhere on the M23, probably chucked in a rubbish bin in a service station. After it's been stamped on."

Rob asked with interest, "How did the killer get your personal number?"

Arla said, "My house was burgled, remember?"

Rob said, "I know. But did you have your number written down somewhere? Maybe on your laptop? If they could get into your laptop, that is."

"Hang on," Arla said, thinking. "Rob's right. My personal number's not anywhere at home. Really only my close contacts have it." She looked at all of them, then at Harry.

He nodded. "Yeah, I do. For when you call me up to go on wild goose chases in Brixton."

"Lisa, you do as well, right?"

"Yes." Lisa was frowning. "And no, I haven't given it to anyone, if that's what you're thinking."

"I know you wouldn't," Arla said soothingly. "Not without asking me, anyway. But could anyone have handled your phone?"

Lisa thought hard. "My partner answered it once, and it was a call from work. Nothing to do with you."

Lisa was in a same-sex relationship with Sandra, a woman Arla had met a few times. Neither of them, she knew, could be a suspect. Sandra was a full-time mum, looking after their two-year-old son, Nicholas.

James said, "I don't have your number."

"I know," Arla said. "And neither do you, Rob?"

"Nope," the portly detective sergeant said.

"And switchboard wouldn't give out your personal number, guv. That's against the rules. All calls are monitored," Harry said.

"Then it's a mystery," Arla said, her brow knotted.

"And the caller was in the area. The signal was picked up by our mast, for Heaven's sake. Cheeky bastard," Rob said.

Arla had a deep frown on her face. "When they sent me that photo, they might have made their first mistake so far. Do we have triangulation data?"

Lisa spoke up. "It gets interesting here. Of the three sectors in our mast, only one sector got this signal. Hence we don't really have triangulation, as only one sector's zone was activated. That zone is two miles from here, in the south-west."

Arla said, "How could only one sector have got the signal? I thought all phone signals activated all three sectors in every mast. That's how phone signals move around, right?"

Harry said softly, "Unless someone knew what they were doing."

No one said anything for a while. Arla broke the silence. "I want all of you to know, I don't hold anyone in this room responsible for what's happening. Harry, Lisa, you had my number, but all these years you have kept it private. If you wanted to give it away, I guess you would've done it by now."

There was a gentle murmur of approval.

Arla said, "I need to speak to the Burroughses again." She sighed. "This time, the job will be much harder."

"They need to come and identify the body. Best if they come tomorrow, at the morgue," Harry said.

"Yes. But we have to break the news to them. Is Johnson here?"

"I saw him just now, getting a drink."

As if on cue, the door to Arla's office flew open.

CHAPTER 39

"My office, now," Johnson barked. He pointed at Arla. "Only you."
Arla shrugged into her coat. "Prepare the incident room," she told
Lisa. "We need to update the others about Maddy. Is that OK, sir?"
She looked at Johnson, who pursed his lips then nodded.

Arla followed the tall, lumbering form of Johnson as he clopped his
way up the stairs, ignoring the lift.

He thrust the door to his office open and pointed at the chair
opposite his own high-backed leather seat. "Sit down."

Arla did as she was told. Johnson picked up a copy of the *Evening
Telegraph* and slapped it down in front of Arla.

"Look at the bottom of the front page."

Arla complied without replying. An ominous feeling of dread was
spreading inside her. She closed her eyes after she read the headline
occupying the bottom third:

US Diplomat's daughter missing in gang-related incident.

She couldn't bear to read the rest. She heard a knock on the door,
and two more people came in. DAC Nick Deakin, and another man
Arla had never seen. He wore a suit and clutched an iPad.

Johnson introduced them. "This is Martin Jones, of the MPA Press
Bureau." Arla knew MPA stood for Metropolitan Police Authority,
the body that governed the administration of the London Met.

Arla shook hands with Martin, who was short, going bald, and red in
the face. He looked like a stocky, barrel-chested rugby player whose
gut was heading south as he climbed the fourth decade of his life.

After they sat down, Nick Deakin asked Arla without preamble,
"Who leaked information to the press?"

"None of my team, sir. I can vouch for all of them."

"But you can't vouch for the members of that… mob that day, can
you?" Deakin was referring to the crowd that had come to protest at
Paul Ofori's arrest.

"I guess no one can, sir."

Deakin's features hardened, a glint appearing in his slate-grey eyes.
"You are the SIO in this case, DCI Baker. While I cannot hold you
responsible for the actions of the protesters, you are in charge of how
this case is conducted. Under whose authority did you arrest Paul
Ofori and Mark Dooley?"

Arla's mouth went dry. She didn't have a search warrant when she had gone to Dooley's house that night. She was acting on a hunch, and it had proved to be the right one. Since when were police officers not allowed to act on their instincts?

Aloud she said, "I called Trident and got information about Dooley, sir. I knew that Paul was involved with him, so I put two and two together."

Deakin asked, "Did you get authority from Johnson?"

Arla noted that Johnson and Deakin didn't exchange a glance, and she knew instantly they had discussed this already. She looked at Johnson, who avoided her gaze.

Deakin continued. "Your arrest of Paul Ofori, on what appears to be a vigilante night-time raid on a civilian's house, has inflamed the local community. Is that not correct?"

Anger flared inside Arla, but she managed to keep her cool. "I was told to get results on this case, sir. Sooner, the better. Is that not true?" She looked at Johnson pointedly.

Johnson cleared his throat. "Yes, but I told you to be discreet."

"Discreet doesn't mean I can't do my job, sir! The entire case hinged on finding Paul Ofori who, as you know, evaded arrest the first time."

"The young man who you have since let go," Deakin noted.

"Because he wasn't guilty. I did discuss this with the DCS." Arla looked at Johnson, who nodded in agreement this time.

Deakin said, "And are you sure that protest movement didn't colour your decision in any way?"

Arla stared at Deakin, aghast. She realised her mouth was open, and shut it quickly. Deakin was angry: she could tell by his stiff, upright posture. He was trying to needle her on purpose. What the exact purpose was, Arla thought, she would find out soon.

"I am a ten-year veteran of the SCU, sir. Not a duty sergeant," she replied, struggling to maintain her cool.

"That doesn't mean we don't take the wrong decisions under pressure," Deakin said.

"It wasn't the wrong decision. If you had taken the time to look at the evidence…"

"Arla!" Johnson raised his voice. "Watch your tone."

"Sorry, sir." Arla bit her tongue. Why couldn't she stop talking sometimes?

Deakin was seething, she could tell. He leaned forward and pressed the words out from between his teeth.

"You acted like an emotional wreck in front of the Burroughses. You acted on a hunch and raided the Dooley residence in Brixton. Then you let the main suspect go after one day. DCI Baker, you are coming across as impulsive and out of control. What the hell is wrong with you?!"

Heat spread like a fan across Arla's face, and with it, a rising sense of indignation. "Impulsive, sir? Because of me, we have eliminated one suspect, and that is a big step in this investigation. Without arresting Paul Ofori and Mark Dooley, we would have made no progress at all in this case. Apart from me, did anyone else have any leads in this case?"

Silence met her question. Arla continued. "And before you say it, the two suspects couldn't have killed Maddy. They were in custody when the murder was committed, and also when the message was sent to my personal phone number."

Deakin appeared to be slightly mollified. "I am aware of the circumstances. Why does the killer seem to have a vendetta against you?"

Arla rubbed her forehead. "I don't know, sir."

Johnson said, "It could be anyone who has a grudge against you, Arla. God knows you have a few enemies."

Arla shook her head. "This isn't some random enemy, sir. They know intimate details about my family. Closely guarded secrets. How they got this information, I don't know."

Johnson asked, "Did SOC find anything at your house?"

"No. That would be too easy. This person is well organised, and has some technical expertise. They are using cellphone masts in very clever ways, and that's not possible by some random criminal."

Johnson tutted. "Are you saying it could be someone in law enforcement?"

Arla's silence was enough to cause consternation to spread across the faces of the two senior officers.

"I am not saying it's within our team, or even the police. It could be someone who works for the telephone companies, or the National Crime Squad, or even the Armed Forces."

Johnson said, "But we have no proof of this, of course."

"Not yet," Arla said.

Martin Jones cleared his throat. Deakin glanced at him, then at Arla. Martin said, "The news is out, and we are now in damage limitation mode. I need to issue a press release today, and to prevent further distress to the family, I suggest we include details of the death as well."

Johnson asked, "So we have no idea about who leaked the news?"

"Take your pick," Arla said. "From the crowd that came the other day. We will never know, and it's not going to change anything, so I suggest we move on."

Martin nodded. "DCI Baker is right. The newspaper won't divulge their sources, but they will now send their reporters sniffing around. Chances are these new hounds will speak to members of the team involved in the case. You know what they're like."

Everyone nodded. No one needed reminding of the lengths a reporter would go to. From installing listening software in witnesses' phones, to stalking the houses of policemen.

Martin said, "So I suggest we move on. DO we have a formal ID of the body?"

Arla said, "DNA samples will verify it, and the photos are identical to the deceased. The family will do an ID, hopefully today."

Martin said, "Then I can do the press release for later this afternoon. I want to do it ASAP, before we get more salacious headlines. The Home Office is furious, quite understandably."

Deakin clamped his jaws. "And the minister is on my back to sort this out." He focused on Arla with a piercing gaze. "This goes to the highest level, DCI Baker. Do you understand me?"

"Yes, sir, I do. But I am not responsible for the media leak."

"That might have been beyond your control, but your actions need to be modified," Deakin said.

"Modified, sir?"

Johnson gestured towards Arla. "What the DAC is saying is that you need to get my approval before starting things. That way, if there is a fallout, then we are more prepared."

Arla felt a mountain of denial rising up inside her. If she had to beg Johnson for approval each time, would she get anything done?

"In that case, sir, is it OK if I tell the family about their daughter's death?"

Johnson's eyes flickered, trying to gauge if Arla was joking. "Yes, you may," he said.

"Let's hope there's no fallout from that, eh, sir?" Arla raised her eyebrows.

Deakin's voice rang out across the room. "DCI Baker! Take this as a formal warning." He raised a finger. "If I hear about any more impulsive actions from you, you will be suspended from the case. Never mind being SIO, you won't take any part at all, and will be suspended on full pay. Do you understand?"

Arla met his withering gaze full on. "Yes, sir. I understand."

CHAPTER 40

Arla stopped by Harry's desk on the way to her office.

"Good, bad or ugly?" Harry asked, noting the stormy expression on her face.

"Ugly." She told Harry about the newspaper article. He swore and stood up, hitching his trousers up. That movement brought him very close to Arla. So close she could reach out and touch him. She didn't step back.

"Do me a favour," she said, ignoring the brief tremor low in her belly at Harry's proximity. "Call up the National DNA Database and get a match for Maddy. It's a weekday, and they should be able to turn it around in two hours."

"Really?" Harry was sceptical.

"Tell them whose sample it is, and that the Home Secretary is involved in the case."

"I guess that's true," Harry said, reaching for the phone.

Arla left Harry and walked into the incident room, where the rest of her team and the other detectives were waiting.

"Madeleine Burroughs was found dead today, at the same location from where she disappeared. This cannot be a coincidence. Someone thinks they are clever, and is playing games with us. With me, in particular." For the staff not in her team, she relayed the story of the photo sent to her phone.

There were whistles and exclamations. Arla said, "The deceased was an American diplomat's daughter, so you know how softly we have to tread. Unfortunately, the press know already. We need to be very careful about reporters approaching us. They can try to entice you with money. I don't have to tell you what happens if any news is leaked to the media."

She turned to Lisa. "The artefacts we got from the deceased's clothing – the necklace. Any forensic clues from it?"

Lisa shook her head. "Gone to a specialist lab, guv. Forensic anthropology. Way too early…"

Arla verbally slapped her forehead. Centre for Anatomy and Human Identification, CAHID, in Dundee. They were perhaps the UK's largest centre of forensic anthropology. Would Professor Sandra Hodgson not do a personal favour for her?

"Has the specimen been sent over?" Arla asked urgently.

"No, it's still in secure storage, but going later today…"

"Lisa, I am authorising you to get the specimen, and courier it to CAHID in Dundee."

"Dundee as in Scotland, Dundee?"

"Yes. I'll give you the address and details in a moment, just go and stop it from being sent anywhere else."

Lisa looked mystified, but rushed off to follow her order.

"The stakes are higher now," Arla addressed the rest. "I want a door-to-door of all the houses within a two-mile radius, with photos of Maddy. Same photos, blown up, as posters all over South-West and South-East London. Get CCTV images of the cul-de-sac, and I want reports on all cars and people on it."

Arla paused. "Yes, I know this is a lot of work, and an avalanche of calls. I will tell switchboard myself to set up four dedicated lines for this. All of you have overtime authorised from today, till we find our suspect. Drop what you have. This is priority one."

A buzz filled the incident room as Arla stopped speaking. Harry walked in, holding a piece of paper.

"DNA match?" Arla asked hopefully.

"Not yet, but they faxed over a number to call. And they will text me as well."

"OK." She turned back to the room. "Get cracking, everyone. We meet here at 18.00 to exchange notes."

Harry let her drive for once. Arla pulled the sunlight screeners down and put her shades on. The sun was winking off passing vehicles, melting the tarmac. All the cement and steel around them was expanding in the heat, the city buckling at the girders, changing shape. The open space on the Common provided some much-needed relief, the breeze rushing through them like air in the city's iron lungs.

Arla drove around the bend of the Common, in the avenue of palaces, and indicated left for the Burroughs' residence. Harry's phone buzzed and he answered. He spoke briefly into it and hung up.

"Amazing what mentioning the Home Secretary does," Harry said. "We have a match with the deceased's DNA and Maddy's."

Arla pulled the car up into the drive. There was no need for discretion anymore. The worst had already happened. With a sinking heart, Arla knew that whatever the outcome of this case, there would be no solace for the devastated parents.

Arla knocked on the door, and the elderly housemaid answered. They waited while footsteps sounded again, and the door opened fully.

Jenny Burroughs stood on the porch, her cheeks more sunken than before, her eyes receding into the sockets. She had lost weight, the cords of her neck sticking out.

"May we come in, please?" Arla asked.

A brief look of hope fluttered across the woman's eyes. "Is there any news of Maddy?"

Arla repeated her question in a low voice, and a look of fear passed over the woman's face. Arla hated this part of her job. It was the worst thing anyone could do to a parent. There was no good way to break bad news, no matter how many lectures they received on the topic.

Jenny lifted her bony hands, like claws, to her throat. Her eyes bulged. "No," she whispered.

A voice came from behind her. "Honey, what is it?" Conrad Burroughs appeared. In a way, Arla was pleased. He could provide the support his wife needed.

He pulled his wife back, a grim look on his face. Arla and Harry entered and followed Conrad as he almost half-carried his wife into the conservatory at the rear.

When they sat down Arla said, "I am very sorry to say that we found a body this morning, in Brockwell Park. DNA tests have now confirmed that it is Madeleine and…"

The rest of Arla's words were drowned in a howl of agony from Jenny Burroughs. "No!!" she screamed and sobbed, hitting the table as her husband tried to control her. "No, no, no!"

Arla had done this before, but seeing the woman's pain made her throat clog up. She couldn't bear to look at them. Under the table Harry's hand reached for hers and gave it a squeeze.

Harry said, "We'll give you a moment." He stood up and gestured to Arla. They went outside the conservatory, and stood in the giant hallway as the wails and moans continued. When they subsided, Conrad appeared. He seemed to have aged visibly, his shoulders stooped and eyes blank, red-rimmed.

He tried to speak but words wouldn't arrive on his tongue. He licked his lips and said, "We need to see her."

"Yes, of course," Arla said. "The body is at the King's College Hospital morgue. I need to let the pathologist know. When would you like to visit?"

"This evening."

"The pathologist might have left then. Is tomorrow morning possible?"

"Let me ask my wife," Conrad whispered in a flaky voice. He went over, and after some time, called over to them.

Arla and Harry went inside. Jenny had her eyes shut, leaning against Conrad's shoulder.

Arla said, "I am sorry to ask this now. But Mrs Burroughs, I need you to answer something for me."

The woman's eyes remained closed. Arla said, "Can you think of anything that Maddy was wearing that night that we might not have come across as yet? I'm thinking of jewellery, hair accessories, even a tattoo, anything."

Jenny didn't move for a long time and they waited. Finally she sat up straight, opening her eyes. She didn't look at Arla. "She wore a ring on her small finger. It had a skull face on it, on steel. I remember it because I told her to take it off. It didn't suit her."

Arla nodded. "Which hand?"

"Left, I think."

"Anything else you can think of?"

Jenny shook her head. Arla said, "I will leave you guys now. But before we go, for the sake of completion, there is one last favour I have to ask of you."

Conrad's piercing blue eyes looked at her questioningly, but Jenny still avoided her. Arla said, "We need to take DNA swabs from the family members. It's a matter of routine. Would you mind if we took a swab from your mouth?"

Harry dug inside his pocket, and took out the plastic packets with the DNA swab kits.

Conrad had a heavy frown on his face. "You consider us suspects? This is ridiculous!"

"I can only apologise," Arla said. "It's a requirement of the investigation."

Conrad raised his voice. "Well, it's a ludicrous one. Absolutely stupid!"

Surprisingly, it was Jenny who touched her husband's arm, and said, "Darling, they're just doing their jobs. Just let them."

Arla looked at Jenny's tired, withdrawn face and felt a touch of admiration. Her life had been turned upside down, but she had been able to locate a well of strength from deep inside.

"Thank you," Arla said.

Harry stood up and did the honours. When they had finished, Arla asked, "Mrs Burroughs, are there any videos or photos of Maddy that you could share with us? Or maybe watch them yourself, if you can, I mean, and let us know if you see anything unusual?"

Arla continued. "Photos of her school life, or videos of a game or performance, that sort of thing."

Jenny nodded, sniffing. Arla and Harry rose.

"We will be expecting you at the morgue tomorrow morning. Is nine am OK?" Arla asked.

"Yes," Jenny said.

CHAPTER 41

"What are you thinking?" Harry asked as he drove.

"The phone number Maddy rang. We have the location by triangulation, right?"

"Within a hundred metres of the school, yes. It was last used the night before she vanished."

"That means in the school. Could be one of her friends."

"Want to swing by? We're going in the right direction."

Arla pursed her lips, thinking. "Yes, why not?"

The iron gates of the school were tall, foreboding and locked as before. Arla had to press the buzzer several times before she got a response. Lunch hour was finished, and the courtyards were deserted as Arla and Harry climbed up the stairs of the main block to Principal Charles Atkins' office. He was waiting for them outside his office. He seemed tired, Arla noticed, tie loose at the neck, and his eyes were red, as if he hadn't slept or had been rubbing them for a while.

"Busy day?" Arla asked.

"It's post-exam season," he said, "so dealing with A level results and getting students on the right path is never easy."

He held the door open for them, and Arla walked past. She got a whiff of his body odour as she walked past, and scrunched up her nose. Papers and folders were strewn on the desk. Atkins made a show of cleaning up the desk. Arla and Harry remained standing.

"We wish to speak to Maya and Imogen again," Arla said.

Atkins looked dubious. "I heard about what happened with Paul Ofori."

Arla and Harry exchanged a glance. "What did you hear?"

"That he was arrested. Also, it came to our knowledge that he was in a relationship with Maddy."

"Who told you this?"

"His mother. She came to find out if his future at the school was affected by what happened."

"I see."

Atkins looked at them closely. "So, what do you want with Maya and Imogen?"

Arla said, "Paul Ofori is presumed to be innocent of any crime, unless new evidence comes to light."

Atkins looked surprised. "Really? But there was a newspaper article. It mentioned that Paul was arrested after he went on the run, and that he was going to meet Maddy that night. It also said that he was selling cannabis in the school, an allegation that we are looking into."

Arla cursed herself for not reading the entire article. "What else do you know?"

Atkins shrugged. "Nothing else. It seems to me you found your man. I mean, if he was going to meet with her that night, then surely he knew what happened to her?"

Harry said, "Not necessarily." He looked at Arla who nodded. Harry continued. "Maddy was in contact with another person. She called this person several times the night before she went missing. Paul says that she was seeing someone else."

Atkins looked disturbed. "And you trust Paul? What if he is lying to save himself?"

"That phone number comes up regularly in Maddy's phone log. She maintained contact with this person over the last three months. And the last call from that number to her came from within the school."

Atkins' mouth dropped open. He was at a loss for words. "What?" he struggled to speak. "You mean, Maddy had another... another..."

"Lover, or friend, or whatever," Arla said. "Bottom line – we need to find this person, and ASAP. Hence we need to speak to her friends, and check their phone numbers."

Arla stopped and narrowed her eyes. "Including yours, and that of your teaching and admin staff."

Atkins opened his mouth and closed it. "You can certainly have mine, but the others..."

Harry said, "We can get them from your database under the Freedom of Information Act. Or you can ask your secretary to send us a list of the numbers. Up to you."

Arla said, "It's to help with a police investigation. If your staff have nothing to hide, then they will have no objection."

Atkins licked his lips. "No, of course not. But do you have any idea where Maddy might be? It's been almost ten days since she disappeared."

Harry cleared his throat and Arla looked at him. She knew what he was trying to say. To get the principal's full cooperation, a full disclosure might be necessary.

She thought quickly. The press release would be out later this evening. The DNA tests had proved beyond doubt who the deceased was. Everyone would know in a few hours.

"Mr Atkins," Arla said softly, "Maddy is dead."

Atkins' eyes bulged out. His face turned red. He stumbled, holding onto the corner of his desk. There was a stunned look in his eyes as he slowly lowered himself into his chair. He looked from Harry to Arla.

"What?"

"I am sorry, Mr Atkins. But it's true."

Atkins said, "Are you sure it's her? I mean the body…"

"DNA tests have identified the body as hers," Arla said quietly. "I'm afraid there is no doubt."

"Her parents…"

"Have been notified."

Atkins looked like a fish out of water. "Do her friends know? I mean." He gulped noisily. "This is terrible for the school's reputation. There has never been anything like this, I assure you."

Harry asked, "What has happened in the past, Mr Atkins? By that I mean serious issues, like children missing or hurt."

Arla nodded approvingly. It was a good line of enquiry. Atkins looked bemused for a while, then shrugged.

"What happens in every co-ed school with students of a certain age. A pregnancy or two. Yes, a child went missing from the senior school many years ago, but she turned up the next day."

"Nothing else?"

Atkins shook his head vigorously. "No, never. This school takes pride in its pastoral care." His head sank down into his hands. "Oh God."

Arla gave him a moment to compose himself. "Do you now see why we need the staff members' phone numbers?"

Atkins took out a handkerchief and cleaned his forehead and face. "Yes, of course." He reached inside his pocket and took out his cellphone. "Here, this is mine. Feel free to look through it."

"Do you have any other phones?"

"No."

Arla said, "Is it possible to meet Maya and Imogen again?"

"Certainly." Atkins reached out and lifted the receiver of the phone on his desk.

CHAPTER 42

Maya blew a bubble from her gum and watched it pop, going cross-eyed as she did so. Arla sat opposite her in the same room where they had met the last time. This time, Harry sat next to her.

"We don't have much time," Arla said. "Can you answer the question, please?"

Maya did the whole teenage body shrug thing. "If she had another boyfriend? I have no idea."

Arla said, "But she was your best friend. She never told you anything?"

"Nothing apart from Paul," Maya said. "And even that was meant to be a secret. You know, from her parents and others."

"Others like who?"

"You know teachers, school."

"So you have no idea if Maddy had another boyfriend in the school? Someone she kept in touch with regularly."

Maddy chewed the gum again, a habit Arla had always found annoying. "Nope."

Harry showed her the number of the PAYG phone. "Do you know this number?"

"Nope."

Arla said, "Would you like to think about your answer before you reply? You didn't even check it against the numbers on your phone."

"I could, but it won't show anything. Most of the numbers I call are in my head."

Arla needed to say something to shake the teenager out of her bubble. She was acting tough, and there was no way Arla could tell her Maddy was dead. She tried something else.

"Maya, do your parents know you smoke cannabis?"

Maya stopped chewing her gum. "What do you mean?"

"You were besties with Maddy, and you knew he was going out with Paul. I'm guessing you helped them sell cannabis in the school. Isn't that correct?"

Maya's eyes swivelled around. "I don't smoke cannabis. I don't know what you're talking about."

"So you haven't read the newspaper?"

Maya looked blank. Arla told her about the paper article, then said, "And Paul confessed to us as well about selling cannabis in the school. You must have known about that, right?"

Maya tried to act indifferent, but it wasn't working anymore. Arla leaned over the table.

"This isn't a game, Maya. Something really bad is happening here, and we will do anything to get to the person whose phone this is. Now, will you help us?"

Maya nodded. "Yes. Maddy was my best friend. But see, she kept things to herself as well. I swear to you, I know nothing about her having another boyfriend, or this number."

Harry wrote the number down, ripped the paper off the notebook and pushed it towards her.

"Will you at least look at it, and then ask around?"

Maya took the piece of paper quickly. "Yes, and I'll call you?"

"Good girl," Arla said. "I gave you my card last time, have you still got it?"

"Yeah."

Arla slipped her another one, and so did Harry.

"Call us immediately," Arla said.

The interview with Imogen went along the same lines, but Imogen was more scared than Maya. Imogen didn't have a clue about the number either.

As they left the school, Harry said, "This is starting to look like a shot in the dark."

"Maybe. I have a feeling, though. Let's see what happens."

Arla looked at her watch. It was 3 pm. Harry noticed. "What do you want to do?"

She sighed. "I need to go somewhere. You don't have to come with me. Or you could just drop me off."

Harry shrugged and they walked towards the parked BMW.

The cemetery on Blackshaw Road, Tooting, is a long, sprawling space, taking up almost all of the one-kilometre-long road. Harry parked opposite and turned the engine off. Arla looked at his chestnut brown eyes, limpid pools of scrutiny in the pale sunlight. She wouldn't mind if Harry came inside with her. After all, he knew all of it.

Harry said, "I guess you need some time by yourself."

She couldn't deny it. Insanity had besieged her world. From being stalked to a murder that she was being made to feel responsible for. A little space might soothe her mind. Arla nodded.

"I guess I do."

He pointed opposite and Arla saw a working men's café. "I'll be having a skinny latte caramel mochaccino in there."

"This is Tooting, Harry, not Chelsea."

"Yeah, well, they have Starbucks in Tooting now. You go there yourself, remember?"

So she did. Maybe Tooting was becoming Chelsea, and she just didn't know about it. Soon people like her would be pushed out of London, commuting from Kent or Sussex, while London became the exclusive province of bankers, footballers and Chinese millionaires. But they could take her out of London, but would never take London out of her. She had been schooled there, gone to University College London to do her Criminology degree, then joined the Metropolitan Police Force. The Met, as it was known, had become her life. The dark secrets that littered the corners of this city, hidden in its diesel fumes, carried in the millions of lives behind those yellow windows in the evening, pretty like an LED display in the neon night, were what she lived for. Arla Baker didn't know anything else.

"One Starbucks does not make it builders' paradise, Harry."

"We'll see in ten years," he said. "Right, I'll get my designer coffee, and see you in..."

"Fifteen minutes."

Arla walked through the arched double gates, watching the heavy boughs of summer lean over the graves, leaves kissing dead headstones. Dry grass crunched beneath her shoes, heat warming up her body. She removed her jacket and slung it over her arm, lifting her face up to the blinding rays. When she closed her eyes she saw red and black floating spots. It was quiet here, a hush that was strangely comforting.

Arla walked over to where her mother and sister lay. She hadn't got them flowers in the last two weeks, she remembered with a stab of guilt. Neither had she sat by Nicole's grave and had her chat, telling Nicole about how busy she was, how she had no time for a man, no time for loneliness, till she got lonely.

She used to have these conversations in her head for more than sixteen years. Now that Nicole was here, the ache of missing her was still present like a non-healing wound, but at least she knew her sister was here. Dead, but where Arla could keep an eye on her. It was better than not knowing.

Arla sat down on the bench opposite the twin graves, hearing the old wood creak. She put her coat down, then went on her knees, cleaning the leaves away from the headstone, touching the cold surface, warming up in the sun.

"I don't know what's going on, Nicole," she whispered. "I have this crazy case, and this girl, about your age, is now…" Arla felt a heavy weight squeeze the back of her throat, that familiar black shape rising up her neck to the back of her eyes. She blinked, determined not to cry.

"She's now dead, but someone wants to get in touch with me. He left your earrings. Remember those?" Arla finished cleaning the top of Nicole's grave, and swept the leaves into a pile. She took out a packet of tissues and shook one out. She dug them into the letters on the headstone, cleaning them.

"And then, on the girl's body, I also found mum's necklace. Can you believe that?" Arla spoke as she wiped down the back of the headstone. In her mind's eye, she was doing up the buttons on Nicole's dress, curling the plaits on her hair. She stood up after a while, and wiped her wet cheeks. Damn it. Nicole would laugh if she was here. Call her a big girl's blouse.

"Wish you were here, Nic," Arla said. Nicole had hated being called Nicky. It was always Nic for her.

"This person, who knows about you, who could it be? What are they trying to tell me?"

The silent headstone stared back at her, the letters and numbers engraved in black on white marble. It was weird that Nicole was in there somewhere. And not out here, standing next to her. Arla's brow creased, the pain sprouting leaves, bearing poisoned fruits in the heat. Nicole would never be there again. She would have to live like this – God, live with this pain of not having her sister – for the rest of her life. It cut deeper than anything else, making her life seem worthless.

Yet, someone was trying to bring the past back to her again, in a bizarre, macabre fashion.

"I'll find who it is, Nic. I swear to you I'll find out, and when I do, I'll make them tell me why."

CHAPTER 43

Arla moved to the headstone next to Nicole's. Her mother, Katherine Mendonca. Arla had mixed feelings for this grave. If anything, her mother's life was more poignant. Arla knew little about her. The only woman in her earliest memories was her Nana Moon. And Nana telling her that her mummy had gone away. That was the night she remembered. She cried till Nicole came and slept with her. The other memories were fleeting, vague. A flash of summer here, a few carols at Christmas. Memories of her father were much more robust. Shame they tarnished so much later on. All she remembered now was him being always drunk and arguing with Nicole. Arla shook her head, banishing the memories. They never left the box, and it was one of the reasons she stayed away from her dad. She blamed him for Nicole running away.

Arla cleaned her mother's headstone as well, then sat back down on the bench. It was then she felt the presence. She turned to the left and saw the figure standing beneath a tree. Breath froze in her chest. A weird mix of concern and revulsion swept through her. A yucky, strange feeling, like picking up a piece of fruit she really wanted to eat, but was scared of the thorns that stuck out from it.

She turned her head away and felt the figure shuffle its way up to her. He walked across her vision like a slow shadow, then sat down next to her, exhaling.

He was silent for a while, staring at the gravestones.

"Hi, Arla," Timothy Baker said.

Arla had no time for him. She wanted to get up and walk away. And she hated feeling that way. She wanted to feel different. But she couldn't.

"What do you want, Dad?"

He didn't reply till some time had passed. "Nothing. It's good to see you."

She sniffed. "You weren't expecting to see me here today, were you? We come on different days for a reason." She closed her eyes, hating the way her voice sounded.

"I wanted to see you, Arla. I care about you, and always will." His old voice was hoarse, croaky from booze and too many cigarettes. Apparently, he had given up both. She wondered what he lived on now. Guilt, probably.

"Like you cared about Nicole." The words had slipped out before she could stop them.

She watched from the corner of her eye as his head folded down over his chest. The corner of her lip shook. She wanted to reach out and touch him. She balled her fists instead, turning the knuckles white.

"I'm sorry." The whimper came from deep within his chest. "I have to live with it as well, you know? I miss her, too."

Arla clenched her jaws tight. "That won't bring her back."

Timothy shook his head, still bent. He mumbled something incoherent. Slowly he lifted his head. Arla felt the force of his attention as he turned his gaze upon her. She glanced at him. Timothy Baker had been handsome once. He had twinkling blue eyes, a shock of light brown hair that he used to wear long, hanging over his eyes. Arla used to swing from his strong arms, screaming happily under bright blue skies. It all changed after her mother left. The cloud of alcohol turned their days to rust.

Now deep lines criss-crossed his face like scars. His eye sockets were prominent, with a hollow, fractured look in his eyes. The thousand-yard stare of a man who has lost everything.

"You know." His voice was like a coat being scraped across the pavement. "I feel so proud when I see you. To see what you have become." He leaned forward to face her as Arla looked away. "I just want you to know that, Arla."

She didn't say anything. What did he expect her to say?

Thanks, Dad. If it wasn't for the foster family, I would have been sold to social care like Nicole, who ran away.

Arla gathered her coat up. "I have to go."

"I need to tell you something," he said. "I saw someone."

Arla stopped and turned to face him. "What do you mean?"

"The person was standing on the street, looking at my window. It was late at night, and the street was empty. I get up at night and look out of the window when I can't sleep."

Arla knew her father lived in a block of flats next to Balham train station. "What did they look like?"

"I couldn't tell their features. It was one person. He or she was dressed in black, and wore a hoodie over their heads. They stood in the shadow of a shop's awning, but were definitely looking up at the flat."

"They might have been looking for someone else."

"No. They did it for several nights. Then I saw them in the street. The same man. He followed me."

"What?" A sense of dread trembled through Arla. She sat down on the bench. "You sure he followed you?"

"Yes. He did it a few times. Making it obvious. Only…"

"Only what?"

"His body shape was odd. He was short and chubby like a kid. And the shoes he wore… Odd. They were pumps with heels on them."

Arla raised her eyebrows. "It could be a woman, then."

Her dad nodded. "I think so. Then I found this." Her dad took something out from his pocket. Arla stared at it. It was the same purple earring that Nicole had. The one left in the steel box at her home.

Her voice shook, a numbness flowing into the tips of her fingers. "Where did you get that?"

"It was left for me on the dining table."

"You mean…"

"Nothing else was taken. The flat was undisturbed. Just the earring was left on the table. I think I recognise it. Didn't this belong to your sister, or to you?"

"To both of us, yes." Arla's brain was whirling around in loops, like a washing machine in a never-ending spin. She felt dizzy.

"How often do you leave the house, Dad?"

"Not much. I do my shopping, then in the afternoon go to the library. Twice a week I meet with the bridge club and play cards in the community hall."

"This person was watching you, to establish your pattern. Then they broke into your flat and left the earring."

"But why?"

Arla didn't reply. She was deep in thought, leaning forward on her elbows, staring at the ground. She straightened abruptly.

"Dad, it's not safe for you to live there anymore."

Timothy stood up, too, much slower, his joints creaking. "What?"

"You need to move."

He shook his head. "You think it's that easy to move? Besides, I'm an old man. When you get to my age, not much scares you. I'm not moving anywhere."

"But Dad…"

"No, Arla. I am not moving. If they want to come for me, let them come."

He lifted his faded blue eyes and they locked with Arla's. She saw an emptiness in them, but also a flat, barren determination. She knew he wouldn't budge. That much, she knew, she shared with her dad. He walked past her, then shuffled down the path, his walking stick making a sound as it hit the ground.

Arla watched him go, then clenched her jaws. Her nostrils flared in anger.

Her conflicted emotions about her father didn't mask one obvious truth. He was the only family member she had left. This had been personal all along. Now it was hitting closer to home.

CHAPTER 44

Harry was back in the seat by the time Arla came back. He tapped his watch.

"Yeah, sorry," Arla said. "Met up with someone there."

Harry started the engine. "Who?"

"My dad." She lapsed into silence, grateful that Harry didn't probe. They were close to Clapham when she opened up.

"Someone left the same earring on my dad's dining table."

Harry took his eyes off the road, but the car maintained a straight line. "The same as your sister's?"

"Yes."

"Did you get them?"

"Yes. But I think my dad's prints will be all over them."

"The lab can still dust for others."

They drove in silence for a while, and Harry opened his mouth to speak, but was silenced by his phone buzzing. It went from the Bluetooth into the car's radio speakers.

"Hello?" Harry said.

There was a hiss of static, then Lisa's voice came on the line. "Guv, where are you?" There was a hint of panic in her voice and it got Arla's attention immediately.

"What's the matter?" she snapped before Harry could reply.

"James is in hospital. He chased after a man who threw down a parcel for you at the carpool, then took off on his bike. James was parking his car: he saw the man and chased."

"Shit!" Arla fumed. "Is James OK?"

"I don't know. We called an ambulance for him. He caught up with the guy, then grappled with him. He knocked James out."

"Which hospital?" Arla asked.

"Charing Cross, guv." She looked at Harry, whose mouth was set in a tight line. He nodded in silence.

"See you there in fifteen," Arla said. Harry thumbed the dashboard and turned the siren on.

The traffic parted reluctantly, and Harry ducked and weaved, showing off his driving skills that would normally exasperate Arla, but on this occasion she was grateful. He parked in the ambulance yard and kept his lights on. At the main reception in A/E Arla showed her badge, and an Asian doctor took them to the cubicle where James was. He was lying flat on the bed, a saline drip snaking its way into his body above the elbow.

Arla felt a surge of guilt. He was a young, impressionable lad, and thought he was doing the right thing.

The lights were dimmed in the room, and James had his eyes closed, breathing softly.

Arla asked the doctor softly, "Can I talk to him?"

The doctor nodded. "He's had a mild sedative, but that was over an hour ago. He was a bit agitated when he arrived, but some painkillers soon sorted that. He kept going on about the parcel." He turned to look at Arla. "Whatever that means."

Arla clenched her jaws and went forward to the bed. She touched James' arm. There was a bruise on the left of his face, a black left eye, and a bandage around his head.

"You can wake him up," the doctor said from behind. Arla shook his arm gently, and James opened his eyes. He seemed groggy, then he sharpened as he recognised Arla. He tried to lift his head, but Arla pressed on his shoulder.

"Take it easy."

Harry came back into the room with two chairs. They sat down. The doctor said, "I'll give you a moment." He was closing the door when Arla said, "The rest of my team will be arriving soon. If they ask, please send them in." The doctor nodded and left them.

James was up, and licked his dry lips. Arla gave him a glass of water from the plastic jug on the bedside table.

"Tell us what happened," Arla said, when he settled down.

"I was parking my car. The barrier was just lifting when I saw the parcel hit the side. I got out of the car, and saw your name on the parcel in big white letters. 'DCI Arla Baker', it said." James frowned. "Below that, he had written, 'From Maddy'."

James stopped and took another sip of water. He seemed tired from the effort. He settled down on the bed and spoke with his eyes closed.

"He was biking off, but not too far away. He had his head covered in a hoodie, and the same tracksuit covered his whole body. Anyway, I took off, sprinting after him. Caught up with him as he stopped at the traffic lights. Pulled him from the back, that's when he turned and punched me."

Harry asked, "Did you get a look at him?"

"There wasn't much time, guv. He wore black sunglasses that covered his face. He turned and punched me real quick, then sat on my back when I fell. So I didn't get a good look."

Arla said, "If he was that well covered up, can you be sure if it was a man or a woman?"

James smiled ruefully. "If she was a woman she must be an Olympic weightlifter. No, this was a man, guv. I felt his strength."

Arla was thinking of the person her dad had described. Covered from head to toe, eyes covered in black glasses. The description fitted. Maybe it was the same person.

An expression of pain crossed James' features. He winced as he tried to sit up.

"Not sure if you should be doing that," Arla said, trying to help him.

"The painkillers must be wearing off. My neck and chest hurt."

Arla looked at the back of his neck where an ugly blue and black bruise was spreading. There was a knock on the door, and Lisa came in with Rob. They spoke to James for a little while longer.

"It should all be on CCTV," Arla said finally. "We should leave James alone now. How soon can we get the images, Lisa?"

Lisa craned her neck back from James' bed. "These are our images, guv. We should be able to get them immediately."

Arla spoke to the doctor once again when he came into the room with a nurse. Lisa and the others waited outside. The nurse changed the drip and started a new one.

"How long will he be in for?" Arla asked the doctor.

"He lost consciousness and has a head injury, so we would like to observe him for 48 hours. If he is well then, we can let him go without the need for a CT brain scan. But if he worsens, then the stay could be a lot longer."

The drive back to the station was a silent one. The sunlight had turned to dust in Arla's eyes, a yellow putrefaction of rotting flesh and decaying leaves. She stalked into the office with fire in her eyes, leaving Harry in the parking lot.

Lisa was at her desk already. She hung up on her phone and looked up at Arla. "AV say they can send us the images but it might be quicker if we pop into their office."

"Let's go," Arla said. They were joined by Harry, and walked down the labyrinthine corridors to the audiovisual technical room. Three sergeants sat in front of a bank of screens that took up one whole five-metre wall. One of them clicked on buttons, and pointed to the top left. The large screen was divided into panels. He enlarged the box and the image was cleared.

It showed a car at the barrier gates. The bar was lifting when a bicycle shot past, and a black object flew out, landing next to the car. James ran out from the car and picked up the parcel, then left it and ran after the bike.

"Next camera," Arla snapped.

They saw an image of the street that came off the parking lot. James was running, and his back was visible. The cyclist was a smaller dot.

"Can't you zoom in?" Arla fumed.

The man froze the image and zoomed into where James had caught up with the cyclist at the traffic lights. In slow motion, they saw an arm extend and catch James on the side of the head. He crumpled to the pavement and the cyclist jumped on him, straddling his back, as James had mentioned. All the time, the hoodie never came off his head.

"That's not enough for an ID," Arla said, feeling frustrated. "Can you show us one of the street cameras?"

"Luckily, guv," the sergeant said, "those cameras belong to us as well."

They stood in silence as the black and white images flickered to life. It showed the same events, but instead of a rear view, they now had a front-on angle.

"Zoom in," Arla said, folding her elbows on the desk and getting closer. The man's face was visible this time. He had a beard, but the big glasses didn't afford a good view of his face. He was smaller than it had seemed in the previous images. But he still punched hard, and Arla winced as she watched him hit James again as he straddled the young sergeant. Then he got up on his bike and raced off.

"Which way did he go?" Arla asked.

"He got up to Coniston Road, here." The sergeant showed them. "And then he disappeared. He knows which streets have CCTV, guv. Clever bastard."

Arla shook her head, the tension still keeping her taut. "So we got precious little. Send the images up to the lab. See if they can get anything from his clothes, the bike, anything."

She turned to Lisa. "Where is the parcel?"

"In your room, guv," she said solemnly. "It's not been opened as yet."

CHAPTER 45

The parcel was A4-sized, covered in black plastic. Arla's name was written on it with a white marker pen. Her breath caught when she saw the words below.

From Maddy.

What the hell did that mean?

Arla closed the door to her office. Several heads lowered when they saw her. Arla pulled down the blinds on her window that faced the office and sat down at her desk. She put on her gloves, and, with a pair of scissors, cut along the side of the black plastic. She had taken Harry's suggestion of wearing a surgical mask, in case a poison like anthrax spores was present inside.

Gingerly she removed a compact steel case, with a ring on top. It was similar to the one left in her garden. Breathing faster, Arla put her finger on the ring. There was no going back. She lifted the ring and the lid rose with it. No gas wafted out from inside. No spores. Arla pulled the ring more and lifted the lid completely.

The interior was lined with green felt, again similar to the last box. But this time, there was a standard-sized photograph, instead of a pair of earrings.

The picture showed a large house. It was in a state of disrepair. Half the roof had caved in, and the windows were boarded up. The eaves had broken and dropped off, but the building had once been an imposing one: that much was obvious from the elaborate woodwork. As Arla lifted the photo close to her face, memory ignited like a fireball at the back of her mind. Her eyes bulged out and her mouth opened in shock.

The photo dropped from her hand and she sat down heavily on the chair.

She didn't know how much time had passed, or hear the knocks on the door. She became aware of a head poking in, and then Harry's large form sliding inside the office. He was on his knees, by her chair, grabbing her arm.

"Arla." His tone was soft, but urgent. "What is it?"

She looked at Harry without speaking, her mind a whirlwind of thoughts. Who would know about this? Any connection to her had been suppressed in the media. Harry knew, so did Johnson. She suspected Lisa did, too, and her father. The others who knew were dead.

She stared at the photo on the table. This person knew Arla's secrets like they were out in the open. Secrets she kept buried deep, out of reach. And he was bringing them out to hurt her, one by one, slowly eroding her sense of safety till she was fully exposed.

Harry picked up the photo and looked at it, his brows knitted together in confusion. Then they cleared.

"This is the house opposite Clapham Common, right?" he murmured.

The shocked expression on Arla's face was answer enough. Where her sister had been found.

Harry picked up the black plastic cover, then put it down. He rested his buttocks on the table.

"They're trying to link what happened to Nicole with Maddy," he said in a matter-of-fact voice. Then he glanced across at her. "You OK?"

Arla felt she couldn't breathe. The past was hemming her in, earthy fingers of dirt closing her nose, covering her mouth. Her chest was fit to burst all of a sudden, and the air in the room was close, humid. She took a deep breath but the only sound that came from her mouth was a croak.

She shot out like a catapult from her chair and turned to leave, almost knocking Harry over. He shouted her name, but she had flung the door open and was running out of the office, oblivious to the eyes following her.

Arla ran into the corridor, then out of the double doors to the back section. Colleagues stared at her as she ran past them, and then at Harry as he ran after her. She came out of the back, and into the carpool when Harry caught up with her. He grabbed her by the sleeve but she had stopped already.

They were both panting. Arla stared up at the sky, her forehead clammy. She took a deep breath, then let it out slowly. She inhaled cigarette smoke, and opened her eyes to find Harry holding a lit cigarette to her. She took it from him greedily and pulled on it. Her first taste of nicotine in years. It felt strange at first, a scratching at her throat, then the old rush returned. It made her head lighter, after a few long pulls. Arla shook her head, wanting to sit down. The head rush would pass soon, she knew that.

"Feel like a walk?" she asked Harry. He nodded. She followed him as he stepped out onto the road, matching his long strides with fast steps of her own. Clapham Common Station was surrounded by art deco apartment complexes from a bygone era, now used as council houses for those on the poverty line. Which, for anyone paying rent and living in London, was a fine line indeed.

They smoked in silence as the buildings loomed around them, a forest of human habitation in a city of lost souls. Arla looked at the windows as she walked past them. How many secrets lay behind them?

"You know what he's doing," Harry said at length. It was a statement, not a question.

Arla didn't reply, so Harry continued. "He wants to break you down. With that photo he achieved exactly what he wanted – bring you to meltdown point."

Harry stopped and so did she. They were standing beneath the shade of a tree, sunlight dappling on its leaves. She was glad of the shade, and aware of Harry standing so close to her, she could touch him. She wanted to lean into him and feel his arms around her. No she didn't. It would just complicate things. God, weren't they complex enough already?

Arla felt her brain swelling, about to explode. She closed her eyes and rocked on her heels.

Without a word Harry unfurled his long arms and she allowed herself to fall into him, into that comfortable smell of aftershave and faint cigarette smoke, into the soft cotton essence of his familiarity. She hugged him, feeling his strong, protective arms around her, and a whimper died in her throat. A pain blew across the scarred remains of her heart like a coruscating, scathing wind, ripping her wounds open.

She stayed like that for a while, clinging onto him, listening to his heartbeat. It felt like the only home she knew. She disengaged, not looking at him, aware that something had passed between them. It didn't need words, and she knew he felt it, too.

"You can't let him win, Arla. His whole game plan is to keep pushing till you explode. Surely you can see that?"

Their eyes met. The chestnut browns were glistening with a softness she hadn't seen before.

She said, "I know. But he knows how to hurt me."

Harry lowered his head. "Exactly. And that's why you need to ignore what he's doing. He's getting cocky. He made a mistake by delivering that parcel in person. James almost caught him."

At the mention of James' name Arla felt a fresh injection of guilt. He was only doing his job. But for her sake, he had harmed himself. Arla had to make it back up to him.

"You're right," she said. "I can't let him get to me. Throwing me off the investigation is exactly what he wants. I reckon it's the same person who killed the victim, I mean Maddy."

"More than likely. If it wasn't the same person, they wouldn't be on your case night and day. He knows that if he succeeds in distracting you, then the chances of him not getting caught are higher."

Arla nodded. "He's a psychopath. Maybe malignant narcissistic personality disorder. Not that I'm a psychologist, but you know what I mean. He gets off by taunting me, showing how superior he is."

"Yes, Dr Baker," Harry said with a smile.

CHAPTER 46

Arla looked at the assembled incident room. The usual jocularity and relaxed nature of the meeting were absent today. Bodies shifted in their seats, and avoided her eyes when she looked at them. Most of them had witnessed her outburst. Arla felt embarrassed, but also knew she owed them an explanation. She couldn't expect them to do their jobs wondering if she was hiding something.

She looked at Wayne Johnson standing next to her. She had spoken to him on the phone after she came back from her walk with Harry. He had agreed, things had gone far enough. It was time to make everyone aware what the dangers were, and then move on towards finding Maddy's killer.

"You might have been aware that Detective Constable James Bennett is in hospital after a run-in with a suspect. This individual was dropping off a parcel meant for me. James intercepted him, but the suspect assaulted him, leaving him unconscious." Arla gave them an update on James' condition.

"The parcel had a photo inside." She told them about the building, and what it had meant to her. "This person knows a lot about my sister, it seems, and about how she died. He is using that to put pressure on me, because he is aware I saw it as a failure, not knowing what had happened to her."

There was total silence in the room, and Arla could hear the ticking of the clock on the wall, and the faint whirr of the fax machine as it printed out paper. No one moved.

She told them how she had found Nicole, and who her mother had been. The raised eyebrows came as she knew they would, and the looks of concern. Arla had never wanted to burden them with this. She had carried the weight around, and now that she was sharing it, it felt like she was giving a part of herself away, a part that she had kept safely hidden and secluded.

It was weird, but she had to do it. It was her duty. She felt the killer's hand at the back of all this, at her forced confession. She had wanted to keep Nicole's death a secret all her life. Until now.

"I know that you will have many questions. But please believe me when I say this. I have no idea who this person is, how they got my number or gained access to my house. Why they are, quite literally, hounding me."

She paused and tucked a stray hair back. "But I take it personally that James is in hospital now. And I don't want any of you to do what James did. If you see my name mentioned in anything to do with this case, then please don't take action. Even if it seems like the right thing to do. Come and tell me, or DI Mehta, or DS Johnson."

Several heads nodded. Arla sat down, and picked up her much-needed cup of coffee. She took a long sip.

Johnson said, "As always, this information stays between us. No one speaks to the media about DCI Baker. We move on with finding Maddy's murderer. Speaking of which, how far have we got?"

Rob Pickering put a hand up. "Sir, before we start, I need to say something about DCI Baker's house."

"Speak," Arla said, putting her cup down.

"You told me to get in touch with Prof Sandra Hodgson at CAHID in Dundee about the earrings, and I did. She got them this morning by express courier: they were flown to her. She rang me back in the afternoon."

"Good work, Rob. And?"

"She said they were definitely copies of the original. Very good copies but not the real thing. These were recently made, not from the 80s. At the back of the pendant, when the central stone was removed, she found an engraving. It said, 'RD'."

It didn't mean anything to Arla. "What does that mean?"

"They were engraved in a certain style, which meant it was probably the designer's initials. Now, there are thousands of designers with those initials. But one of them is a huge workshop called RD Designs, which specialises in remaking 80s jewellery. They are based in Nottingham."

Arla couldn't suppress her admiration. "You did well, Rob."

He blushed, which Arla thought was cute. He said, "It took a while, but of the many RD Designs, this place stood out."

"Have you contacted them?"

"Yes, and I spoke to their head designer. He had a look at the photo of the rings and confirmed that it is a style that is familiar to them."

"And did they have any requests recently to make them in that style?"

"Well, they make loads of them. So he needs to check through his records to see if anyone asked for this specific type."

"OK, stay on it." She felt herself deflate a little. If they were producing the earrings in bulk, there was no chance of finding a specific buyer. Unless this design had something different.

"When will they get back to you?" Arla asked.

"I told him by tomorrow. He needs to check his catalogues and see if this one fits."

"Do they have e-fit or does he have to do it manually?"

"Nope, they are in the 21st century. He can use the photos I sent him to do an e-fit."

"Good. Any progress on the cars?"

John Sandford put his hand up. "James was dealing with it, guv, and I was helping him. He is getting frustrated, I have to say. There are hundreds of images we have to go through."

"SOC found blood and clothes fibre at the site where she went missing, before the dead body appeared. Any DNA traces?"

Lisa shook her head. "Nothing on the databases, guv. Of course that only means our perp hasn't been caught, yet."

Arla nodded. She was frustratingly short of leads here. Aware that everyone's eyes were fixed on her, she turned back to the whiteboard. Maddy's face when she was alive stared back at her with a sultry pout, posing in her pink dress. Next to it was a close-up of her face, blue and mottled with death.

A thought struck Arla. She swung back to Lisa. "What about the necklace we found on Maddy's body? The one that belonged to... Katherine Mendonca. Is that a replica as well?"

Rob raised his hand. "Prof Hodgson hasn't got back to me about it as yet, guv. By the way, she wants to speak to you as well about something. Could you please give her a call back?"

Arla nodded, wondering absent-mindedly what Prof Hodgson had to tell her that she couldn't tell Rob. She looked at her watch. It was almost 18.00. So much had happened in the last few hours. One shock after the other. What was left to come?

She thought of Banerjee, in the morgue with the body. She turned to Lisa. Poor Lisa was having to do more running around now that James was in hospital.

"Could you please ring Banerjee, and tell him that I want a report by later tonight? We can't wait till tomorrow morning."

Lisa raised her eyebrows, but shrugged and left. Arla asked the team, "What happened with the door-to-door in a two-mile radius from where the body was found? And the Crimestoppers poster of Maddy? Any call-ins?"

John Sandford said, "A few calls came through. The usual pranksters. We think the body was left there early in the morning, just before dawn. Not many revellers in the park then, guv. Sorry."

"Not your fault, John, thanks for trying."

Apart from the design company in Nottingham, not much to go on as yet. She wanted to speak to the Burroughses again, and ask the wife if she had seen the recent school videos of Maddy.

"Skull-shaped ring," she said to herself.

"What?" Harry asked.

"Maddy had a ring with a skull on it. She wore it on her left middle finger. That's what her mother said," she told the team. "Can we ask the SOC team to see if they find anything nearby?"

"I will, guv," said Rob.

CHAPTER 47

Cindy was wearing blue overalls, with a peaked blue cap she kept pulled low over her face. She concentrated on pushing the broom along the pavement, brushing up stray leaves. During her work at Lambeth Council, she had paid a cleaner a hundred pounds to claim her uniform as lost. Cindy wore the spare uniform now. It was a great way for her to get close to the police station, and keep an eye on things. The two detectives walked close past her, so close she could have tripped them up using her broom. That would be nice, she smirked, seeing the female detective sprawled on the floor. They walked up the road, Arla Baker walking faster than the tall male detective. She saw them stop beneath a tree, and smoke. She leaned forward suddenly, and they were hugging. Cindy narrowed her eyes. She stayed behind a bus stop, and watched them. They disengaged after a while, but slowly. This wasn't a normal hug that colleagues gave each other occasionally. This was more tender, and Cindy breathed faster. Was something going on between them? Had she missed something? She had been to Arla's house once, and she needed to increase the frequency of her visits.

The man spoke to her, and Arla seemed to listen with rapt attention. Cindy became angry. She curled her lips, thinking of Gary being close to her. She missed him. He could make her feel good, he always had. Now this bitch was able to have a life and be with her man, but Cindy had to carry on, planning her operation.

It wasn't fair.

It's not her who should be suffering, it was Arla Baker!

Cindy turned away, on the verge of losing it. She was gripping the broom hard. She had a brief vision of the broom being a knife, and she could charge them, tearing Arla Baker to pieces with her knife...

No. She had to stop. Visions were no good for her, when she couldn't control her mind she got into trouble. That's when the sleepless nights came, and the need for the medications. Cindy had to see her doctor at some stage, but she didn't have the need or the time. Psychiatrists didn't know the half of it. They liked to act arrogant, as if they knew, really knew, what she had been through. Cindy started scrubbing with the broom again as the detectives walked back, passing within five feet of her.

She followed them at leisure, knowing they wouldn't go far, as they weren't in a car. They went inside the police station.

Cindy made her mind up. She left the broom behind the shed of a derelict single-storey house, where she had found it. She walked to Clapham Common tube station. Within ten minutes she was in Tooting. She got to Hoyle Road, and walked past number 35, Arla Baker's address. She walked backwards and forwards till she found what she was looking for. An alley between two houses, opposite number 35. She looked carefully at the houses on either side of the alley. One had lights on, the other dark. Like every other house in the neighbourhood, this one was divided into a ground- and upper-floor maisonette. As Cindy watched, lights came on in the ground-floor bay windows. Hurriedly, she moved on.

Cindy thought as she walked. She could keep an eye on the front of Arla's ground-floor apartment, but what about the back? The bedroom and the kitchen faced the small garden. Cindy walked around the block, taking a left at the next road and doing a full circle till she came to the row of houses that stood opposite. She took an approximation of where Arla's apartment was in relation to these houses.

She found one with not only the upstairs maisonette lights off, but also the front windows boarded. Her heart raced. A discarded house. She waited ten minutes to make sure the pedestrians were minding their own business. Casually, she loped up the black iron staircase that looked like a fire escape. Armed with her two sliding knives, she was inside within one minute. The place smelled musty and old. She stood listening for a while, and letting her eyes get used to the dark. Then she switched her flashlight on, keeping the beam pointed to the floor. The place had been cleaned out. Her footsteps creaked on the bare floorboards. Gaps on them gaped like broken teeth, showing the rafters underneath. A mouse scurried in the corner, past the skirting board. Confident the place was empty, Cindy marched to the rear. There was a bathroom at the back, and a bedroom next to it. The window was boarded up partially with slats of timber that had been screwed in. Working with her screwdriver, it was painstaking work taking the slats off, but thankfully there were only a handful. When she looked out of the window, she was greeted with a sight that filled her with happiness. She looked upon the rear façade of the houses on Hoyle Road. She counted the numbers down, and got to 35. The upper-floor maisonette had lights on, but the ground floor was dark. Arla was at work. Cindy could still make out the kitchen and the rear bedroom window.

Cindy smiled. An ideal place for her to sit and wait for Arla Baker to come home.

CHAPTER 48

Lisa came back as the meeting in the incident room was coming to an end.

"Sorry," she said. "I couldn't get through to Banerjee. He said he could get some prelim reports for you in an hour's time. But the blood reports would take two or three days at least."

Arla nodded. "Thanks for trying. We might still head down to the morgue. Banerjee will have something for us."

Arla finished some last questions with the team, then left with Harry. Evening was deepening with mauve shadows dragged across the horizon like a shroud. Headlights glowed like eyes of a giant centipede, its metallic legs crawling over a river of black asphalt. Diesel fumes and neon lights coloured the electric night a pulsating cobalt and red. Arla put the window down to feel the warm breeze, saline with sweat, on her tepid forehead. Voices from a dozen different nationalities floated in from the pavement. The pot was melting, overflowing, a rich concoction of hopes, dreams and tragedies.

Harry was silent as they drove through the tortuous streets of Brixton into Denmark Hill, where King's College Hospital, one of the largest teaching hospitals in England, was situated. They parked in the visitors' car park, and walked past the massive sprawl of Accident and Emergency to the mortuary. It was well signposted. They took the elevator to the basement level two. When they knocked on the door, they were buzzed in after they were seen in the camera overhead.

Banerjee, looking less like Columbo and more like Quincy now with his surgical gown and cap on, called out to them from a steel gurney he was leaning over.

"Get dressed, my lovelies. She's right here, you made it in time."

Arla and Harry put on their gowns without bothering to change their shoes. Banerjee's Chinese postgraduate medical student, Xinxin, helped them with a smile on her pretty, cherubic face.

Arla looked at the lifeless, cold body of Maddy, and looked away. She wasn't any stranger to dead bodies. It was part of the job. But that didn't mean she had to enjoy it. This case was hitting closer to home than she had imagined, and it was making her more sensitive. She forced herself to listen to Banerjee as he talked.

The old pathologist's eyes travelled down the Y-incision he had made to open up the ribs, then carried on down to slice the abdomen open.

"Let's start at the top," Banerjee said. "Hair fibres have been pulled off, and there is a haematoma on her scalp, which indicates some scalp trauma. Nothing heavy, just from pulling and maybe a punch or two. It definitely didn't kill her."

"Nothing in the eyes or oral cavity. Teeth are all intact. So is the tongue." He lifted up one wrist. "Ligature marks on both wrists and ankles. She was tied up, and the depth of the marks shows they were not just to restrain, but to imprison her."

He continued. "Oh, and these." He pointed to some bruise marks across the ribs and flank. They were flat and broad, and stood up in angry, broad welts.

"What are they?" Arla asked.

Banerjee seemed to ponder. "Well, they were made by something pressing down on her for prolonged periods. For my money, I would say restraining belts, like you see in a straitjacket."

Harry said, "To tie her down on a bed?"

"Yes," Banerjee said. "Many moons ago, I was a psychiatry resident as a junior doctor. Whenever a patient became boisterous, he was sedated and then clamped down with big belts on the bed. Those methods are prehistoric now that we have much quicker-acting sedatives, but the old brute method can be used."

He lifted a hand before Arla opened her mouth. "Before you say anything else, I would add that the rest of her is surprisingly pristine. No trauma, no sexual abuse."

"You sure?" Arla asked.

"As sure as I am she's dead."

Arla frowned. "How did she die, then? No trauma or strangulation…"

Banerjee intercepted her. "Actually I told you a lie. There is one type of trauma." He grinned. "But only because someone doesn't know how to give injections. The poor girl had multiple intramuscular injections on her arms, in the shoulder region. Left her with loads of bruises."

"Injections of what?"

"Million-dollar question. But I am pretty sure they were meant to sedate her."

"How can you be sure?"

"Because intramuscular injections are crude and quick. The chemical gathers in the muscle and slowly diffuses. I took a little sample and sent it to the lab. It came back as a benzodiazepine. Like Valium. In high enough doses, they will flatten a human being. Too high a dose, and it causes breathing to arrest. The process can be speeded up by putting potassium chloride into the mix, which can cause the heart to stop. Total cardiorespiratory arrest."

"Is that how she died?" Arla asked.

"Her muscles show a huge amount of flaccid paralysis, and delayed rigor mortis. I would say yes. But toxicology reports will prove it."

Harry said, "A lot of Valium and that potassium stuff: isn't that what they put into a lethal injection? Many American states dole out the death sentence that way."

"Yes," Banerjee said. "But they add an anaesthetic as well."

Arla was thinking. "So if we could find out where they got the chemicals from…"

Banerjee shook his head. "You can try, but unfortunately these days with the dark web it's all too easy to get hold of drugs. If you have the right software to access that part of the internet, then you can get hold of anything."

"Hold on," Arla said. "I know from the cyber security guys this is about downloading the Tor software browser, then using it to access the dark web."

"Even if you do, there will be hundreds of sites these drugs could have been brought from," Banerjee said.

"I know. But the drugs had to be posted to a UK address, and if we can find that address, then…"

Harry said, "That sounds good in practice but in reality it will be a needle in a haystack." He caught the determined look in Arla's hazel eyes. Then he sighed. "Alright, I'll get in touch with the Cybercrime Unit."

Arla gave him a smile and turned back to Banerjee. "Anything else?"

"Yes. There are signs of sexual activity. They seem to be consensual as there are no bruises or laceration in the genital areas. I have isolated some sperm from the vaginal vault. Sperms are dead of course, they only live for 72 hours, which means the sexual intercourse was earlier. But the DNA is isolated and is being put through the national database as we speak."

"Good," Arla said, her spirits lifting, but shadowed by darker thoughts. They had DNA samples from the cheek swabs of Paul Ofori, Mark Duggan and Maddy's parents. She expected to find Paul's DNA sample, or even Mark's. The other didn't bear thinking about, and she wondered if she would have to widen her net of DNA swabs from Maddy's contacts.

Momentarily, her mind was cast back to the vivacious, smart, confident girl in the photos, dressed to the nines. The dead body on the slab before her was utterly alien, divorced from that warm image full of life and promise.

But Maddy had a dark side, too. She liked pushing boundaries, checking limits. She wouldn't be the first intelligent person to do so, but she had paid for it with her life.

And that wasn't fair. Something tightened inside Arla's chest. Nicole had been smart, too. She used to coach Arla before her exams. Nicole sailed through hers with minimal work, and Arla was the plodder, envious of her elder sister.

"Arla?" Banerjee said.

She blinked and swung her head back to Banerjee, to find that both he and Harry were looking at her with concerned faces.

"What is it, my dear?" Banerjee knew her well enough to ask that question.

Why does so much of this case remind me of my own life? Arla thought to herself in silence.

Aloud, she deflected. "Time we headed back. Thanks for this. Will you let us know about the toxicology, and if you find anything else?"

Banerjee studied her for a while. "Yes. Look after yourself, Arla."

CHAPTER 49

It was almost 9 pm by the time they left the morgue and headed back. "Shall I drop you home?" Harry asked.

"I can take the tube," Arla said, her voice neutral. She knew something had passed between her and Harry. She didn't want to admit it, but knew there had always been a ripple, an undercurrent of attraction. Like a silent river it had flowed between them. They had stood on either bank, opposite each other, watching, waiting. It was summer, and the waters were warm.

"Too stuffy," Harry said. "The Met has given you a carriage and a driver. Might as well use it."

"Chauffeur, you mean. Doff your cap to me next time."

"You just want to see me in a uniform."

"In your dreams," Arla smirked.

"Yes," Harry said, his voice suddenly serious. "That's right."

She was aware that he was glancing at her. She looked out of the open window as a flock of birds weaved and ducked between the trees on the Common.

Without further ado, Harry took the straight road down towards Balham that carried on towards Tooting.

Arla said, "If someone came into my house, we should see something on CCTV, right? Not on my road, as there are no cameras, but on the High Street."

"The problem was the lack of cameras on your street, remember? Tooting High Street is busy. There's a tube stop, pubs, bus stops, and a load of restaurants."

Arla nodded. They had had this conversation already. Tooting was South London's curry mile. Rows of Indian restaurants, curry houses all of them, ran from Tooting to Balham. Easy for someone to get lost in the crowd.

I just want to know who you are, Arla thought to herself.

Harry found a parking space three doors down from her ground-floor Victorian conversion. Arla stopped at the porch before she went in. No signs of break-in, but there hadn't been any last time either.

"I'll be off, then," Harry said. He took an imaginary cap from his head and did a mock bow.

"In recognition of your efforts, I shall reward you with a glass of wine," Arla said. She turned the key and opened the door. The alarm cable hadn't been fixed as yet: she didn't have the time. Her fingers brushed the wall for the light switch. She stepped inside, followed by Harry.

Arla stiffened immediately. She could hear a voice, and it took her a few seconds to locate it. Harry shut the door and the voice became clearer. Fear tightened like a razor ball in her guts. She listened and realised it sounded like the TV in the living room. Her panicked eyes met Harry's. He put a finger to his lips and she nodded.

Was there someone in the living room, watching TV? That was absurd. But you could never tell…

Arla flattened herself against the wall, and inched over to the door frame. The door was open, and she could see inside the living room. It was dark, apart from the glow of the TV, casting an eerie light inside the room. Arla switched the light on. The room was empty. She stepped inside, looked at the windows and beneath the table.

"I'll check the rest," Harry said, shuffling over to the bedroom. She heard the bedroom light go on, but her mind was suddenly far away, transfixed on the TV screen. The same programme was on a loop, and it was about the body found inside a deserted house on Clapham Common. The TV news from last year, when it had all happened. When she had found Nicole's body. Wayne Johnson's face appeared, giving the TV interview. Arla's name was not mentioned. Her eyes snaked over to the DVD player, connected by a wire to the TV. The screen showed the images repetitively: the house, street, the room… Arla reached over and turned the TV off, then kicked the DVD player on the carpet like it was cockroach. She whipped around to find Harry, a similar shock on his face, having seen the TV.

"There's no one here," Harry said.

Arla grabbed her hair and pulled. "What the hell is this? What the fuck is going on?"

She brushed past Harry, not waiting for his answer. She charged into her bedroom, throwing open the wardrobe doors. She riffled inside her long dresses, then opened the sideboard drawers. She didn't know what she expected to find inside. The bed was made by her before she left, but she pulled the duvet up, finding nothing.

"Arla," Harry said from the doorway.

She stormed into the kitchen and used the key to unlock the garden door. With her torchlight she looked around, at the potted plants, under the barbecue, and the small garden table. Breath heaving in her chest, and an impotent rage gathering steam, she stared at the fence separating her from the house opposite. She rushed to it, shoved the Maglite in her back pocket, and tried to climb the fence. She felt a strong arm grab her elbow and pull her back. She fought Harry, kicking, pushing, hissing out the words from her lips.

"Let me go, damn it! There's someone over the fence…"

"There's no one over the fence," Harry said between clenched teeth, struggling to hold her. Arla was five-nine, wiry, and worked out when she working. Running and yoga kept her limbs strong. But she wasn't any match for Harry's long arms. He gripped her across the chest and lifted her up, turning around to put her back on the ground. He held her as she fought, making them both kneel on the floor.

"Shh," he whispered in her ear. "This is what he wants you to be like. He wants you to lose control. Can't you see that?"

"Let me go!" she screamed.

Harry moved his arms away and she stood up, panting, sweat running down her head. Harry stood up slowly, his features set in stone, his chestnut eyes melting. Arla stared at him with fire in her eyes, holding it back, feeling it pulse like a volcano against her throat.

"Why?" she asked him, and her voice broke. "Why me? What have I done?"

Harry reached out and she stepped back, feeling her leg hit one of the garden chairs. She sat down on it heavily. Harry joined her, sitting opposite. Arla shivered, despite the heat, sweat cooling her body.

"Let's go inside," Harry said. He held out his hand and Arla took it, lifting herself up. She shut the door securely behind her, locking it. With Harry, they went through every nook and cranny of the apartment, Harry using her screwdriver to remove panels from the wall, checking the heating pipes and stopcock. There was no evidence of a listening device, or a camera. Surveillance cameras could be the size of postage stamps these days.

When they were done, Harry said, "We need to get SOC to come back. That DVD player will be useful."

Arla swept her hair back, scratching her scalp. She was beginning to recover herself. Harry was right. She was being pushed to the edge, but she couldn't go over. She walked to the kitchen, and took out a bottle of white wine. It hadn't been opened. She had been good with alcohol recently. She put two more bottles in, and turned to Harry. "Drink?"

They took their glasses and sat down on the sofa, staring at the TV. The familiar black screen now looked weird, teeming with secrets. Arla knocked her drink back and stood up. She felt unsteady. Harry was standing next to her. She stared at him for a few seconds, his eyes unfathomable. She leaned over to him, and their lips met. Harry removed the glass from her hands.

She grabbed his hand and they stumbled into the bedroom.

CHAPTER 50

Cindy was watching with barely concealed glee as the female detective and her lanky boyfriend ran amok in the garden. From her actions, the detective must have found the little gift that Cindy had left behind. The DVD player had been brought from a car boot sale outside London, for cash. There was no chance the police could track it down to Cindy.

She watched as he restrained her, and then together they went inside. She could see them through the kitchen window, Arla Baker opening the fridge to take out a wine bottle. Then they disappeared from view as they went down the hallway to where Cindy knew the living room was.

The bedroom curtains weren't drawn when the light went on, and she saw them kissing feverishly, hands roaming over each other's bodies, touching and groping. Then Arla broke off and pulled the curtains. There was still a triangle at the top where the two curtains met, and Cindy watched the light shining through till it went off. She imagined their bodies entwined on the bed, and a longing for Gary grew inside her. She hadn't been with him for so long. This operation had better finish soon, and she knew it would be worth the wait.

Maybe I should have put a camera in every room, Cindy mused to herself as she stole down the stairs of the derelict apartment. That way, she could have sent Arla Baker some juicy photos on the phone.

As she walked down to the tube station, Cindy focused. The next stage was starting now, and she already had the victim in her sights.

CHAPTER 51

James Bennett shifted his position inside the Honda Accord passenger seat, and winced. Lisa was keeping an eye on Mrs Ofori's house. She glanced over at James sympathetically.

"Ribs still hurt?"

James had an expression of pain on his face. "Yup. But it's getting better."

He looked outside at the sunlight-dappled but quiet cul-de-sac. "What are we looking out for?"

"Anything and everything. DCI Baker thinks Paul could give us clues to who killed Maddy, even though he's no longer a suspect himself."

James nodded in silence. "What he said about Maddy two-timing him was pretty impressive."

"Impressive?" Lisa arched an eyebrow.

James gave a boyish smile. "I mean, you know. She knew what she was doing, right?"

Lisa shrugged. "If that's what you want to call it. If you ask me, she brought a lot of this trouble down on herself. Poor girl."

James nodded in agreement. "No one deserves to go like that. But at least she had it easy."

Lisa frowned this time, facing James. "What do you mean, easy?"

"She wasn't tortured, was she? Wasn't strangled to death, and the path report didn't say anything about being sexually abused. She went quietly, by an injection."

"She's still dead before she could reach eighteen. I wouldn't call that easy, either on herself or her parents."

James didn't say anything for a while. Then he spoke. "I was in the Army for one year before I joined the Met."

Lisa hadn't known that. "Really?"

"Yes. Infantry regiment, stationed at Kandahar in Afghanistan. We used to do all these patrols in our armoured vehicles. One day we saw two men approaching our vehicle. Sounds silly now, but over there, everyone's a potential suicide bomber. So we called out to them to stop. We kept screaming, but they wouldn't stop. Before you know it, one of the squaddies opened fire. Both men went down. When we got closer, we saw two kids, neither more than sixteen years old. Their dress and headgear made them look taller from a distance."

Lisa shook her head. "That's pretty rough."

"Yes, it was. One of the boys lived, but the other was shot through the chest. And that's not the first time I've seen a kid take a bullet, either."

Lisa said, "That's why you said Maddy had it easy."

"Yes."

Lisa remained silent. She sneaked a glance over at young James, wondering how many more deaths he had seen during his time in the Army.

When she looked back at the road, a man dressed in a suit caught her eyes. He emerged from the end of the cul-de-sac, near Paul Ofori's house. He walked straight down, past their car, in the direction of the main street. Lisa tried to think where she had seen the man before. Then it dawned on her.

She turned to James. "What was the principal of Brunswick High doing here? Mr Atkins, I think his name is."

James was looking at the rear-view mirror. "Yes, that's him alright."

CHAPTER 52

Arla couldn't remember the last time she had a lie-in. Good job the team had been briefed last night. She lifted herself on one elbow and peered at Harry. He had an arm draped over his eyes. Memories of last night came back, making her blush. He had been good, much better than she had hoped. She had reciprocated as well: it had been too long. She felt content, warm, basking in the residue of a busy night's lovemaking.

"What you looking at?" Harry asked without removing his arm. She tickled him in response, at the tuft of hair on his belly, extending down his midline. He grabbed her arm and she fell on his chest, her naked breast brushing against his chest.

"For that, DCI Baker, I might just have to arrest you," Harry murmured as they kissed.

"And put me in handcuffs?" Arla teased.

"As I recall, you quite liked that last night," Harry said, beginning to kiss down her neck onto her chest.

Arla panted, "Maybe we should try it again, then."

And they did. When it was over, they lay in each other's arms, getting their breath back. Arla looked at the watch. Almost 9 am. Her head was a nice, fuzzy blank, a big change from the pressure, the hard edge she had been walking recently.

That thought brought the present back, crashing. Maddy's killer was still out there. Some lunatic was still out to get her as well. Maybe they were the same person. Arla sat up in bed, the thin bedsheet wrapped around her midriff.

"You OK?" Harry asked.

"Yeah." She turned around to face him. "How about you?"

He nodded, holding her eyes. Arla said, "This stays between us."

"Definitely."

"I don't want any hassle," Arla said softly.

Harry picked up her hand and kissed it. "Last night was great. And yes, I do care about you. I always have, Arla."

"Me, too. But we keep it simple, OK? We both have jobs, lives."

"I know. All I want is another night like last." Harry smiled.

As they were getting ready, Arla said, "Will you take me over to the Burroughs house? I need to speak to Mrs Burroughs once again."

Arla rang the station, and got the phone number of the Burroughses and rang in advance. It would be on their way back into work. Arla looked around in her apartment in the unflinching morning light. Nothing had changed, and apart from the DVD player on the carpet floor in the living room, there was nothing to suggest her home of the last several years had been violated yet again. Twice in the space of one week.

Harry found the number of an alarm company, and called them to make an appointment.

"If you can't be here," he said, "then I will. Either way, we get the CCTV and your alarm sorted now. It's beyond a joke."

Arla wrapped the DVD player in a plastic bag, as the specimen bags weren't big enough. Harry was talking to someone in the kitchen, and he came out presently.

"I called for a uniform car to be present in front of your house," he said.

Arla frowned. "There was no need for that."

"Oh yes there is. You could get a nasty surprise when you come home late one night. Don't want that on my conscience."

They drove to the Burroughs house. Mrs Burroughs was expecting them. She took them inside a different room on the ground floor. The sofa in the corner alone was probably the size of Arla's apartment. There was a huge, flat-screen TV on the wall. Mrs Burroughs picked up three DVDs and handed them to Arla. Her features were more haggard than before.

"These are some of the videos of her play at school, and the final of the inter-school volleyball tournament. Can I have them back when you are finished, please?"

Arla took the DVDs with thanks. "Are you coming to the morgue?"

Mrs Burroughs bit her lower lip. "Just waiting for my husband to come back."

Arla nodded. "We will see you there."

All life seemed to have been sucked out of Mrs Burroughs. She stood there, withered like a winter leaf as Arla said goodbye.

Banerjee was hovering inside his office, dressed in a suit.

He glanced at Arla and Harry as they walked in. "Is the family here?"

"They will be soon," Arla said. "While we are waiting, can we use your TV and video player? Want to look at some videos of Maddy."

"Feel free." Banerjee waved them towards the TV in the corner.

Arla grabbed a chair while Harry put the DVDs into the player. The first video was of the school play, where Maddy had played Lady Macbeth. She looked stunning in the costume, much older than her seventeen years. She acted convincingly, but it was a home video, taken mostly from an angle. Harry fast-forwarded through most of it. The volleyball match was boisterous, hordes of screaming girls and their families jumping up and down in the stands. Arla spotted the form of Charles Atkins, the principal. He was shouting encouragement from the sidelines. Brunswick High won, and the girls went into a prolonged group hug. Mr Atkins had a flushed, happy face, and he spent some time talking to the girls. The video changed to more images of the girls, singing and waving.

"Wait, go back," Arla said. Harry rewound.

"Stop, stop."

"What are you looking at?" Harry demanded.

"Give me the remote," she said, and took it from his extended hand. She rewound, then forwarded. She stilled the image on where Mr Atkins was talking to one of the girls.

"Isn't that Maddy?" Harry asked.

"Looks like it."

Something about the image bothered Arla. It was a teacher speaking to a student, but they were standing very close. She pressed the play button and saw it immediately. For a second or two, so fleeting it would have been missed in all the bodies rushing around, Atkins' hand touched Maddy's waist. The fingers of his right hand snaked around her waist, and were visible on the camera from behind. Then they were gone.

"See it?" Arla asked, her voice tight. Her head felt dizzy. She rewound, then paused it.

Harry stared at the screen. "Son of a bitch," he said under his breath. He got closer to the screen. "There's something on his fourth finger. Like a ring. Wrong hand for a wedding band. He's married, right?"

"Yes." Arla was seething. She thought back to the way Atkins had been the second time she went back to see him. Tired, stressed. Had he known Maddy was dead? Arla scolded herself for not being more alert to his body language.

"We need to send that image to the AV guys, see if they can blow up the finger to see what sort of ring it is."

"Then bring him in?"

"Not sure: we need his DNA first. But as soon as we do that, he might know the game is up."

Harry stared at the TV, then back at Arla. "You think he could be the other lover that Paul mentioned?"

CHAPTER 53

A buzzer penetrated the silence in the office before Arla could reply. Banerjee, seated behind his desk, rose to answer it. A minute later, Mr and Mrs Burroughs walked in. Harry switched the TV off. Banerjee introduced himself, then took them around to where Maddy's body lay. They would only be shown the face. The sound of a wail reached their ears in a few minutes, and Arla knew the dreadful formality was over. A really useless part of her job, and also one of the cruellest. But it had to be done.

The couple appeared soon, Conrad supporting his wife as they walked back. Arla nodded at them and they walked off outside, holding each other.

Arla said goodbye to Banerjee, and they raced back to the station. James was back, Arla noted happily. She gave him a peck on the cheek.

"Back to normal?" she asked.

"Is this place normal?" He grinned. "Thanks for asking. Getting better by the day. By the way, Lisa and I were trying to get hold of you."

"I was in the mortuary basement. No signal there. What's up?"

Lisa had walked around, her face excited. "Guess who we saw near Paul Ofori's house?"

Arla's face tightened when she heard. She told them about the video. Harry was still with the AV guys, getting a blow-up done while he waited.

"We still need to keep an open mind. Atkins could be checking up on Paul. There could be a number of reasons, in fact, why he was there."

James shrugged. "To score drugs? I mean, it's the wrong side of town for someone like the principal of Brunswick High, isn't it?"

He had a point. Why was Atkins there? And Arla knew what she had seen in the video. The earnest, almost emotional look on Atkins' face, and then the touch on the waist. Maddy had her back to the camera, but she hadn't made any effort to move away.

Arla sighed and closed her eyes. Could this really be happening?

Harry came up behind them. He had an envelope full of photos in his hand. He took them out and handed one to Arla. The photo was a close-up of Atkins' hand when it had appeared around Maddy's waist. The ring was more visible now. It was a steel ring, with the shape of a skull on it.

Arla's heart raced and her mouth went dry. The ring that Mrs Burroughs had told her about. A ring that Maddy used to wear every day. A steel ring, shaped like a skull.

Harry looked at her. "What?"

She told them. Harry said, "None of us have actually seen the ring, have we?"

Arla conceded. "No, we haven't, but there is one person who would have."

"Mrs B."

"Yes," Arla said to Lisa and James. "Can one of you head down to their house and show Mrs B the photo? If she identifies it we have the makings of a case."

To Harry she said, "You and I are going back to school. Make sure we have a DNA swab kit with us."

Arla couldn't stop thinking as Harry drove. Maddy had signs of sexual activity, but not recent, Banerjee had said. And it had been consensual. Did 'recent' mean longer than ten days? That was when Maddy had been abducted, ten days ago. Was it an abduction or had Maddy gone missing on purpose, aided by her lover? And then he killed her?

"My God," she whispered to herself. She turned to Harry. "We need to speak to Atkins' wife as well. We know where he lives?"

Harry nodded. "Got the house number as well, if you want to call her."

Arla took Harry's phone and rang the number. Mrs Atkins answered, and agreed to the detectives coming around.

She handed Harry his phone back. "That was easy," he remarked. "She sounded relaxed. Let's see what she's like, then head over to the school."

Mr Atkins lived in Stockwell, up the road from Clapham. There was a pub in the corner opposite Stockwell tube station, and they drove down the road to find once stately homes built before the First World War now converted into apartments. The Atkinses lived in the first floor of a conversion, and Mrs Atkins buzzed them in through the door almost as soon as they knocked.

Arla and Harry trudged up the darkened stairs. A door opened at the top, letting in a shaft of sunlight. Mrs Atkins stood framed in the doorway. Arla shook hands with the petite woman, who was almost half the size of her husband.

"Thank you for seeing us at such short notice," Arla said.

"No problem," the woman said. "Call me Laura, by the way."

Arla detected an Irish accent. They sat down on the sofa, and Arla had her first proper look at her. She was much younger than Arla had originally assumed. She put her age at mid- to late-twenties, which seemed a lot less than Charles Atkins, whom Arla put in his forties.

"Dreadful business, this girl dying at the school," Laura said. Arla noticed she wrung her hands as she spoke.

"Did you ever meet Madeleine Burroughs?" Arla asked.

"Oh no," Laura said quickly. "I just saw the news."

"Did you ever go to the school?"

"There has been the odd occasion. For the summer ball and things like that, you know."

"Did you meet any of the students?"

"No."

Arla noticed Laura wasn't good at maintaining eye contact. She answered the question, smiled, then looked away towards the window. The bay window had its blinds down against the blinding sun, and muted sounds of traffic came from Stockwell's main road at the end of the street.

Harry said, "Did you ever meet the Burroughs family?"

"No."

"Where were you the night of 3rd June?"

"At home, actually, just watching TV."

"On your own?"

"Yes."

Harry asked, "And your husband?"

"He was here with me." Laura looked at the floor.

Arla and Harry glanced at each other. Was Laura going through the motions? Arla remembered Charles Atkins' statement – he was at home as well on that evening, and they could alibi for each other.

Arla asked, "How long have you been married?"

"Seven years now," Laura said with a slight smile. "I moved from County Derry in Northern Ireland, and met Charles while I was living up north."

"Laura," Arla asked with emphasis, "has your husband ever mentioned Maddy, or any other student to you?"

Laura shook her head. "Not specifically. He talks about work, but he didn't mention any student."

"Do you have any children?" Arla asked.

Laura shook her head. A shadow passed across her face and she stared at the light bouncing off the window blinds.

"Would you mind providing a DNA sample? It's a simple mouth swab, and we have to do it as a matter of routine."

A puzzled look flashed across Laura's face, and then she shrugged. "I don't mind."

Harry took the kit out and handed it to Arla. She took the sample, put the swab back into its sterile container and snapped the lid shut. She gave it back to Harry who put it in the specimen bag.

They said their goodbyes, then walked down to the car.

"She's hiding something," Harry said as they got into the car.

"Maybe." Arla buckled herself in. "The body language was weird, there's no doubt."

CHAPTER 54

Half an hour later they were sitting in Charles Atkins' office. He looked the same as last time, tie undone, suit crumpled, a definite departure from the suave and polished image Arla had seen before. He could do with a shave, and his eyes looked like he hadn't slept for a long time.

He opened the door when Arla knocked, and stood staring at them for a while. He didn't know they were coming.

"Can I help you?" Atkins asked, his tone hostile.

Arla walked in without being invited, followed by Harry, who stared down at Atkins as he went past him.

Arla perched herself on the desk and Harry guarded the door. Atkins looked from one to the other like a trapped animal.

"I'll make this easy on you, Mr Atkins. Let's go back to the beginning. Where were you on the night of 3rd June?"

Atkins licked his lips before replying. "I told you already…"

"I know what you told us!" Arla snapped. "We have new evidence which casts serious doubt on your statement. I'll ask you once again. Where were you that night?"

Atkins rubbed his forehead. "I have nothing more to add, DCI Baker. Now, if you will excuse me…"

"We saw a video where you put your hands on her waist," Arla said softly. "After the inter-school volleyball match final. Remember?"

Atkins looked at her, a haunted look in his face. He sat down on a chair. Arla continued. "You also had a ring on your right hand fourth finger. A skull-faced ring. That was hers, wasn't it? She gave it to you."

Atkins shook his head. His face was pale and drawn, but he made his voice authoritative. "I don't know what you're talking about, DCI Baker."

"You are the lover that Paul Ofori was talking about. You met Maddy that night in Brockwell Park, outside the Wrangler's Arms pub. You waited for her, then took her…"

"No!" Atkins shouted, standing up. His face was still pale, but pockets of colour appeared on his cheeks. "You have this all wrong. I never met Maddy that night."

Harry said, "Then why don't you tell us what happened?"

"There's nothing to say." He slumped back on the chair. His legs shook. "Nothing at all," he repeated.

Arla said, "We need to take a DNA swab from you, Mr Atkins." Atkins looked like he would crumble to dust if he was touched.

"What for?" he asked in a shaky voice.

"For the investigation into Maddy's murder, for which you are now a suspect. Are you refusing?"

Atkins hung his head. "No," he replied, his voice almost inaudible.

Harry stepped forward and took the swab. "Now you need to come with us to the station, to give an official statement," he said.

Atkins looked around the room like there was a solution to his problems hidden somewhere. He finally looked at Arla. "Are you arresting me?"

"No. But if you resist coming down to the station I will be forced to."

"On what grounds?"

"For being the prime suspect in Madeleine Burroughs' murder, and for resisting arrest."

Atkins looked like he had been punched in the gut with a sledgehammer. "My God," he whispered, lips barely moving. "This cannot be happening."

Harry stepped forward and put a hand on Atkins' elbow. "Come on, Mr Atkins."

Atkins shook Harry's arm off. "I want a lawyer," he said, glowering at Harry.

CHAPTER 55

Detective Superintendent Wayne Johnson and Deputy Assistant Commissioner Nick Deakin faced the soundproof double-glass screen that separated them from interview room 2. Johnson fidgeted nervously and glanced at Deakin. His superior officer was wearing his uniform as usual, and looked calm, in control. Johnson wished he felt the same way. This case was shaping up to be one of the biggest of his career. Only a quick conviction now would bring it to a smooth conclusion. And Johnson, being the overall officer in charge, needed a smooth conclusion.

Because the investigation had been anything but smooth. He had put Arla Baker as the SIO, against his better instincts. She ruffled feathers, but no one got results like she did. This time, however, the chaos had been widespread. For some reason, the killer was nagging Arla. Johnson had thought long and hard about who it could be. Someone who had close personal knowledge of Arla, and a vendetta against her. One by one, he had eliminated all her colleagues.

Johnson had taken a personal interest in the triangulation of the phone message that had been sent to Arla. The photo message showing Madeleine Burroughs' dead body. A pay-as-you-go phone that no doubt had been destroyed as soon as it was used, as the SIM card was never used again.

The photo was sent to Arla's personal phone. How did they get hold of that number? It hadn't been the switchboard: Johnson had checked.

He sighed. Whatever. It seemed like the psycho was finally in their grasp. As he looked at the suited, dishevelled form of Charles Atkins, a feeling of nausea passed over him. Johnson had teenage children, a boy and a girl. To think the principal of a school could stoop to such lows was unnerving.

But was he the man who was chasing Arla as well? The one going to such extraordinary lengths to remind Arla of her turbulent family life?

Johnson didn't know. If he was, then that meant Charles Atkins was a deep, dark mind indeed. Bringing him to justice would be a big notch on his career post. And, he thought with relief, bring this whole fiasco finally to an end. After all, he was only one month away from being promoted to a Deputy Assistant Commissioner role as well. Mandy had already given his measurement to the Met tailor. Neither she nor Johnson could wait for the day to arrive.

But at the back of his mind, a sense of doubt kept niggling away. Johnson knew something was wrong about this case still, and he couldn't put his finger on it.

Nick Deakin leaned closer to Johnson. "Do you think he's our guy?"

Johnson nodded. "The evidence is stacked against him, sir. Absolutely stacked."

CHAPTER 56

Harry pressed the button and did the introductions for the recorder. Arla looked at the two men opposite her. Charles Atkins was slouched against the chair, his lean, athletic figure now looking wasted, shrivelled. His cheeks were sunken, but not as much as his eyes, which seemed to be receding further into their sockets each time Arla looked. She couldn't muster much sympathy for the man. He had lied, misdirected them, and was guilty of sex with a minor, who was a student as well. But was he guilty of murder? That was what Arla had to figure out now. She had to keep an open mind. Of course, it had been natural for him to lie. It would have been the end of his career if he had confessed at the beginning. She looked down at the DNA report that had arrived just before they went in. It hammered in the final nail in the coffin for Charles Atkins. His DNA matched the DNA found inside Maddy. All the other DNA samples they had taken – her parents, close friends – turned up negative.

Next to Atkins sat a portly, bald-headed man wearing a blue and white Oxford rower's tie and black suit. He was Malcolm Hindmarsh, a well-known adversary, who had frustrated many a police case by representing the rich and famous.

Arla began her questions. "Mr Atkins, where did you first meet Madeleine Burroughs?"

He licked his lips before replying. "When she joined school two years ago."

"When her parents moved from USA. She was fifteen years old then."

"Fifteen and a half," Atkins said.

Arla looked at him, a feeling of revulsion rising up inside her. What kind of man, what kind of *teacher,* acted out his base fantasies on his students?

"Where exactly did you meet her personally?"

"I am the president of the girls' volleyball club. She was the captain, and I had to approve the girls' choice."

"So it was the night of the vote?"

Atkins nodded. "Do you remember the date?"

"Early September, 2016. I cannot remember the exact date."

Arla wrote it down. "How often did you meet her after that?"

"Every now and then… Look, Maddy wasn't your average shy teenage girl. She was much more confident and mature. She knew how to have an adult conversation."

"What do you mean by adult conversation?"

Hindmarsh leaned towards Atkins, and the two had a whispered conversation. Arla got the impression Atkins was being scolded. Atkins said, "By adult I mean a grown-up conversation about politics, news, that sort of thing. She was a remarkable girl who was very aware of the world around her."

"What did you talk about?" Arla felt an uneasiness, a slimy repulsion slide down her skin. This man and Maddy locked in solitary conversation was not an image that came easily to the mind.

"She was passionate about climate change, the ozone layer. She also felt strongly about the way African Americans and Native Americans had been treated historically, and so on. Like I said, she was quite political."

"Then you started to have a relationship with her?"

Atkins face went red briefly, then he blew out his cheeks. Arla stared at him intently. Hindmarsh moved in and did his lawyer thing, then moved away.

"What do you mean, relationship?" asked Atkins stiffly.

"Let's not play games here, Mr Atkins. Your DNA was found in the genitals of the deceased. Do you admit to having a sexual relationship with Madeleine Burroughs?"

Another hushed conversation followed, and Arla waited patiently. Atkins finally straightened in his chair. "Yes, I did."

Arla glanced at Harry, relief evident on her features. One step closer. The question she really wanted to scream at him lay silent in her soul.

Are you the one ripping my life apart?

But she knew she couldn't ask that question yet. Certainly not here, in her official capacity, and not now. She swallowed and continued. "Did you have relations with any other girls, like you did with Maddy?"

A look of incredulity, then of irritation passed across Atkins face. Arla tried not to smirk. He was acting righteous here? Really?

"No, of course not."

"Are you sure of that, Mr Atkins?"

His face was suffused with colour now. "Listen, I am not some pervert…"

Harry raised his voice, speaking over him. "Just answer the question, Mr Atkins."

Atkins stopped and looked from Arla to Harry, his jaws locked tight. "No. Never."

Arla said, "So if we dig up all the schools you have worked in, we will not find any evidence of inappropriate relations you had with other girls?" This was a trick question. The team had already checked: no scandals had been uncovered at the three other schools that Atkins had tutored in.

"No."

"Did you ever think about the consequences of your actions?"

"Yes, of course I did. But it just happened, you know. Couldn't help it. It was she who started it, by the way."

Arla frowned. "But you are the adult here. It won't be the first time a teenager has a crush on a teacher."

"Yes, I know." For a while Atkins looked downbeat.

Arla was warming up slowly. It would be time to move in for the kill soon. "You enjoyed your career, didn't you?"

"Yes, I did."

"And your wife was proud of what you achieved?"

"I guess she was, yes." Atkins' eyes narrowed slightly at the mention of his wife.

"If news about your relationship became public it would have ended your career. Isn't that right?"

Atkins looked around him, then his lawyer touched him on the sleeve. They had a quick chat.

"What do you mean?" Atkins asked.

"I am the one asking the questions here, Mr Atkins, and you know perfectly well what I mean."

Malcolm Hindmarsh cleared his throat. "We are not in a court of law, Miss Baker, and I would remind you my client is not bound to answer your questions."

Arla ignored him and stared at Atkins. He swallowed, his Adam's apple bobbing up and down.

"If anyone knew, your life and career would be destroyed. She could have told her boyfriend, Paul Ofori or any of her close friends. So you abducted her, didn't you?"

Atkins stood up from his chair. His face was flushed red and a vein was throbbing in his temple.

"No! No! I didn't take her, and I didn't kill her!"

"Sit down, Mr Atkins," Arla said, not raising her voice. He sat down, breathing ragged and heavy. He looked at Arla, his face earnest. "I didn't kill her. I didn't."

CHAPTER 57

The incident room at Clapham Common Station was packed to the gills. The four air-conditioners were working full blast, but many of the detectives and uniforms packed in the room were pulling at their collars and rolling up their sleeves. Arla was at the whiteboard. A photo of Charles Atkins had been stuck to the top, and below it, a smaller one of his wife. Arla updated the team about the day's events. It was 15.00 already, and she was beginning to get a headache. Wayne Johnson was in attendance, and all calls to the desks had been barred by the switchboard.

Arla said, "His lawyer confirms that Mr Atkins will plead guilty to sex with a minor, and misleading a police investigation." She looked up at the hushed room. "But not guilty to the charge of murder." Murmurs broke out among the crowd and got louder. They were subdued when Arla raised her voice.

"You should note that Charles Atkins' fingerprints were not found on the deceased's clothes. He was not seen at the Wrangler's Arms pub the night of the abduction. His DNA was also not found at the scene. Another set of DNA was seen in the grass, but not his."

"He didn't have to be in the pub, guv," James Bennett said from the front row. "He could have been hiding in the park."

"Absolutely," Arla said. "And he had motive, didn't he? A very strong one. Protection of his reputation, career and family life."

She continued. "But he does not possess a car. And our working theory is that Maddy's body was transported using a car." She turned to James and Lisa, sitting next to him. "How is the car ID coming along?"

"Slowly," James said. "My accident hasn't helped."

Arla hid her frustration by speaking up to the rest of the group. "Mr Atkins remains the prime suspect and he is in custody. But we cannot hold him for longer than 48 hours. This is crunch time, guys. Anything we can uncover at this late stage can make or break this case."

Arla had a strange premonition that she was close to solving this case. She didn't know why. She wondered if Atkins was indeed a serial predator on teenage girls, or if he was telling the truth about himself – an extreme lack of judgement in an otherwise well-respected teacher.

"We need to send an SOC team to his house, folks. Search warrant has been issued. I will speak to his wife and make sure she spends the night somewhere else as we turn the place upside down. With care of course. While that is happening, I want to know everything about Charles Atkins. Who his childhood friends were, where he went to college, partners, favourite food – you get the picture."

"He was born in Nottingham, guv," Lisa offered. "We are in touch with Midlands Constabulary already."

"Good. I want a door-to-door of his home town. Also of the towns where he lived. Someone will know something. As always, the truth lies in open view while we hunt in dark corners. So let's not forget the obvious places."

Arla broke the meeting up. As chairs were scraped back and bodies stretched, she walked back to her office. Within ten minutes she was joined by Harry and the rest of the team. Johnson came in, too, and shut the door.

"Well?" Johnson demanded.

Arla was leaning against the prefab UPVC window behind her desk. "Hand on heart, I don't think he's the killer, sir."

She could see the visible disappointment in her boss's face. "Why not?" he asked.

"He confessed to sleeping with her, sir. Now surely, if he was guilty, he would have hidden that fact when I told him Maddy was dead?"

Johnson pondered this and Arla continued. "An admission to a relationship with Maddy is admission of a motive for him. It was in his best interests to carry on denying it."

Johnson said, "How could he with the DNA evidence?"

"Sure, but he all but admitted before we took the DNA sample from him. His alibi checks out with his wife. Unless she is lying, of course. Then there is the actual process. Did he hire a car or have an accomplice? Where was Maddy kept for almost nine days while we turned London upside down looking for her?"

The room was silent. Arla said, "We will keep on looking, and maybe something will emerge, but I doubt it will point to him being a killer."

Johnson closed his eyes and rubbed them. "We need a conviction, Arla. The press is aware of this arrest. It will be front-page news tomorrow. Can you imagine what it's going to look like if we let him go?"

Arla bristled. "I know we need a conviction, sir, but we need to find the right person first! I know Atkins is a creep, but is he a killer?"

Harry said to Arla, "Then there is the small matter of your stalker, guv."

Arla nodded without looking at him. She didn't want to give anything away in meaningful glances. Harry was doing the right thing by not calling her name.

"A prelim search of his house does not reveal any notebooks or materials about you. We have his laptop, and Cybercrime are going through it as we speak," Lisa said.

There was a knock on the door. A uniformed sergeant poked his head through. "Message for DCI Baker."

"What is it?" Arla asked.

"While you were in the incident room, there was call for you at the station, man called Timothy Baker, your father?"

"Yes, that's right. What did he say?"

"Nothing. He asked for you to get in touch with him."

A tingle of unease nudged inside Arla. Her dad never bothered to be in touch. It was normally she who made contact. The memory of her stalker being in her dad's apartment was unnerving.

"Thanks, I'll call him back."

Arla checked her phone quickly. No messages. They broke the meeting up. Arla went to the technician's office, where the software on her phone was checked.

"Anyone who calls you now," John, the technician, said, "will have an electronic tag on their number. We can use that to listen to their conversations. And of course, your conversations as well. So let your peeps know."

Arla grimaced. "My peeps mostly live in the station, John. Like me, they have no life."

Harry was waiting for her back at the office, flanked by Lisa, James and Rob.

"You all know what you have to do, folks," Arla said.

"Guv, don't forget to call Prof Hodgson from Dundee back. She wanted to speak to you, and said it was urgent."

Damn it, Arla thought. She'd become so busy of late she had no time. "Yes, I will." She turned to Rob. "Is the folder on Atkins back now?"

"Yes, I emailed it to you."

"Good," Arla said, sitting behind her desk. "I'll stay for a while and prepare a report for the top brass. See you guys tomorrow."

Harry yawned. "I'm headed home. Goodnight, guv." Arla suppressed a grin. She knew exactly where home was tonight for Harry. Not only did she feel safer with him there, he also made the nights far more interesting.

CHAPTER 58

Timothy Baker heard the buzzing sound and turned around. He muted the TV and stood up stiffly from his armchair. His mobile phone was buzzing. He picked up the phone and squinted at the screen. It wasn't a number he recognised. He hesitated for a while, thinking. He remembered what his daughter had said about the earring left in the apartment. Someone was watching him. The phone was insistent, buzzing in his hand.

He pressed answer and held it to his ear.

"Dad, it's Arla," a female voice said. Timothy could hear traffic in the background.

"Arla, are you OK?"

"Yes, Dad, are you alright? I heard you tried to contact me at the station."

"That's right." Relief flooded through Timothy. Although she was calling from a new number, it had to be her, as she knew about the message he had left.

"What's the matter?" Arla asked.

"I think I was followed again," Timothy said, peering down the third-floor window of his apartment. The windows of the living room faced the street. Traffic crawled up and down the busy intersection of Balham train station, and the road below the railway bridge.

"Dad, you need to listen to me now. This is going too far."

"Hold on," Timothy said. He couldn't see down to street level with precision without his glasses. He found them inside their box after moving some magazines off the table surface. He put them on, then picked up the phone. Although he had called about his stalker, Timothy was glad of the opportunity it gave him to speak to his daughter. It was ironic that he had to be in danger in order to finally spend some time with her. A warmth filled him inside, and a glow of emotion. How long had it been since he had a proper conversation with her? It always led to bitterness and recriminations, but it didn't have to be that way. He would die one day soon, and he had plenty of regrets already. Having some sort of a relationship with his own flesh and blood would mean he died with less heartache.

He suspected Arla felt the same, but her anger at him clouded her mind. Oh God, how could he blame her? And yet, all his living life he had tried to make amends. And he would continue till his days on earth came to an end.

"Go on, Arla," he said, pressing the phone to his ear. He listened in silence as his daughter told him about arresting Charles Atkins.

"But I think the killer is still around, Dad. And it's not Atkins. So you have to be careful. But we need to meet, Dad, and speak face to face."

"Of course. When do you want to meet?"

"Well, I'm driving down to Balham as we speak."

"Are you coming up to the apartment?"

"No, can you come down to the street, please? I will park up, then we can drive to the café, and talk over a cup of coffee."

Splendid, Timothy thought to himself with enthusiasm. A morning coffee with his daughter would be the ideal way to start his day. When was the last time that had happened?

"OK, just call me when you get here."

"Do me a favour, Dad."

"Yes, of course. What is it?"

"Don't answer your phone if it rings again. The stalker has my number: it's possible he has your number as well. That's why I'm calling from a phone box, and not my phone. Not sure if he is tracking my calls. Do you understand?"

Timothy frowned and nodded slowly. "This is serious, isn't it?"

"Yes, it is. We have to be careful, because he could be watching you even now. But don't worry, I doubt he will try anything in daylight with all these people around."

"If you say so."

"Just wait for my call, then come downstairs."

Arla hung up. Timothy went to get dressed, a strange feeling in his heart. He had a spring in his step as he got ready, but he was weighed down by the gravity of the situation.

He tried to read on his Kindle but his attention strayed. Beams of sunlight burst in through the windows, motes of dust swirling in them. Timothy waited, his feet tapping on the carpet. He almost jumped when the phone rang on the table. He snatched it up.

"Come down, Dad," Arla said. "I'm in a black VW Golf."

Timothy closed the windows and locked the door. He had left a key to his front door with Arla many years ago. She had visited once or twice. He took the elevator down to the ground floor, and stepped out into the noisy street.

The old brick and cement bridge creaked above him, belching out dust as a train rolled in from London Waterloo. Timothy looked around a while, till his eyes fell on a black VW idling by the kerb. He set off for it, his gait shuffling, slower after the knee replacement he had ten years ago. As he got closer to the car, he could see the driver. Arla's long, brown hair hung past her shoulders. He could see her white hands on the steering wheel.

He got to the passenger door and opened it. He sat down, wondering why his daughter kept her face averted from him, and from the rear-view mirror.

"Hi, Dad," Arla said. Her voice sounded very different from the phone.

The next few seconds were a blur to Timothy. The door opposite him opened, and a man jumped inside. As soon as he slammed the door shut the car took off with a squeal of tyres, pressing Timothy back against the seat.

"Arla, why are you…?"

His voice froze when he caught sight of the pair of eyes in the rear-view. The woman who was driving was definitely not his daughter. She was shorter, more stocky, with a wide neck. Fear clutched his throat as the woman ripped off the wig from her head. She gave a cackling laugh, throwing her head back.

Timothy turned his bulging eyes to the man sitting opposite him. The man was observing him with a smile on his face.

He said, "Timothy Baker, please don't try to open the doors, they have been locked."

"Who… who are you?" Timothy asked in a shaky voice.

The man kept smiling. "Someone who has wanted to meet you for a long time."

CHAPTER 59

Arla was having one of the best lie-ins for a long time. It was true what they said about sex in the mornings – it was much better. It lasted longer, and she had barely recovered from a toe-curling orgasm when Harry was on her again. When their sweat-stained bodies collapsed back on the bed, panting, she felt flushed, alive. This sure as hell beat her morning running and yoga routine.

She glanced at the bedside clock. She sat up straight almost immediately. It was close to nine am! She kicked Harry and got off the bed.

"What?" Harry said drowsily.

"Look at the time, sleepyhead," Arla said, pulling the bathrobe around her. Harry did, groaned and flopped back on the bed.

"Damn it. I was just getting my third wind…"

He was cut off by Arla's phone ringing. She rooted around in her handbag and got it out before the line disconnected. Her heart sank when she recognised the number. She had to answer.

"Where are you?" were Johnson's first words to her.

"On my way, sir."

"You better be. Have you seen *The Daily Telegraph* this morning?"

"Not yet, sir, I was just…"

"Deakin is here, and we are going into a meeting with the MPA Press Liaison, so you better hurry up, Arla." Johnson hung up.

Harry had sensed something was up, and he was in the shower already, so she went and joined him. Which was a bad move, as it only served to delay her further.

It was close to 9.45 am by the time Arla scrambled in to work, rushing through the double doors. John Sandford, the uniform sergeant at the desk, stopped her. Before he could open his mouth, Arla saw Conrad Burroughs and his wife rise up from the plastic chairs by the wall. Conrad's face was like a storm, and he shook a newspaper in her face.

"You catch the man who abused my daughter and don't have the decency to tell me?" he thundered, his face inches away from Arla's.

Arla said, "Mr Burroughs, we were about to inform you, but someone leaked news to the media. We have not done a press release as yet."

"You think I give damn about your press release? The guy you have in jail is the principal of her school, for Heaven's sake!"

He thrust the page in front of Arla. She saw a photo taken with a long-distance lens, of Charles Atkins coming inside the police station, led by herself and Harry. There was an inset photo that was a close-up of a younger Charles Atkins, smiling. The lurid headline was splashed across the top:

Principal of £30,000 a year school in sex scandal with 17-year-old student

The photo meant they had been under surveillance from when Atkins had been arrested. Who had tipped the police off? Or did the media vultures now have cameras covering the station all the time?

She swallowed the discomfort in her throat and faced the irate Mr Burroughs.

"We only came to the conclusion yesterday, and brought Mr Atkins in for questioning very quickly. Hence we didn't have the time to inform you."

"He killed my daughter!" Conrad exploded.

"No," Arla shook her head firmly, trying to control a situation that was going from bad to worse very quickly. "He did have sexual relations with your daughter, but we think it was consensual. It is too early to say he was the murderer."

Conrad looked at her, his face aghast. His wife stared at Arla. "What did you say?"

"I said there is no proof at this moment that Charles Atkins was the murderer, Mr Burroughs. Look, would you like to come inside, please, where we can talk in private?"

"I would like that more than anything else."

The internal doors opened and a flustered-looking Johnson stepped out. He had obviously heard about the commotion involving the family, and come to check. He extended his hand to Conrad, who shook it without enthusiasm.

"Who are you?" he barked. Johnson introduced himself. Very quickly, Arla and Johnson herded the Burroughses through the doors into the corridors of the station.

"I want to know exactly what's going on," Conrad said as soon as the door shut. Arla let Johnson do the talking, and took the time to observe Jenny Burroughs. The woman cast a baleful gaze back at Arla, and she shivered under it.

"This is all your fault," Jenny Burroughs said suddenly. The words cut through what Johnson was saying. Everyone stopped speaking and looked at her.

Arla was at a loss for words. Jenny said again, "Why don't you admit it?"

"I can't see how you can say that, Mrs Burroughs."

"Someone who's after you took my Maddy away." Jenny voice was ugly, accusing. "That's why they left that note. Then they sent a photo to your phone. This is down to you!" She literally screamed the last words.

Arla felt a cold weight settle on her chest, a numbness that froze words on her tongue. She opened her mouth but no words came out. Jenny Burroughs stood up, and approached Arla slowly. Her face was changing colour from pale to blood red.

"Who are you?" she hissed. Arla stood her ground, chest heaving, mouth open.

"You bitch!" Jenny lunged herself at Arla, who sidestepped, and held her from behind. The woman kicked and fought, and Arla held her as Johnson and Conrad got involved. Between them, they managed to restrain Jenny and sit her back on the chair.

Johnson pointed to the door. "Get out, Arla. Now."

"Sir, let me explain to her what happened."

"Now is not the time, Arla. Leave, now!"

Arla's blood had curdled to ice in her veins. She opened her mouth to speak, but no words came out. She turned on her heels, and went out of the door, slamming it shut.

CHAPTER 60

Shaken, Arla walked quickly to the drinks machine in the rear corridor, and grabbed a glass of water. As she downed it, she saw Harry and Lisa approaching. From their faces she knew they had heard about the Burroughses coming to the station.

"You OK, guv?" Harry asked, keeping a respectful distance.

Arla gripped her ice-cold fingers and shoved them in her trouser pockets. "I need a fag."

Lisa said, "I got one."

They went outside and puffed in silence. Arla inhaled the nicotine gratefully. Right now, she didn't care if she was sliding back into a smoking habit.

Both Harry and Lisa maintained a diplomatic silence. Arla studiously avoided Harry's eyes, resisting the urge to melt into his arms.

She asked Lisa, "Have we been through Charles Atkins?"

Lisa nodded. "Laptop, phone and bank details are all out. I put together a CV, and the whole thing's on your desk."

Arla needed to work just to get her mind off things. Johnson would be back soon, and she knew that Deakin was upstairs, waiting. She stubbed the cigarette under her heel.

"Let's find out more about Charles Atkins."

Arla leaned back in her chair and put her feet up on the desk, crossing them. She was looking through Atkins' CV, trying to find something.

"He graduated from Nottingham Queens University, then did some odd jobs before becoming a teacher. One of his first teaching jobs was to children in social care." Arla looked at the address, with the dates when Atkins had worked.

"That was a good ten years before he came down south," Harry noted. He had a copy of the papers in his hands as well.

Arla leaned her head back, a mental itch at the back of her mind. She wished she could reach inside and scratch her brain. It suddenly came to her in a flash. She sat up in her chair.

"Nottingham."

Harry and Lisa looked at her, bemused. Arla stared at them with shining eyes. "Nottingham," she repeated.

"What about it?" Lisa asked.

"Remember the necklace that was found on Maddy's body? The one which was a replica of my mother's?"

"Yes," Lisa replied slowly.

"Well, Rob had tracked the maker down to a firm called RD Designs in Nottingham. Where is Rob?"

"Not at his desk, guv, I have to check."

Arla was chewing her lower lip. "I want to speak to the social care home where Atkins used to teach." She looked up the name. "Beaverbrook Children's Home."

She Googled the name, and it came up in the top hit. Arla dialled the number from the screen, using her table-top phone. When she introduced herself, after holding for a while, she was put through to the administration office.

"This is Sharon Stevens, Matron in charge of Beaverbrook."

"Hi, I need some information about a teacher you might have had ten years ago. His name was Charles Atkins."

There was silence on the other end. Sharon, who had a heavy Irish accent, only breathed. After a few seconds, Arla ventured again. "Hello?"

"Just a minute, Miss Inspector, I am having a look like, you know." Arla heard the click of buttons. Sharon said, "I must say the name strikes a distant bell, but it was a long time ago. I have been here for almost fifteen years."

Arla raised her eyebrows at Lisa and Harry, who waited patiently opposite her. Finally Sharon returned on the line.

"Yes, I found him. I do remember him now. Thin guy, well dressed. I got the impression he was destined for better things in life."

"Sounds like him," Arla said.

"He was here for one year, and then he left. Is he in trouble?"

"Afraid I cannot disclose anything at this moment, Miss Stevens. Do you have any staff members from that time who will remember him? I need background information on what he was like. Did he get into any trouble? Did he ever have any issues with the children?"

"What do you mean issues?" Sharon's Irish twang was suddenly sharper.

"Abuse of any kind," Arla said frankly. "Did any of the girls or staff ever complain?"

There was silence again and Arla heard buttons clicking. Sharon said, "There's nothing in his records. And to be honest, something like that would stick in the mind, like, you know."

"Yes."

Arla could hear Sharon breathing down the line. She said, "Sharon, why don't you ask around about him, and I'll call you back tomorrow? I need to know, you see. It's important."

Sharon agreed. Arla gave her the personal number, then hung up.
*****

After half an hour, Arla was sitting in Johnson's office on the fourth floor, with a panoramic view of South London's skyline. Johnson was stone-faced behind his desk, and Deakin was sitting to his left, without his uniform for once. Martin Johnson, the short, corpulent press officer from the MPA, was clutching a folder, and Harry was sitting in one corner.

Johnson said, "Who leaked the story to the media?"

Arla shook her head. "Don't know, sir. In the paper, the photo is of me and Harry coming back with the suspect. It was taken in the rear car park with a telephoto lens, which means they were waiting for us."

Johnson slapped the desk with his hand and swore. "This is beyond tiresome now." He looked around and composed himself when he realised Nick Deakin was observing him closely.

"Any new leads?" he asked Arla in a quieter voice.

"We are looking carefully into Atkins' background, sir."

Deakin spoke up. "His lawyer, Malcolm Hindmarsh, has been in touch already. We need to let Atkins go tomorrow morning if we don't charge him with murder. For the other charges, he will plead guilty and get a non-custodial sentence."

Both senior officers stared at Arla. She spread her hands. "We are looking. His bank account shows usual activity. He has admitted to having the pay-as-you-go phone that Maddy called the night before she vanished. She was calling him to arrange a meeting, but he refused. She kept calling back as she was angry."

"You believe that?"

"I don't think he killed her, sir."

Deakin said quietly. "He had every opportunity to do so, Arla. And he had the motive. What makes you so certain he's innocent?"

Arla composed herself before replying. "The killer is stalking me as well, sir. Atkins knows nothing about me. I have never seen the guy before. He certainly doesn't have my personal number. If Atkins is the killer, then who sent me the photo of Maddy lying in the park?" There was silence for a while.

Johnson said, "If we don't charge him, do you know what the US Consulate and our Home Office will do?"

Arla couldn't help herself. "Seems like you care more about what they think than the truth."

"Shut up, Arla," Johnson growled. "Do you know how long I spent calming the Burroughses down? The husband was threatening to call the CIA, for Heaven's sake."

Deakin said, "I got a call from MI5 yesterday. It's actually MI6 who maintain close contact with the CIA, but for this case, MI5 have been approached by the CIA, as it's a domestic matter. I can only refuse them for so long. The questions they ask are pertinent, I think."

Arla frowned. "What questions?"

Deakin shrugged, but Arla noted that he wouldn't meet her eyes and looked evasive. "Just questions about the case?"

"Sir, have they been forwarded case files already?"

"This is a bureaucratic as well as criminal matter…"

"Sir!" Arla raised her voice, something she had never done before in Deakin's presence.

"Arla," Johnson warned.

She softened her tone. "Can I please have a straight answer? Have the case files been sent to MI5 already?"

Deakin cleared his throat. "Yes."

Air seemed sucked out of the room. A moment intensified, thoughts and gasps colliding in a silent choke, like that moment in an action movie when a bullet smashes into a sheet of glass in slow motion. The news was like a blow to Arla, almost bending her double. She felt fractured, cracked fingers spreading through her like a web.

"What?" She wasn't aware that she was standing up.

"Sit down, Arla!" Johnson said. Arla couldn't hear through the roar in her ears. She shook her head, the sunlight outside suddenly blinding. She squeezed her eyes shut, then opened them.

"My personal history is tied in with this case. Has it now been revealed to MI5?" Arla managed to stutter out.

Both of her senior officers looked at the floor. Deakin grasped his palms together, and met her eyes. "Arla, sit down. Please."

She didn't. Something else was bothering her. She turned towards Johnson. "Sir, you said there would never be a file on me. Not with Nicole in it, or my family."

Johnson moved his neck up and down, doing everything but meeting Arla's eyes.

It was Deakin who spoke. "There is a file on you, Arla. It is top secret, and marked for the eyes of Johnson, and the Commissioners, only. Don't be alarmed. For most of the London Met, such files don't exist. No one can access them without our knowledge."

Arla said to Johnson, "You lied to me."

Johnson had the courage to meet her eyes. "No I didn't. Not when you asked me. Later on, it was an operational necessity. For a day like this, actually. Think about it. If someone was trying to blackmail you, what better way to do it?"

CHAPTER 61

Arla couldn't believe her ears. "I don't think you did this out of concern for me. It was to keep me in check. In case…"

"In case you get blackmailed or harassed, like you are now," Johnson said. He seemed to have recovered his composure. "Despite the killer trying to involve you in this case, I kept you on as SIO. To give you a chance."

Rage was boiling inside her, and it emerged scathingly in her voice. "You call this a chance? You have undermined all my efforts by feeding case details to MI5."

Johnson sighed. "That's not true." He slid a sideways glance to Deakin that Arla didn't miss. "MI5 only have reports, they are not yet actively involved in the case."

Arla mouthed the words. "Not *yet*?"

Deakin said, "Given the importance this case could have to bilateral relations between the USA and us, I have to tell you that if we don't have an arrest by tomorrow, then we have to hand over the case to MI5 officers."

Arla felt like she had been slapped in the face. She tottered on her flat shoes, and sat down on the chair behind her. Harry was looking at her. His face was calm, but she could see the turbulence in his eyes. She turned to Deakin.

"An arrest by tomorrow? But that's only a few hours away."

"Yes, I know," said Deakin pointedly, staring back at her.

Incredulity surfaced inside Arla, spewing out of her mouth in a wave. "You want me to arrest Atkins on a made-up charge of murder?" She looked from one officer to the other. "This has already been decided?"

Johnson spoke in a soothing voice. "Nothing has been decided. You need to consider the implications here, Arla. If we arrest Atkins, it shows we are making progress. No one is saying that Atkins will be convicted if he is not guilty. The investigation can continue. But at least we can show the Americans we are getting somewhere."

Arla raised her hands and flapped them down. "We keep coming back to the same thing. Sir, this is nothing but showboating. Don't you think the Americans will think we are incompetent when Atkins walks away free? Hindmarsh is one of the best lawyers in the CPS."

"By that time we will have more evidence and other suspects."

"You want me to arrest him on a fake charge to buy us time," Arla said.

It was a statement, not a question. Colour blossomed in Arla's cheeks, and fury gritted inside her teeth, hardening her jaws. How stupid were these men? Especially Deakin, the most powerful man in the room. Her eyes settled on him.

Deakin said slowly, "Our jobs are never simple, Arla. If you do this for us, it shows you as capable of making difficult decisions. Senior management will not forget that. Charles Atkins is not being sent to jail. As you said, we are just buying time…"

Arla said, "I am not doing it, sir."

"Arla…"

"No! This is hogwash, sir, and you know it. We have no evidence!" She was shouting again but she didn't care anymore.

Johnson held his head in both hands, and Deakin looked at him. Arla had the strange feeling that Deakin had just won, and Johnson lost. Johnson didn't raise his head, or look at Arla. Deakin swivelled his gaze back to Arla.

"In that situation, DCI Baker, I have no choice but to remove you from the case. You are not being suspended, and you will maintain your rank. But as of today, you will cease to play any further part in the Madeleine Burroughs murder enquiry."

Arla felt like she had been punched in the gut.

CHAPTER 62

She stared at the two officers in disbelief. Johnson stared down at his desk, and when he did look up, avoiding her eyes, she saw regret in his features. Deakin, on the other hand, was icy calm.

"In your absence, DS Johnson will be taking over the case, and he will be assisted by DI Harry Mehta and the rest of the team." Deakin glanced at Harry, who stared stonily ahead, and gave a slight nod of his head to acknowledge the news.

Arla looked at Johnson. She felt no pity for him. He wanted to get his senior rank, and would do anything that Deakin demanded of him. She realised now that Deakin had always wanted her off the case, and Johnson had fought to keep her in it.

There was nothing more to say. She had made her position clear. She looked at Harry once, then turned and left the room. He followed. She went down the steps quickly, not looking back up. She got to her office, slammed the door shut, and locked it.

Arla paced around a while, held in a cocoon of anger and revulsion. She took her phone out, and thumbed through messages. Nothing so far. No more photos of dead teenagers. She had a horrible feeling Maddy was not the last one, and it was frustrating that she had just lost the authority to lead the case.

Well, she didn't care. Johnson had to come down here and take over. Till then, she would do what the hell she wanted. She opened the door and called Harry and Lisa in. James and Rob had arrived, and they followed.

Arla looked at the pensive faces. Harry looked the most disturbed, and she avoided looking at him.

"I have just been taken off the Burroughs case," Arla said, her voice tight. She lifted up a hand when Lisa started to talk. "Don't go there. Johnson is SIO now, and Harry is his sub."

Everyone turned to look at Harry, who spread his arms and spoke to Arla. "Guv, you know I don't care. Just tell me what to do, and I'll do it."

"Just the response I was hoping for," Arla said without mirth. "Get Charles Atkins in the interview room. I want to question him before they slap the murder charge on him and he clams up completely."

She turned to James and Rob. "Anything more from the laptops and social media accounts?"

Both of them shook their heads. James said, "He seems to be normal in every way. Paid his rent and taxes on time."

"What about the pay-as-you-go phone?"

"He used that to contact Maddy. Apart from her number there aren't any others. And he's deleted all of the messages anyway."

"Photos?"

"Deleted as well." James crossed his arms and leaned against the wall.

Lisa said, "There was another number on the phone call list. It was caller ID withheld."

"Did we trace it?"

"Yes," Lisa said. "They were from phone booths over South-West London. Brixton, Streatham, Clapham, all mixed. The calls never lasted more than two minutes."

"What about the voice data?"

"Waiting for the phone company."

Arla sighed. Phone companies moved to their own timetable, and slowing down urgent police investigations seemed to be their speciality.

"Boss," Lisa reminded her, "don't forget to call Prof Hodgson back. She called again while you were upstairs."

Arla mentally slapped her forehead. "Thanks, Lisa, I will today."

When they left, Arla took some time to compose herself. She called her father, but he didn't answer. She left a message, hoping he would call back. She checked the time. She had to hurry. If Johnson came down and saw she was questioning Charles Atkins, that would be the end of it.

They met with Atkins in the interview room. Harry did the introductions, and they started. Harry said he was the SIO for the case, and Arla winked at him. He looked relieved. Hindmarsh was on his way, and Atkins seemed nervous without his lawyer.

Charles Atkins looked as if he was on the diet of his medical namesake from California. The Atkins Diet might have been proved to be a fad, but it was working on the defendant. The man had shrunk to a shell, his shoulders cowed in submission, head bent over his neck. Arla couldn't help feeling sorry for him this time.

"Mr Atkins, I have to ask you some questions."

"Go ahead," he mumbled. Fight seemed to have drained out of him.

"I was looking at your CV, and it seems you worked for more than a year at Beaverbrook Care Home for children in Nottingham. Is that right?"

Atkins looked up, a frown on his face and he stared at Arla. "Yes, that is right. That takes me back years."

"Did you enjoy that job?"

"It was challenging work, teaching teenage students from impoverished and neglected social backgrounds."

Arla glanced at the paper on the desk. "Then you moved to a school called Radlington in Brent Cross, North London. That was a public school, and must have been very different."

"Yes, it was."

"You stayed there for more than three years, rising to deputy head for science. Do you remember any students from those years?"

Arla observed him closely. Atkins' body language was key now. He maintained eye contact with Arla, his hands remained folded on the desk, still. His feet didn't tap, his body didn't move.

"You are asking me a lot, Inspector. There are a lot of faces from that time."

"Anyone special?" Arla asked.

Atkins' eyes widened, then narrowed. "Is this about Maddy?" A light appeared on his face. "Oh God. You think I'm a paedophile. Is that what this is about?"

"No," Arla said. "We are keeping an open mind. Can you please answer the question?"

Atkins appeared uncomfortable, but then gave in. His head sank back on his chest. Arla gave him some time. When he looked up at them, his eyes glinted with a light.

"Yes. There was a boy and girl from my year in Nottingham. I got to know the girl first. She was fourteen, and had a horrible life. Her mother had died at birth, and her life had been a succession of foster homes. She had been abused several times, in horrific ways. She was the most damaged child in Beaverbrook while I was there."

"What was her name?"

"It was a long time ago, but I think her name was Sally, or Cindy, something like that. She had a boyfriend while she was in Beaverbrook. I got to know him, too. He had a similar life to the girl, but not as bad."

"What was the boy called?"

Atkins shook his head. "I cannot recall at all, sorry."

"Any other children that stuck in your mind?"

"Various academically gifted ones. But that couple from Beaverbrook were my first taste of how challenging behaviour can be in relation to getting educated."

Despite herself, Arla was intrigued. "How do you mean?"

"The girl, and the boy's, level of psychological disturbance was so deep it touched their personalities. They suffered with depression and anxiety. They had to take medication for it. But, despite that, they were clever."

Arla pursed her lips, something bothering her. An image flashed on the back of her mental retina. The necklace found on Maddy's dead body had been made in Nottingham. There couldn't possibly be a connection. Could there?

She asked, "What happened to the boy and girl?"

"I don't know. I left Beaverbrook after one year. They were still there at the time."

"OK." Arla changed tactic. "An undisclosed number called your PAYG phone occasionally. We will get the voice data soon. But can you tell us who it might have been?"

Atkins stiffened. There was a knock on the door and Hindmarsh walked in. The veteran lawyer was red in the face. He pointed a finger at Arla.

"How dare you question my client in my absence?"

CHAPTER 63

Hindmarsh was seething as he sat down. He picked up the pink handkerchief from his immaculate black suit's breast pocket and wiped his forehead.

"I hope you realise, Miss Baker, whatever my client has said so far cannot be treated as evidence."

"He's not said much, I assure you."

Arla said, "Tell us about the ID withheld number that called you, Mr Atkins. Was it always the same person?"

Hindmarsh stopped Atkins from speaking and leaned close to him. He smiled eventually and moved away. Arla didn't like the smirk on the lawyer's face.

Atkins looked troubled. "I was going to mention this to you sooner. But I wasn't sure if it was the right thing."

"What is?"

"That same number called me several times."

"It did?"

"Yes. Somehow, the person who spoke to me knew about Maddy and me. He or she was trying to blackmail me."

Arla sat bolt upright, sensing Harry do the same. "Was it a man or a woman?"

"I don't know. The voice was disguised by a machine. At first I thought it was a prank call, but then they left threatening messages about telling the papers about me and her. Apparently, they had photos of us together. They sent me one. I deleted everything."

Arla shook her head in disbelief. "And you didn't tell us this?"

Atkins wasn't finished. "The person also told me when you guys were coming. I was told to deny everything."

Harry asked, "What did they want from you? Money?"

"That was the funny thing," Atkins said. "They said I would know when the time was nearer. I was kept waiting. Then Maddy vanished." He looked down at his lap, a stricken look on his face.

"After she went missing," Harry asked, "did the calls stop?"

"No. They came about once every other day. If anything, I was more nervous after Maddy disappeared. If someone found out about us, they would think I had taken her."

Maybe that's exactly what they wanted us to think, Arla thought to herself.

Arla sat back in her chair, her brows furrowed. Hindmarsh was looking even more smug. He said, "Surely you can now see that my client was being blackmailed."

"It's too early to reach conclusions," Arla snapped. But she couldn't deny that the dynamics of the case had changed. Atkins being blackmailed reminded her of the dilemma she was in. She wondered if it could be the same person who was responsible.

She nodded to Harry, who concluded the investigation.

When Atkins was taken back to his holding cell, Arla and Harry rushed down the corridor to the office.

"I think it's all linked," Arla said.

"How do you reckon?" Harry asked.

"The killer is manipulating us. I think he knew it was only a matter of time before we caught Atkins out. If we didn't, the killer would have exposed Atkins eventually."

Harry pondered in silence. Thoughts were swirling around in Arla's head like clothes in a tumble dryer.

"My stalker is intelligent and resourceful. Do you think he'd make a schoolboy error like leaving the name of the designer engraved on the necklace he planted on Maddy's body?"

"I guess not. He knows we can trace it."

"He *wants* us to trace it, Harry. He's trying to tell me something." They had arrived back in the office. Arla's eyes fell on Rob. "Did you get in touch with the manager of the factory at RD Designs?"

Rob's face brightened. "Yes, guv, it's in my report but I'll tell you now. The bloke said they make lots of designs like that, but this necklace was a one-off, and they only made one thousand of them. To put that into perspective, they make millions of their other 80s design jewellery – mainly necklaces, earring and rings."

"Have you got this guy's name and number?"

"Yes."

Arla thought hard, biting her lower lip. She thought of Sharon Stevens at the care home in Nottingham. An idea struck her. She had to make two phone calls. One to Sharon, another to Prof Hodgson. She took her phone out, and her eyebrows creased. Her father had tried to call her twice. Her phone had been on silent while she was in the interview room.

She called him back, but it went to answerphone.

"Harry is the new boss, so take orders from him now. I have to go and see my father." Amid resigned calls of frustration, she closed the door. She made sure the door was locked, then picked up the receiver of the phone on her desk, and used the secure line to call Prof Hodgson at CAHID.

"Hi, Arla how are you?" Sandra Hodgson sounded pleased to hear her voice. Arla remembered the time she had spent with her, and became sombre. CAHID had been a deeply impressive place, but Arla's moments there had been laced with pain. Yes, she had gained closure on Nicole, but that didn't mean the regrets ever stopped. "Good, and thank you for your help with the case. You wanted to speak to me?"

"Yes, I did." Arla detected a deepening of her tone, and a pause. "What is it?" If the matter was related to the case, Arla didn't understand Sandra's hesitation.

Sandra said, "I went back to Nicole's skeleton as my work wasn't finished."

Arla clutched the receiver tighter. She listened to the static for a while. "Why not?"

"I felt the lower half of the skeleton needed more examining. So I did some MRI scans and looked at them in detail. Turns out I was right."

Arla swallowed. "About what?"

"I had missed something. It was in the base of the spine, at the bottom near the coccyx. There was a shallow indentation made in the lower vertebrae."

"What does that mean, doc? In English, please."

"The smooth depression in these have been made by a weight pressing against the vertebrae for a period of months. Large tumours at the base of the spine can do that. At the age of sixteen or seventeen, it is virtually impossible Nicole had such a big mass inside her, and she didn't suffer with ill health."

"Then what could it be?"

As soon as she asked the question Arla had a fearful premonition. She closed her eyes. No. Please, no.

Sandra said, "A gravid uterus. She was carrying a baby."

Breath left Arla's chest in a painful gasp. She felt hollow inside, eviscerated. Sandra continued.

"The bones of the pelvis have a widened brim as well. Which shows they had been stretched."

Arla couldn't speak. Eventually she licked her lips and asked, "What does that mean?"

"It means the baby was delivered. I would say at full term, or nearby. Nicole gave birth before she died, Arla."

CHAPTER 64

Cindy leaned over the body strapped to the bed. The old man's fearful eyes were open. He was strapped to the bed the same way the girl had been before him. Thick belts enclosed his torso and upper legs. His hands were shackled to the sides, and his feet were tied together. Duct tape covered his mouth.

Cindy said, "I will remove the duct tape from your mouth. If you shout, no one will hear you. We are in a remote area. But shouting, or fighting, will only mean I dose you with this." Cindy lifted up a hypodermic needle with syringe attached. She watched with satisfaction as the old man's eyes widened.

"Do you understand?"

Timothy Baker nodded twice. Cindy reached over and pulled the duct tape off. Timothy shouted in pain as a few hairs of his stubble came off. He glared at Cindy, who stared back at him with interest.

"Do you know," Cindy said softly, "how long I have waited to see you?"

Timothy's eyes narrowed, then became worried. "Who are you?"

"You will soon find out."

"Why were you following me?"

Cindy gave a short laugh. "What is this, Twenty Questions? I ask the questions here, not you." Her expression became serious. "I'm going to untie your legs, and one hand. The other stays in the handcuff."

She pointed to the floor, and Timothy craned his neck. He could see a plate of food – bread and soup. He felt nauseous and had no appetite whatsoever. Next to the plate, there was a dirty bucket with a handle.

"You wee in the bucket, and then eat. I will close my eyes while you wee, and stand behind you with the needle against your neck. Try anything funny, and the needle's going straight in your neck. Agreed?"

Timothy nodded quickly. A wee is what he definitely needed. He fought the rising bile in his mouth. How long had he been here? The man in the car had wrestled him to the seat, then he had felt a sharp pain. Then he remembered nothing. He imagined the same needle as the one the woman held now had been used to subdue him. Timothy thought about his chances. Once one hand was free, he could grab the hand holding the needle. Or he could try to elbow her with his back turned. Then he could use one leg to kick her. But if she had the needle pressed on his neck, how far would he get?

Cindy seemed to read his mind. "Thinking about an escape, are you?" She jumped forward suddenly, surprisingly quick for a woman of her short, stocky frame. She grabbed Timothy's shirt collar and pressed him against the bed, choking him. His windpipe was crushed, and veins stood out on his forehead. He made a choking sound, unable to breathe.

"Listen, Mr Baker," Cindy said, getting her face very close to Timothy's. "I have waited a long, long time for this moment. I promise you, anything you try will only prolong your pain. So I'm telling you one last time. Don't try it."

She let go of his neck and stood up, chest heaving with the effort. A tangle of brown hair had fallen over her face, and she tucked it behind her ear. Timothy spluttered and coughed. He cleared his throat, making a rasping sound. Cindy watched him warily. She didn't want the old man to die. Her job was only half-done. There was a long way to go still, and he would only get his full reward when all the chips were aligned.

Timothy coughed a few times more, then gasped. Saliva drooled down the sides of his mouth. His throat and neck felt raw, bruised. He felt the woman touch his legs, then remove the cords that tied one foot to another. He wiggled his toes gratefully, trying to get some sensation back in them. He blinked, and was surprised to find water escape the corners of his eyes. He needed to clear his head. The woman was impulsive and dangerous. But there would be a crack in her armour. Somehow he had to locate it.

"Which hand?" Cindy asked. "Remember you have to eat with that hand as well."

"Right," Timothy croaked.

He folded his legs and sat up in bed, surprised when the woman helped him. She brought the bucket around, then stepped behind him. Timothy was taller than her, so she stood up on the bed, and he felt the sharp needle prodding him in the neck as she reached over. He was leaning to one side, left hand shackled to the bed. It was bloody uncomfortable, but it was a relief to be able to urinate. Once he had finished, the woman jumped down and grabbed the bucket handle. She stepped backwards, watching him.

"Sit down on the floor and eat. I will put the bucket behind the door and return. I can still see you."

She didn't turn her back on him. Timothy crouched gingerly on the hard stone floor. For the first time, he had a look around himself. The flagstone floor extended to the corners of a timber structure, with a window on each side. Rafters crossed the ceiling. The room was big, twenty by ten feet at least, he thought. There was no straw or farm utensils, but he wondered if it could have been a barnyard for a farm in its original state. There was a dry, musty smell in the place, as if the windows had not been opened for a while. The odour mingled with another, a fetid mix of sweat, urine and vomit.

He ignored all of it and focused on the woman. She had kept her eyes on him, and her stocky body was approaching him fast. A shaft of sunlight fell on her, and he caught the glint of something on her belt. It was a long kitchen knife blade, and the sight of it made him catch his breath. He got a good look at her as well. Her cheeks were podgy, and a scar was visible on her neck. The small, dark eyes were focused on him, as was the frown on her face.

"Why aren't you eating?"

"I'm not hungry."

"I want you to eat." She removed the knife from her belt. It caught the sunbeam again and winked. Timothy swallowed.

Cindy stepped forward. "Now."

Timothy looked down at the plate. Two rolls of bread and a bowl of green soup, bits of vegetables floating in it. Despite the nausea, his stomach rumbled as he inhaled the still steaming soup. He could eat, after all, and maybe he needed to keep his strength up.

Once he had finished, the woman guided him back on the bed. He lay in silence as she strapped his legs together after shackling his hands.

"Are you the same person who's stalking my daughter?" he asked.

He felt the woman stop, then carry on tying the rope.

"You are, aren't you?" Timothy repeated. The podgy face appeared in front of him, staring down. The evil eyes glittered at him. Her brown hair fell over her face, but she made no attempt to brush it back. Beads of sweat had gathered on her forehead.

"So what if I am?" she asked.

Anger flared inside Timothy's chest. Arla didn't speak to him much, but he could see how stressed she had been the last time they met. He tried to raise his head, neck muscles quivering.

"You leave her alone, you hear me!?" he shouted, mustering as much strength as he could.

Cindy smiled tauntingly. "And if I don't, what will you do? Helpless old git."

"Take my shackles off and I'll show you what I can do," Timothy gritted through his teeth.

"I can kill you anytime I want, old man. Just remember that. And your daughter's not going to be far behind."

"No," Timothy gasped, seeing the fanatical smile on Cindy's face.

"Oh yes."

"If you touch her, I'll kill you."

"Not if I kill you first."

Timothy narrowed his eyes. This woman was disturbed, warped. Maybe he should try something different. "Then I will haunt you. I'll return as an evil spirit and inhabit your body, occupy your dreams. You will never sleep again, you stupid bitch!"

"Shut up!" Cindy shouted, but her eyes were scared all of a sudden. She stared at Timothy.

"My face will burn in your eyes. Your life will be a hell." Timothy was overdoing the drama act, but weirdly, it seemed to have the desired effect.

Cindy panted through an open mouth. "Don't say that."

"I will. My curse will ruin your life."

"NO!" Cindy screamed, putting her hands over her ears. Then she bared her teeth, and hit Timothy on the jaw. His head snapped back, and she hit him again and again, drawing blood.

CHAPTER 65

Arla felt a weightlessness inside her, like she was made of wool. Her body seemed to float, Sandra Hodgson's words hitting her like bullets, passing through her without contact. There was a pain between her eyes, and she rubbed it hard, trying to regain focus.

"Arla, are you there?" Sandra's voice was concerned. "I'm sorry. I know this is disturbing for you. I wanted to see you in person, actually, but we're so far away. Hence I've been trying to call."

Arla tried to tether herself back to reality, but it wasn't happening. As if her sister's untimely death wasn't enough. Now this.

Somehow, she wanted to go to sleep, close her eyes and drift away. Maybe dreams would be better than this reality, even though her dreams were dead, driftwood in an ocean of despondence.

Not only had she failed Nicole. She had also failed her child.

A candle lit in a dim corner of her mind, like a light in a frozen attic.

"Sandra?"

"Yes, I'm still here."

"You're saying the baby was delivered, right?"

"It would seem so, yes. The tension and marks in the bone suggest extreme stretching of the pelvic floor muscles and ligaments, and a woman only gets them during childbirth."

"Where would the baby have been born?" A foolish question, Arla knew. Nicole's life had been so chaotic…

"Where was the body found?"

"Here, in the old care home. But that is in ruins now, and there are no records of what happened there."

They thought in silence, both reaching the same conclusion. "It could have been anywhere," Arla said almost to herself. "But if she was pregnant, she wouldn't have gone far, would she?"

Sandra said, "You don't know what. If she was in trouble, or danger, she would have gone anywhere to keep the baby safe."

That made sense, too, Arla thought. In fact, Nicole was in danger when she was in London, Arla knew that for a fact. She would have moved away for the childbirth. Maybe she went to a hospital outside London. But her body had been found in London, Arla reminded herself. So she must have come back.

Did she come back with the baby? Arla doubted it. Then where had she left the baby? Was the baby even alive anymore?

A heavy shroud of sadness draped itself around her shoulders. She slumped on the desk, receiver falling from her hands. She picked it up and said, "Thank you, Sandra. I'll be in touch."

Arla hung up, and remained head down on the desk for a while. She tried to think through the fog of regret that clouded her mind. There was only one person left alive who might have known about Nicole's last days. Her dad. Even he might not know it all, but he was all Arla had.

She picked up her keys and went out of her office. She stopped in front of Harry's desk.

"I need the keys."

Harry looked up at her, and knew instantly something was wrong. "Are you OK, guv?"

"Yes." She bit her lower lip, forcing herself not to look at him. Harry knew everything about Nicole. She didn't trust herself to have a conversation with him now, and not break down.

"Keys, please." She stretched her hand out. She could feel his eyes on her.

"What did Prof Hodgson say?"

"Nothing. Keys, please, Harry." She let impatience creep into her voice, while she checked a mark on her shoe.

"Want me to come with you?" Harry asked in a tight voice.

"No."

He handed her the keys in the end, and she snatched them off his hands, turned and left as quickly as she could. Several heads watched her leave, then shrugged, looking at each other.

The heat hit her like a wall as soon as she came out into the parking lot. It prickled her hair, eyes and back. The air was thick, yellow with air-brushed pollen and sunshine. Normally, she would welcome it. Now it felt like a weight on her shoulders.

She got into the car and drove to Balham train station. A train rumbled overhead, and traffic snorted like a herd of bulls on the road. Arla stared at the Victorian house where her father lived, and at the window of his apartment. The curtains had been pulled back, and she could see the white ceiling. She crossed the road, and pressed on the buzzer. After five tries, she had no luck. She cursed and rang him. It wasn't his day at the bridge club, but he might have gone out shopping. He didn't answer.

Arla paced around for a while, feeling idiotic. She had a key in her apartment in Tooting, and should have got it before she came here. An old woman ambled over, her bent knees moving slowly. She had a walking stick, and with the other hand pulled a trolley bag. She approached the house. Arla walked towards her.

"Do you live here, ma'am?"

"Who are you?" The old woman looked at her suspiciously.

"My father lives here. Mr Tim Baker. Know him?"

The old woman thought for a while, then her face cleared. "Oh, yes, I do. Tim who plays bridge."

"That's the one."

"So you must be Arla, his elder daughter."

Momentarily, Arla was taken aback. How did this woman know her name?

She looked up at Arla and smiled. "Your father always speaks about you. I play bridge as well. You are the high-ranking police officer, aren't you?"

Arla didn't quite know what to say. She felt touched that her dad talked to others about her. She never spoke to anyone about having a living relative.

"Can I come inside, please…?"

"Edith, my dear. My name's Edith. Can you help me with the bag, my love? Gets heavier for me every day."

"Of course." Arla grabbed her trolley bag as Edith took her key out and walked to the front door. Arla dropped Edith off at her door, and went up to her dad's third-floor apartment. It was locked, as she thought it would be. She knocked and hammered, to no avail. She wished Harry was with her. His heavy boot would have come in handy. The door was a single sheet of timber, but what grabbed her attention was the frame running around the door. From her very basic knowledge of DIY, Arla knew that the lock and door jamb were in the door frame. She pushed the door, and it rattled against the frame. She pushed with her lean weight on it, and saw the door move back, giving her a view of the lock. She had a credit card, but fiddling with it seemed like a waste of time.

Sorry, Dad, she thought. You could be inside having a deep sleep. She went to the end of the corridor, then ran at full tilt at the door, and smashed into it with her full body. Her shoulder and ribs stung from the blow, but she heard a loud splintering sound, and a creak. The thin frame was hanging by screws to the old plaster on the wall. Arla took three steps back, and used her right boot to hit it. It moved again but didn't cave in. The second and third kick did that, the door suddenly flying open and slamming against the wall behind it.

"Dad!" Arla called out as she walked in. Her boots crunched on bits of plaster and timber. She repeated her call, but only silence answered her back. A panic was starting to rear its ugly head inside Arla's stomach. She fought it down. She went through the one-bedroom apartment with a toothcomb. It was empty. She looked out of the window in the sitting room. All the windows were shut. The TV was off. In the bedroom her dad's clothes were all hanging in the wardrobe, and his suitcases were beneath the bed.

Mr Baker was not planning on a trip anytime soon. Her phone beeped again, and she pulled it out, praying it was her dad. A photo message had been sent to her. It was the picture of a man lying on a bed. As Arla stared at it, the colour drained from her face. Her heart jackhammered against her ribs, and waves of nausea cannoned against her gut. With a sharp cry, she knelt on the floor.

It was her dad, tied to a hospital gurney, his eyes closed.

Beneath the photo, the text read: *We have your father. How long he lives is up to you.*

CHAPTER 66

DI Harry Mehta had a unique problem. For the first time in his life, he couldn't look a criminal in the eye. Not because the criminal was free of guilt: far from it. His lack of judgement was extraordinary, and he would bear a cross for the rest of his life. No, Harry couldn't look Charles Atkins in the eye because he didn't believe Atkins was guilty of the specific crime for which he was about to be charged. It wouldn't be the first time that Harry had misgivings about a case. But ultimately, he knew it didn't matter. The defending team would blow holes the size of Clapham Common in the prosecution's evidence. This man would one day walk free. Which didn't lessen his current ordeal.

Harry pushed the charge sheet across the table to Atkins and Hindmarsh, his lawyer. Hindmarsh snatched it up with the alacrity of an eagle seizing its prey. He raised astonished eyes to meet Harry's. "Murder?" the pinstriped lawyer's face was livid with rage. "How can you be serious?"

"It says on the charge sheet, doesn't it?" One thing Harry did find amusing was the righteous anger of lawyers. Especially Hindmarsh, who had made a career out of protecting rich clients who were as guilty as mud on a white wall. Money made his world go around, not justice.

"This is a waste of the Crown Court's time and money," Hindmarsh spat. In silence, Harry agreed.

Atkins' face was the colour of the green lino on the floor. Harry rose, went to the water machine and poured him a glass of water. It stayed untouched on the table. Harry held it in front of his face. "Drink," Harry said. "Then go home." He looked at Hindmarsh. "Your client is allowed home till his court hearing date. He cannot make external calls unless they are to first-blood relatives. He cannot leave London. He has to surrender his passport and not leave the country on a false one. He will attend this station once a week on Wednesday at 12.00 hours. Please confirm that you understand." Hindmarsh was staring at Harry like he was rotten. Atkins took a sip of the water, then Harry took the glass off him. Atkins stared at Harry like he had never seen him before.

"This is insane," Atkins said.

Yes, it is, Harry felt like saying. It is also politics. Aloud he said, "Do you agree to the terms?"

"Yes, we do," Hindmarsh said between clenched teeth.

Atkins signed the relevant forms, and with once last, withering look, Hindmarsh shepherded his client out of the door.

*****

The cab drove away, leaving Charles Atkins staring at the terraced house in Stockwell Road. The lights were off in the upper-floor bay window, which meant there was no one home. Charles wondered if his wife was still living there. The few short conversations that he had with her, saying he was sorry, and that he wasn't guilty of the murder, seemed to have fallen on deaf ears. Apart from the odd monosyllable, she said nothing, then hung up.

But the apartment was in both their names. It made sense for her to stay there and change the locks. He felt for the key in his pocket and approached the door with trepidation. To his relief, the key turned in the lock. He opened the door and stepped inside. The narrow hallway and staircase were dark. He fumbled for the switch on the side wall. He flicked it, but nothing happened. If the electricity had been cut, his wife must have left.

Atkins trudged up the staircase, his body and soul weary. He reached the landing, and with the key, opened the door to his apartment. A hand shot out, grabbed him by the shirt collar and pulled him in. Before he could catch his breath, his back had slammed against the wall, and an elbow was pushed against his neck. His trachea was bent almost in two, starving his brain of oxygen.

Atkins' eyes doubled in size and his face was suffused with blood. He tried to shout but only a croak was heard. A light flicked on, and he saw the face of his attacker.

"Remember me?" the voice said.

Atkins stared at the face in wide-eyed terror. His mind was running loops, but nothing came to him. The figure leaned forward and whispered in Atkins' ears.

Atkins frowned, trying to drag through his memories. Then he remembered.

"Yes," the figure said, "it's me."

The pressure on Atkins' throat lessened for a second. "But... but, I helped you," Atkins stuttered.

"You were the same as the others," the voice hissed. "You only helped yourself."

Atkins opened his mouth to speak, but the elbow slammed back into his neck, pushing him against the wall. The back of his skull exploded in a shower of pain. Atkins felt something sharp enter the soft of his neck, and his body was convulsed in agony. He screamed, but nothing left the vortex of his black mouth. His eyes rolled and he sagged limp to the floor.

CHAPTER 67

Arla breathed in short, shallow breaths. Her fingers pressed reply on the screen and she thumbed, "Who are you?"

With the other hand, she whipped out her work phone and called the station. Switchboard answered. Arla kept a desperate eye on her personal phone, willing it to buzz. It remained silent.

"Switchboard, this is DCI Baker. I need Signals, please, ASAP."

A sergeant from the Metropolitan Signals Intelligence answered. Arla explained her situation quickly. "I need a live trace on calls to my tracer phone." Mentally, she thanked the time Rob had taken her phone to the technicians to have the tracing software installed on it. "And tell the DI Harry Mehta I am in Balham, at my father's flat."

Arla put the phone down. "Come on, come on," she whispered, staring at her own phone. If this person now sent her a text back, that signal would be traced. The previous one would also be traced, but it would take time to get the location by triangulation. A live or warm trace was much more valuable to a police officer chasing a suspect. Nothing happened. No buzz and no blinks, apart from the green light on top of the phone. Ten minutes passed. Arla paced the floor, seething. Why hadn't she answered her dad when he called the first time?

She heard a sound on the landing, and then running steps. She went to the door to see James Bennett burst in, his face sweating. His eyes were wild with worry.

"Are you OK, guv?" he said. "DI Harry sent me to make sure you're OK."

Harry would have given the young sergeant the address. Something important must be keeping Harry at bay in the station.

"Don't worry. The bastard's already been and gone." She tried to stem the tide of panic threatening to engulf her. She needed to move, stay active, get things done. If she stopped to think she'd fall apart. She swallowed, realising her throat was parched dry.

"Jesus, guv, you did this?" James looked at the door literally hanging off the frame.

"Yes." Arla tried to quell the shaking of her hands, but it wouldn't work. Silently, she handed James her phone. The young man took it with a question in his eyes, then frowned as he looked at the screen. "Who…?"

"That's my dad," Arla said. Her throat closed over. Even now, she realised what her stalker was trying to do to her.

You couldn't help your dad, just like you couldn't help your sister.

"I need to get to the station," she told James.

He nodded, handing the phone back to her. He looked at her, his gaze steady. She found a cold determination in his eyes. "I'll drive, guv. Leave your car here."

Arla swallowed, trying to slow her surging pulse rate. Probably best she didn't drive with her state of mind.

James drove a black VW Golf. He gunned it down the road, dodging past traffic. "Do you mind if I stop by at my house, boss? I left my pager at home. I need to get changed as well. You can come in for a quick cuppa if you want."

Arla hid her impatience. She was in his car now, she couldn't turn back.

James lived close by, between Balham and Clapham. He screeched to a stop outside a house with a garage. He reversed and put the car on the drive, then up to the mouth of the garage, which was shut. "I live in the ground-floor apartment," he explained. "The garage came with it. I'll be ten minutes. Sure you don't want to come in? You look like you need a cup of tea."

Arla had to agree. She needed a triple gin and tonic, in fact, but for now a cup of tea would do. She got out of the car and followed James inside. He turned the alarm off as he went in. The apartment was small, but neatly furnished for a single man. Well, she thought he was single.

The hallway opened out to a living room at the end, with two doors leading off the hallway. James went into the living room, and Arla followed. There was a kitchen opposite, and he went inside.

"Milk and sugar?"

"Yes please," Arla said, plonking herself down on the sofa. James was out very quickly, bearing a hot, steaming mug in his hand. Arla took it from him gratefully. He turned the TV on and gave her the remote.

"Make yourself at home, guv. I'll be out in two ticks."

He padded down the hallway, and she heard him shut the front door. Arla sipped the tea, inhaling the fragrance. It was a nice cuppa. She flicked out her phone, and gave Harry a quick call. It went to answerphone. Mentally she ticked off what she had to do. She needed to call Sharon Stevens at the Beaverbrook Care Home again, and find the names of the two children Charles Atkins had mentioned. She wondered if Sharon would remember, but if the children had interacted with Atkins extensively, there would be some record.

Arla sighed and massaged her neck. She hadn't realised how tired she was. Last night's poor sleep hadn't helped. Her muscles ached after battering against the door. Arla stood up, stretched and went to the window behind her. There was a table with a laptop and printer on it. Papers were stacked neatly to one side. She looked up to see a bookshelf in one corner. Her eyes fell on one called *Genealogy: Know Who You Are.* She picked up the book and leafed through it. A page had been turned near the beginning. Arla yawned again, and covered her mouth, embarrassed.

She opened the page that had been turned, and stopped. The chapter heading was the same as her last name. Baker. The chapter was devoted to where the Baker clan came from in England. Bennett was the next name that had been earmarked. Arla put the book away, feeling puzzled. Maybe James was looking at where all the B's came from.

A piece of paper sticking out of the laptop caught her eye. She leaned closer. Curiosity got the better of her, and she pulled on it. It was part of a scrapbook. Guiltily, Arla looked behind her. James was still getting dressed. She would put it back as soon as she had a quick look.

She yawned again, silently this time, rubbing her eyes. She picked up the scrapbook. It was made up of newspaper articles that had been stuck together. As she peered at the articles, her mouth opened in shock.

All the articles were about Nicole. From where she had disappeared, to when she had been found. Several lines had been underlined in black repeatedly, as if the reader was highlighting its importance. In the middle of the scrapbook there was a large, square piece of paper. Arla squinted, wondering what on earth was wrong with her eyes. She was seeing double, definitely.

She picked up the scrapbook, holding the square paper close to her eyes. It was a birth certificate. She read the name on the top, and suddenly she couldn't breathe. Her knees almost gave way, but she managed to stand with an effort.

Baby's name was James Baker. Mother's name was Nicole Baker. Father's name was blank.

The scrapbook fell from her hands to the table. Arla put a hand to her forehead, swaying. Her eyes were defocused and hazy. The walls bent, then swirled around like they were being twisted. Arla tried to move, but she collapsed. The scrapbook fell on the floor, and she dragged the laptop down with her when she fell. She held onto the edge of the table and somehow stood up, knees shaking.

Someone was standing a few feet away. It looked like James, but with her eyes now, she couldn't be sure.

"Hello, Aunty Arla," a familiar voice said.

CHAPTER 68

"Where's DCI Baker?" Harry barked as he strode into the room. Lisa looked up from her screen.

"Last I heard she called Signals Intelligence about tracking a warm signal. Nothing came of it, as far as I know."

"That doesn't answer my question, Lisa," Harry sighed. "She said she was going to see her dad, but she should have been back by now."

Harry took out his phone and frowned. Then his face cleared and he swore softly. Lisa stood up.

"What is it?"

Harry's face was ashen. "Have you ever seen Arla's father?" Lisa shook her head.

Harry said, "I have once, and bloody hell that looks like him."

Lisa came forward and looked at the photo carefully. The phone on Harry's desk began to ring. In two long strides Harry was on it, the receiver clasped to his ear.

"Arla?" he snapped.

"Hello, no…" The female voice on the other end sounded confused.

"Who are you?" Harry asked in a harsh voice. Something weird was happening and he needed to get to the bottom of it. He needed to get hold of Arla.

"I am Sharon Stevens, the matron of the Beaverbrook Care Home in Nottingham. The policewoman, Miss Baker, had called me."

Harry was instantly alert. This was the care home where Charles Atkins had worked and become close to two students.

"Yes, I remember. This is DI Mehta. Have you found any new information?"

"Well, it's strange, I was looking through the records, and I found some old folders that Charles Atkins had written about the two children. They were fourteen and fifteen years old at the time."

Harry was impatient. "Do you have their names?"

"Well, that's the strange thing. One of them, the boy, has the same last name as the policewoman. His name was James Baker. On his birth certificate, the mother's name was Nicole Baker. But when he left us, he made a court affidavit and changed his name to Bennett."

Harry sat down heavily on the chair, his heart racing, mind numb. Nicole Baker… Arla's sister. Memories rose up like shadows from a dark crypt, gripping his head.

He spoke with an effort. "Can you repeat that please?"

When she did, Harry beckoned at Lisa. On the phone he said, "And what was the girl's name?"

"Her name was Cynthia Mullins. But everyone called her Cindy."

"Anything else?" Harry cradled the phone on his shoulder and wrote a quick message for Lisa on a piece of paper – *Find James, now!* – then gave it to her. She nodded and went out of the room quickly.

"Yes, Inspector. These two children were very disturbed. They were clever, but God had not been kind to them. They suffered terrible abuse at the convent they came from, and then at the hands of their foster parents."

"But they were friends?"

"More than friends, as they got older. They were very quiet, always kept to themselves. Never bothered anyone. The accident happened just when they left."

"What accident?"

"Sorry, thought you knew. Our old building was burned to the ground. We are housed in new premises now, with the same name. Police claimed arson, and that it was an inside job. But I never believed them."

CHAPTER 69

Arla swayed on her feet, her back against the wall, hand on the table for stability. James went in and out of view, his body merging with the background. She noticed him step forward till he was close enough to touch.

"Wh… What did you say?" Arla said, wondering why her tongue felt so heavy, and why her speech was so slurred.

"I said hello, Aunty."

"Aunty?"

"That's right. I am the son of Nicole Baker. She was your sister?" Arla tried to fight the mist of confusion expanding against her brain, knocking against her skull, and failed.

"Yes, she was. That birth certificate," she had to pronounce the words slowly, "is yours?"

"Yes."

"Then why didn't you come and tell me?"

"Because I was waiting for the right opportunity."

He came closer still, and Arla had her back pressed against the wall. Her anguished mind couldn't think much, but she cottoned on to one thing. She looked at the four Jameses standing in front of her. She squeezed her eyes shut and they became two.

"Did you get my phone number? Is that how…?"

"Yes, that is how those photos were sent to you."

Arla's mouth fell open, and her chest was squeezed remorselessly in a vice-like grip of pain. She croaked and fell to her knees. She retched on the carpet. She wanted to vomit, but only a spit of saliva came out.

Through bloodshot, red-rimmed eyes, she looked at him, standing over her. "But my dad, he's your grandad. How could you…?"

She didn't finish her sentence. James lifted his foot, and kicked her in the chest, knocking her backwards. Arla's head hit the wall, and pain mushroomed in a yellow-orange wave over her eyes. She tried to scream but no sound came. She slumped on her back, unconscious.

James looked at her critically, then bent down and grabbed her by the shirtfront. He began pulling her towards the door.

CHAPTER 70

Harry was standing in front of Lisa's door, agitated. "Where is he?"
Lisa put the phone down. "He's not answering."
Harry gripped his forehead. "Send a squad car to James Bennett's
address, now. Tell everyone he is dangerous, and not to approach
him."
Lisa gaped at him. "Really?"
"Yes." A thought came to Harry. "You worked with him, didn't
you? On that CCTV stuff?"
Lisa pursed her lips. "Yes, I did. And I did surveillance with him,
when we camped outside Paul Ofori's house."
"What was he like? Did he say anything?"
A frown appeared on Lisa's face as she thought. "Come to think of
it, we were speaking of Maddy's death. He talked of being in the
Army. He was an infantry soldier."
"He was in the Army?"
"That's what he said. Stationed in Afghanistan. He talked about how
one day a teenager was killed, mistaken as a terrorist."
Harry swore and gripped his forehead. He needed to think, but panic
was suffocating him all of a sudden.
"Where's Rob?"
"I don't know…"
"Find out, now. Rob and I will go to DCI Baker's father's flat.
That's where she was last seen."
"What's going on, guv?"
"I don't know. But it seems James Bennett was actually DCI Baker's
nephew. His mother's name is certainly the same as her sister's."
Lisa digested this in silence. Harry said, "And given how much her
stalker knew about her family, I have a very disturbing feeling about
this."
Lisa nodded, looking shocked. Harry continued. "We also need to
locate one Cynthia Mullins. She was close to James when they were
growing up. Look in IDENT1, and then anyone with that name
living in London."
"Why London? She could be anywhere."
"She could. And her name is common so we might have a huge
search on our hands. But if she was close to James, chances are she
still is. We have to presume she could be in London."

Harry suddenly remembered the person following Arla's father around. He had described them as short and stocky. He passed on the message to Lisa.

Rob bustled in from the doorway. "Guv, you wanted me."

"Yes, you and I are off to DCI Baker's dad's house. Lisa, can you please bring up the CCTV images from Brockwell Park, at Maddy's last location."

Harry checked his phone again. Nothing from Arla. He dashed to his table and rang Johnson's office. When his boss picked up, Harry explained what was happening.

"Good God!" Johnson exclaimed. "And you have a photo from Arla's phone that shows her dad tied up to a bed?"

"Yes, guv. We know from the path report that Maddy had probably been tied up like that as well."

"And what about James?"

"I have sent a squad car around, and will head there myself after checking DCI Baker's dad's place. Hopefully she will call by then to let us know where she is."

"OK. Keep me posted."

Harry hung up and, with Rob in tow, hurried to the car park. The parking lot was a yellow haze, swimming in a soup of sunlight. Rob blinked and pulled at the tie chafing his neck.

"I read somewhere that the pollution from cars absorbs the heat. It can't escape into the sky, that's why it's so bloody hot."

"It would be bloody hot no matter where you were. But yes, our concrete jungle doesn't help," Harry said, turning the AC on full blast.

When they arrived at Balham, they got lucky. A woman with a pram was trying to get out of the door, and they helped her. They raced up to the third floor. It wasn't hard to see the only apartment with the smashed door.

"You sure this is the right one?" Rob asked.

"Yes. But let's have a look inside."

In fifteen minutes, they were outside. Harry chewed things over. There had no other signs of struggle inside, so the bashed door might well have been just Arla trying to get in. Presumably her father hadn't been in, or why would she have that photo?

Harry looked at the shops opposite. "OK, Rob. We ask in every shop opposite. If they have seen an old man like Mr Baker, or DCI Baker herself."

"Right. Old man with a stick, or tall, pretty, brown-haired woman in a black summer coat."

"And anything unusual. Get cracking, be quick, and meet back here."

"Aye aye, guv."

Harry didn't have much luck with the first three shops, but on the fourth one, a newsagent, he struck gold. The turbaned Sikh man looked bored behind his counter, but he faced the street and, as it turned out, his eyes missed little.

Harry flashed his badge and asked about an old man with a stick, and anything unusual. The man straightened when he saw Harry's badge.

"Yes, I did, actually. This old guy, I see him now and then walking up and down. He got into this car. Then all of a sudden, this guy ran across the road, jumped in, and the car took off like it was doing a race!"

Harry took out the photo of Arla's father, zoomed into the face only, and showed the man the image. "Is this him?"

"Yes, that's the guy. Seen him before as well."

Harry's body felt cold. He flipped to a photo of Arla, and showed it to the man. "Seen this lady? She's a police officer."

The Sikh man snapped his fingers. His bored countenance was now replaced by animation. "Oh yes," he stroked his beard. "Funny thing, that. She came out from the same house as the old man. But she was with a younger guy, shorter. They got into a car and he drove off."

"Describe both cars, please."

The man stopped stroking his beard and stared at Harry. "What is it?" Harry asked impatiently.

"This must be a police case," the man said.

"What?"

"Both the cars were the same. I remember now. It was the same car, I think, a black VW Golf, 2014 registration."

"Mr Singh," Harry said, "you should be policeman."

"I have thought about it!" Mr Singh called out as Harry dashed out of the shop.

Harry flipped out his phone and dialled Rob as he ran. When Rob answered, Harry panted, "Get back to the car. Mr Baker has been abducted, and Arla left with a young man in the same car."

"I was just about to call you," Rob said, sounding like he was running as well. "I just found DCI Baker's car. It's parked in a side road by the tube station. It's locked and there's nothing inside."

"RV to my car. We need to drive to James' house ASAP. Do you know what sort of car James drives?"

"A black Golf, I think."

They were at James Bennett's house in ten minutes, blaring sirens through the afternoon traffic. A uniformed officer was leaning against his car, hands in his Kevlar vest as Harry pulled up to a screeching stop.

"Anything?" Harry shouted.

The uniform sergeant looked nervous. "No guv, we rang but the door's locked."

"Anyone been in or out?"

"Nope."

"OK, get the battering ram."

"Sorry, guv?" The sergeant's mouth fell open.

Harry was already at the door, looking through the keyhole. Rob explained to the sergeant, and they opened the trunk of the squad car and took out the short, squat, metallic weapon, which looked like a giant truncheon with a handle on top.

Harry pointed to the door. "Smash it down."

"You have authority, guv?"

Harry was sweating. "Yes, I do. Now do it, for Heaven's sake."

Three meaty blows with the battering ram splintered the door open with a crash. The alarm went off instantly, a loud claxon belting out over their heads as they poured in.

The apartment was empty. The kitchen door led to a narrow landing that opened out into the garage. It was empty, too. Harry and the team started turning the place upside down.

Harry focused on the garage. The shelves on the grey cement block wall were full of old magazines and bric-a-brac. He flung them all down, finding nothing till he stood on his tiptoes and passed his hand over the dusty top shelf. Two DVDs in their covers fell to the floor. He picked them up quickly, wondering why they looked familiar.

The blue and white logo of the National Highways & Motorway Police stared back at him. He opened them up, and looked at the disc with the words 'CCTV' written over the top.

He ran out the garage, shouting at Rob to follow him.

Where are you, Arla? Harry thought as he drove like a madman. His heart was lying in pieces, and a pain had seized him, making him feel ill. His sweaty palms gripped the steering wheel tighter.

Where the hell are you?

CHAPTER 71

Arla could feel herself rising and falling. She was in a fairground ride with her dad, sitting next to him. She screamed with glee as the ride went up and down, making her bounce. With one hand she clutched her dad's jumper, the other white knuckle on the seat handle.

The dream faded, replaced with blackness and a steady drone. But she was still moving, tilting this way and that. Her eyes fluttered open. She was in a warm, dark cocoon. She tried to move her hands. Her fingers crunched, but she felt the plastic cuffs tying her wrists together. She tried to move her feet. Similarly tied.

There was a jolt, and her body lurched to the left of the small compartment she was in, and her head bashed against something hard. She winced, and moved her head back. She was tied up in the trunk of a car, that much was obvious.

Her memory kicked into gear. How long had passed since she had been in James' apartment? The thought filled her with a cold dread. Could this be real? She shook her head. That birth certificate seemed original.

Where had James been living all these years? Where did Nicole run away to to give birth? There were a lot of unanswered questions, but the most pressing one in her mind now was how to escape.

Her eyes got used to the dark slowly. A thin shaft of light came in through a gap in the trunk, and as she looked around she found more tiny stabs of light. They didn't illuminate a great deal. Arla unfurled her long legs, and found she could stretch them out to almost straight.

Her lips were cracked dry and her throat was parched. There wasn't much she could do but lie there, and conserve strength. At least the shafts of light told her it was daytime yet. The fact that the car was moving at constant speed and not slowing down told her she was on the motorway. She closed her eyes, and the movement lulled her to sleep again.

*****

When she woke up the darkness was complete. There were no shafts of light coming in through the cracks. It felt colder and she was stiff. There was another difference. She had stopped moving. Arla moved her neck, and tried to lift her head. It bumped against the hood again, and she slumped down.

Arla listened. It was very quiet, and likely to be evening, or night, given the lack of light. She was still thinking when she heard footsteps approaching. A key turned, and the hood of the trunk yawned open. She took a deep breath of the fresh air, sucking it in greedily. The silhouette of a man appeared, framed against the dark sky. Strong arms grabbed her underneath the armpits, and dragged her up and over. She helped by moving her legs, but she didn't have much leverage.

"I can walk," Arla said as the man tried to pull her across the ground. She stamped her feet lightly on the ground. Her captor stopped. She recognised James' voice when he spoke, and a feeling of incredulity passed through her again.

"Your feet are tied. How will you walk?"

Arla was trying to see ahead of her. Light had faded almost totally, but she felt she could make out the edges of a field. She was out in the country somewhere. The air smelled clean, fresh.

"If you untie my feet, I can walk."

"And let you run away?"

"I can't run far with my hands tied."

"Shut up." He pulled her again, her feet bouncing painfully on the hard ground. Arla looked up at the sky. The first stars were appearing like diamond studs on a black cloth. A bird swooped down from the sky: all she heard was the cry and the flutter of wings. A smell carried to her in the wind, something wet and humid.

They didn't have to travel far. Arla sensed a building around them, and then James pushed a door with his back. There was a stone floor over the doorway, and she heard something new. Another voice. She listened hard, but they spoke in whispers.

Arla felt a sharp sensation against her neck, like a needle. A female voice spoke in her ear.

"If you move, this needle will go right into your neck and paralyse you. We are now going to let you walk. Try anything and you know what happens. Do you understand?"

Arla nodded. The needle became sharper on her neck, till she felt it puncture her skin and draw blood. Arla winced, but didn't jerk her head back. She felt a rope being loosened around her legs, and she could walk all of a sudden. She almost collapsed with the first step, but James held her up.

Sensation returned to her numb feet after a few more steps. The needle stayed constant, a sharp, deadly presence at her neck. They went through a stone walkway, footsteps echoing in the dark. A door creaked open in front, and Arla was propelled into a large room. It smelled dank, humid, musty.

A light came on overhead, and she closed her eyes in the sudden glare. When she opened them, a strange sight greeted her eyes. The room was large, with windows on opposite sides, both boarded up. There was a bed in the middle, with two chairs next to it. On one of them, a familiar old man was strapped to the back. Her heart lurched as she recognised her father's form. His head was drooped over his chest.

"Dad!" Arla whimpered. He didn't respond.

Arla was moved to the chair next to him, and then strapped by belts, which pressed against her boobs and tummy. She called out to her father again, but was rewarded with silence.

"I wouldn't be calling him now," a voice said in front of her.

Arla stared forward. A short, stocky woman stood close to James. She was wearing a T-shirt and baggy jeans. Her hair was tied back in a ponytail. With a flourish, she removed the kitchen knife from her belt. She came close to Arla, grabbed her hair, and bent her head back. Arla gasped.

"Hello. My name is Cindy." Arla shivered as the blade of the knife slide down her forehead to the side of her face. "Now let's see if you bleed the same colour as us."

CHAPTER 72

The incident room at Clapham Common Met Police Station looked like a war zone. Detectives hunched over laptops. Harry and Johnson stood next to the whiteboard, shoulders drooping. Papers were strewn on the floor. Lisa and Rob were typing away feverishly on their PCs.

Lisa was the first one to look up. "Got the CCTV images, guv."

"The ones I got from James' garage?"

"Yup. These are the missing images from the film of Brockwell Park, of the night when Maddy disappeared."

"Good." Harry strode over to the desk. "Can we see them?"

Lisa angled her screen so people could crowd around her table. The projector wasn't working, and they had no time to call IT to fix it. Lisa clicked on the link, and the images came to life as a panel of six screens.

Lisa pointed a finger to the middle screen. "Look."

A black VW Golf had appeared on the screen, and it was coming out of the T-junction. It indicated right, and waited for traffic to let it move. Lisa zoomed into the registration plate.

"Bloody hell," Harry said. "That's James' car. Same reg number."

"All Points Bulletin is out with Highways Police, all ports, docks and airports. Anyone sees the car, they stream us a live link and we jump on it," Rob said.

"Good," Harry said. "Anyone called back from Cybercrime?"

Banerjee had called, reminding Harry of the high concentration of diazepam that had been injected into Maddy's shoulder. Diazepam was available as tablets illegally on the normal internet, but as liquid or injectables it was only available on the dark net. Cybercrime technicians could access the dark web without an IP address, and snoop on the illegal drug traders who plied their trade.

"Yes," Sandford, the uniform officer, said. "Told me to call them when you're free."

"That would be now, John. Call them and put them on loudspeaker."

The crackly voice that came on the loudspeaker of Harry's phone was high-pitched. "Hello?"

Harry introduced himself and explained the urgency of the situation. The high-pitched voice came back again. "My name is Mathew, by the way. So, for injectable diazepam, we found three places in London that had placed orders, one in Scotland and another in Kent."

Harry took down the addresses in London, and Sandford started a search on them. They were scattered around in the north, west and east, nowhere close to south-west. Harry chewed his lower lip. Scotland was too far. That left Kent.

"Whereabouts in Kent?"

"Close to Folkestone, just off the M20. Village called Newham, not far from the English Channel."

"Send us the address please."

"They're all in the same email. Should be hitting your inbox now." There was a sound of running footsteps, then the flushed face of a uniform sergeant banged open the door of the incident room.

"Guv!" he shouted at Harry. "Highways Police are on the line for you. They spotted a black VW Golf, with matching registration plates, heading down the M20 two hours ago."

CHAPTER 73

Arla felt the tip of the knife press close to her left ear and she flinched. Cindy laughed. The knife travelled down her cheek, and nicked her lower jaw. Arla felt a trickle of blood down her neck. "Easy," James said. "Save her for later."

Cindy stepped back, looking critically at her handiwork. "You should see what we did to your dad." She smiled.

Arla looked at her father, who was beginning to stir. His neck was craned back, and there was an expression of pain on his face. The right sleeve of his shirt was ripped open and bleeding, showing a gash on the forearm. Blood still dripped from the fresh wound, gathering on the floor.

"What do you want?" Arla seethed.

James spoke. "What we want? You still don't know?"

Arla stared at the handsome young man. Her breath caught when she saw the lines of Nicole's mouth in his face and the similarity of his stance. How had she missed it?

"No, I don't." Arla's head was aching, and her arms were going numb. "Look, just let my dad go. Please. He's an old man, his body can't take it."

James ignored her. "We want our lives back. All the way to when I was born, and abandoned by your sister."

Arla closed her eyes, feeling a pressure build behind them. "I knew nothing about that. I tried to look for Nicole, but she didn't want to be found."

"And what about me?" James asked.

"You? Believe me, if either I or my father had known that you existed, we would have moved heaven and earth to make you safe."

"But you didn't. I was left to rot, just like Cindy."

"I am sorry for that," Arla said, feeling the blood beginning to soak into her shirt collar. "And I know my apology won't make that right. But don't let this become the end, James. The police will find you. And when they do, there won't be any escape. Please listen to me."

"Only if you listen to me first," James said. He pointed to Cindy. "And then to her."

"I will," Arla said. She needed to keep him talking, buy more time. By now, Harry and the others would know she was missing. Good job she had sent Harry the photo when she did.

"Why did you kill Maddy? She was young, innocent."

James smiled, a sickening, calm expression on his face. "Well, we had to find something to jog your memory. A dead teenager, just like your sister."

Arla's head fell on her chest. She couldn't speak for a while.

James continued. "Besides, we wanted to punish Charles Atkins."

Cindy hissed next to him. "That idiot thought he could be our saviour. He counselled us. Told us to write everything down, and he would take it to the police."

Arla looked up. "And did you?"

James said, "Yes, we did. Guess what happened then? He changed jobs, and that was that."

"You could have contacted the police yourself. Why didn't you tell Sharon Stevens, the matron at the care home?"

A look passed between James and Cindy, and they both smiled. Arla felt a chill run through her.

"She's next on your list, isn't she?"

"Yes. We want to take you two up to Nottingham, and meet up with her. Kill all the birds with one stone," Cindy spat.

James stepped closer. "Enough with the questions. Now it's time you heard our side of the story."

He began to peel back the layers of his first memories. The horrors he had faced as a child, the cruelties inflicted upon him by men and women he trusted. The beatings he suffered as a little boy when he didn't obey the filthy commands he was subjected to.

Tears flowed down Arla's face as she listened. It was unimaginable, incomprehensible, that human beings could be so cruel to a child. But they weren't human. James had been subject to life with evil monsters, and they had shaped him into the monster he had become.

"Stop!" Arla cried, unable to bear it any longer. Her heart heaved with agony. It was awful that he had been through this; what made it far worse was that he was related to her. She shook her head, sobbing. "I don't want to know. Just stop. Please."

Cindy spoke up loudly. "No. It's my turn now." She came closer to Arla. "Do you know the nights I lay awake, hearing children sob?"

Arla said, "Maybe you can help them. We can do it together."

Cindy grinned. "Oh, I help them already. I saved a number of children from their drug-addled parents. I work as a council housing officer, you see." She explained to Arla how she had rescued the children from the homes she had visited.

Arla shook her head, aghast. "You killed the parents? How does that help things?"

"They deserved to die anyway," Cindy said forcefully. Then she carried on with her story, which was similar to James': the untold horrors they had been forced to endure together.

Arla felt sick with pain as she listened. She wanted to cover her ears, but her hands were tied.

James smiled for the first time, a grin that twinkled in the corners of his eyes like a maniac. He turned to Cindy triumphantly. "See, I knew she wouldn't be able to deal with it."

He stepped forward, his face suddenly a mask of hatred. He slapped Arla hard in the face, then again and again. Arla felt pain explode inside her head, her skull rocking back with each blow. Her eyes dimmed, then her head rolled forward, blood streaming from her nose and mouth.

James stepped back, breathing hard. "Now you know!" he shouted. "And this is only a small part of what is to come." He indicated towards Timothy. "Get started on him."

Cindy moved towards the chair, when a loud sound reverberated across the room, shaking the ground beneath their feet. The boarded-up windows rattled. The sound grew louder, and with it came the staccato bursts of a helicopter's wings beating in the air.

A strobe of light flashed outside, bursting in small filaments through the rafters. Over the commotion, a voice yelled from a loudspeaker in the sky.

"This is the police! We know you are in there! Come out with your hands raised, right now!"

"Move!" James screamed at Cindy. He jumped towards the chair, and began to unfasten Arla. Cindy was doing the same to Timothy when James stopped her.

"No, leave him. She is who we want." He grabbed Cindy and kissed her passionately. "Get the car out. We have our route planned."

Cindy kissed him back, then ran out the back. The garage was an extension of the barnyard, with a steel gate that opened out onto a country road that led out over the hills, down the cliffs to join the M20 motorway. Once on it, they were only minutes away from the Folkestone Channel Tunnel.

CHAPTER 74

Harry's face was illuminated blue in the light from the MH-70 helicopter's cabin. He was sandwiched between two armed officers, Heckler & Koch MP5 sub-machine guns strapped to their vests, fingers on triggers.

Lunch rose to Harry's mouth as the helicopter banked sharply, as the man near the exit repeated his warning on the loudspeaker. Good job he was strapped in. He almost fell off his seat, then looked alive as the barn came into view briefly, before the helicopter righted itself. They had lost a lot of altitude already, and now the machine skimmed the roof of the barn as it prepared to land.

There was a frantic shout in their headphones, and Harry winced as his eardrums were pounded.

"Vehicle seen exiting building. Repeat, vehicle to ten o'clock. Black VW Golf."

Harry looked to his right just in time to see the black Golf streak out like a bat out of hell from the barn. He could just make out James driving and a figure next to him. A human shape was laid out on the back seat. It looked familiar. His pulse leaped up into his throat.

"There, there!" Harry screamed, pointing to the car. "Don't land, take the tyres out."

One of the firearms officers calmly crouched on the cabin floor and lifted the rifle to his shoulder. He aimed for a couple of seconds, and just when Harry thought the car would disappear from view, a prolonged burst of bullets were fired. The empty cartridges leaped up in the air, and the smell of burned cordite was heavy. Harry snapped his head back, and watched the car do a crazy zigzag as the bullets ripped open one of the back tyres.

The Golf passed underneath the helicopter and kept moving. It was going down a path that was heading straight for the cliffs and... Harry's mouth went dry.

Right ahead was the English Channel, its inky expanse now the same colour as the sky, the twinkling lights of ferry and cargo ships like spaceships on the calm waters.

The car's headlights were hurtling down the hill path.

"We need to stop it!" Harry screamed.

One of the officers said, "It's not easy to shoot a moving vehicle without hurting the passenger. Let the pilot do his thing."

"Hold on," the pilot's voice crackled on their headphones.

The machine whined and roared, and its wings beat louder than the waves crashing far below them. It went lower still, till it was level with the trees. The car appeared on their left, heading for the cliffs that ended so sharply: there was nothing but a sudden drop to the beach below.

"I cannot hold for long like this." The pilot sounded stressed for the first time. "Any lower and we could hit the trees. You have 30 seconds and counting. One, two…"

Harry counted, feeling each second tick in the loud thud of his heartbeat. The armed officer bent on one knee again, as if in prayer, a stock-still image, the black butt of the rifle rock steady on his shoulder.

The car was weaving its way down the path, heading dangerously close to the jagged cliffs.

A split second was all they needed, but the seconds were ticking down fast.

Please shoot, Harry whispered. *Please shoot.*

"Eighteen seconds," the pilot's voice said in his ears. "Seventeen, sixteen, fifteen…"

The sudden gunfire sent yellow sparks streaking out of barrel, and slammed into the car. Harry saw them hit their mark, and there was an explosion as the second rear tyre blew up, belching black smoke. Now the car slowed down to almost a crawl, the front wheels struggling to keep the vehicle moving.

"Get down!" Harry shouted. "Get down!"

The car's headlights were on, and it showed the driver jump out and open the passenger door. He reached inside and pulled out a supine form, and put it across his shoulders in a fireman's lift. Then he ran for the cliff's edge. Harry saw another shorter, chubbier figure emerge from the passenger side and follow him.

The sound of the helicopter was now deafening as it prepared to land. The ground rushed up, and when they were six feet away, Harry shook off his lanyard and belt, and jumped. He landed with a blinding pain in his ankles, but he rolled over and was up.

Then he ran, pumping his long legs like he never had before. He could see the driver, who was James, running up ahead. Harry speeded up, then felt a glancing blow at his legs, and he tumbled over. Before he could stand up, he saw the glint of a blade flashing in the air. He moved just in time, and caught the hand that wielded the weapon. Harry pulled on the hand and stood up in the same movement. The figure stumbled. Before it could turn, Harry punched it in the face as hard as he could. There was a grunt and the figure toppled over. Harry took out his Maglite and flashed it on.

A woman lay on the ground, knocked out cold. She was short and stocky, and the knife had fallen from her hand.

Harry looked up, and his heart froze. Wind whipped at his hair, roared against his ears. James was at the cliff's edge. The shape on his back was on the ground, and James was pushing it to the point of no return.

CHAPTER 75

Through a mist of pain and nausea, Arla felt cold wind on her face. It jerked her awake. She drew in a sharp breath. She could feel hard ground beneath her flimsy shirt, and stones poked her ribs. In front of her stretched out an unbelievable sight.
She was at the edge of a mountain, and once the slope rolled over sharply, there was nothing. Ahead, she could see twinkling lights, and she didn't know what they were. Arms tugged at her chest, ripping buttons. Arla froze. She couldn't go any further or she would die.
She suddenly realised what was happening.
"James!" she screamed. "Let me go."
He didn't answer. She could see his dark shape, his face dim as it turned away from her, heading towards the edge. Arla looked down at the hands pulling her shirt and fought him, but he was too strong. She opened her mouth wide, then bit down viciously with her teeth, clamping down with every ounce of strength in her jaws.
She drew blood and bit harder. James screamed and his hands let go. Arla rolled away before he could reach for her again, and stood up rapidly. James was now silhouetted against the horizon, huddled and staring at her.
"Let it go, James," Arla said. "Hand yourself in." She spat out the blood in her mouth and wiped her sleeve. He moved, and she realised he was trying to circle around her. She stood her ground. If she circled, then she would be on the edge. James came closer, and lunged for her suddenly.
All those months of running and yoga came in handy. James was bigger but Arla was supple. She twisted out of his reach even as his fingers brushed past her. She bent an elbow, and sent it crashing into his left temple as he stumbled, trying to grab her. He grunted and fell to the floor. He got up and staggered back. He was right on the edge all of a sudden.
"James, stop!" Arla shouted. She heard footsteps running up behind her. She would have recognised the lanky man who emerged from the darkness, his tailcoat flapping in the wind, anywhere. Tears of relief streamed down her face. It was Harry.
She turned her attention back towards James. She couldn't see his face, but Harry's arrival seemed to have changed his attitude. He stood tottering on the edge, not attacking her.

Arla stepped towards him, a pain searing her chest. "James. Come back. Please, come back."

Tears blinded her vision. Without knowing what she was doing, she stretched her arms out. "I couldn't save Nicole. Let me help you. Please."

She stepped closer to him, but couldn't see the evil grin that was spreading across James' face.

"Arla!" Harry's voice shouted behind her.

She was a metre away from James. The wind was pulling clouds and waves in its wake, the distant moon shuddering in an unforgiving sky. Arla felt heavy like a rock, weighed down.

"Come to me, Aunty," James said softly, stepping further back. From the heels of his feet, chunks of earth fell over the edge, blowing out into nothingness.

Arla reached out a hand, and so did James. She felt his warm touch, whispering against her skin, of past regrets and dead dreams, of wounds that would never heal. His hands unfurled to grasp her hand tightly.

CHAPTER 76

Arla felt a colossal weight crash against her from behind and wrestle her to the floor. Breath left her chest, and as Harry tumbled her to the ground, she looked up to see James with his hand outstretched at the sides, rotating madly as he tried to keep his balance.

"No!" Arla screamed.

He looked at Arla, his face calm all of a sudden, a cocky grin on his face, his eyes burning. Arla reached out an arm, sobbing.

James lost his balance, and the grin vanished from his face.

He struggled one last time, then vanished from sight, as if the air had swallowed him up.

Arla was dimly aware of Harry getting up and sprinting to the edge. He stood over, looking down. Three more figures ran up from behind her, and then she saw headlights strobe towards them, lighting up Harry and the others at the edge.

Harry came back to her just as she was sitting up. She wiped the dirt and tears from her face.

"He's gone," Harry said quietly. "It's over."

One of the firearms officers said, "There's an old man in the barn. He's injured, but alive. We're going to take him on the chopper to the nearest hospital."

Arla stood up. "That's my father. Can I come with you?"

"Sure, no problem. We picked up a woman lying unconscious on the ground here as well."

Harry said, "She's an accomplice of the killer. Her name's Cindy Muller, and she needs to be arrested."

"Roger that," the firearms officer said, and moved away.

The wail of sirens filled the air behind them, heard faintly as the wind scattered the sound. Arla shivered. Harry took his coat off, and wrapped it around her shoulders. She looked up at him, grateful.

"Guess you have your uses, DI Mehta."

"At your service, DCI Baker. Anytime."

Arla suppressed a tired grin, and followed them to the waiting helicopter.

THE END

WANT TO READ MORE?

Have you read the first book in the Arla Baker series?
The Lost Sister, Arla Baker Series 1, is now out on Amazon!

FROM THE AUTHOR

If you've read this far, I'm hoping you enjoyed this book. I am a self-published author, and I don't have the marketing budget that big publishing houses possess. But I do have you, the person who has read this book.

If you could please leave a review on Amazon, it would make my day. Reviews take two minutes of your time, but inform other readers forever.
Many thanks
ML Rose.

Made in the USA
Middletown, DE
15 July 2019